Beneath the Stairs

The Douglas Town Chronicles
~ Book Two ~

By Ginger G. Howard

Sequel to: **Under the Tracks**

First Edition

ISBN: 978-0-578-30374-1
Publisher: Gemini Pacific Publishing

For more information, visit the author's blog:
https://gingerhowardauthor.blogspot.com/

Edited by: Angie Gia Bennett and Paul Howard
Cover Design: Copyright© 2021 Riley M. Howard

The stranger at my fireside cannot see
The forms I see, nor hear the sound I hear;
He but perceives what is; while unto me
All that has been is visible and clear.

The spirit world around this world of sense
Floats like an atmosphere, and everywhere
Wafts through these earthly mists and vapours dense
A vital breath of more ethereal air.

Excerpts from *Haunted Houses* written in 1858
By Henry Wadsworth Longfellow

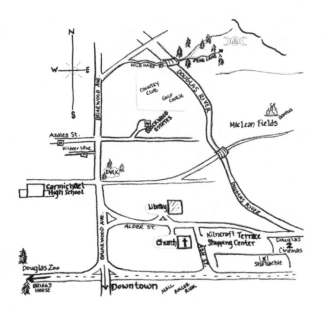

Chapter One
School Daze

Because I worried so much about being late, I was perpetually an early arriver. Thus, that first day at the bus stop, I stood alone in the cool morning air watching as each person ambled over to an invisible designated spot on the sidewalk.

Some people I recognized from middle school, some I didn't. Still, we stood away from each other at a comforttable distance, not making eye contact or acknowledging one another, as more and more tired zombies showed up.

Ruffled prairie shirts seemed to have been the popular choice when back-to-school shopping, as most the girls were wearing a version of one. I felt a little self-conscious in my new outfit. It was a white button-up cap sleeve blouse, tucked into my pleated teal pinstriped pants, a white belt and white Keds. My grandfather had been generous for my birthday over the summer, with his impersonal birthday check, reminding me that turning fourteen only happens once. *Isn't that true for any age?*

I also noted that all the girls were wearing a lot of make-up; some succeeding in the application process better than others.

I think the common denominator amongst us was that we were all coming from a place of: *"Am I supposed to dress this way?"*, *"Is this how high school girls wear make-up?"*, *"Am I going to fit in?"*

The guys at the bus stop were all scruffy hair and bags under their eyes. They didn't seem to give two shits what people thought. I envied that. Chris had not shown by the time the bus pulled to a complete stop and raised its red sign. I had really hoped to see him.

Stepping up into the bus I noticed it was basically the same as the one I rode in middle school. The only difference was that some of teens who got on the bus looked like young *adults* - the guys even had facial hair.

I made sure to sit next to a girl I recognized from a Social Studies class in 8th grade. We weren't close friends, but I think she was relieved that someone familiar was sitting next to her.

The bus ride didn't turn out so bad, because the driver played the radio. Hearing familiar music coming out of the overhead speakers helped ease the nervousness, and created a strange sense of camaraderie among my fellow passengers. That morning it was "Tainted Love" by Soft Cell that caught my attention.

When our bus lined up in the queue in front of Carmichael High School, I stared out the window at the foreign environment. As I waited to be allowed off the bus, my stomach was all tied up in knots. I noticed my hands were sweating, and I could feel my heart pounding rapidly. So on top of being exhausted by the continual onslaught of nightmares since visiting the house, I just felt... gross.

Maybe I'm coming down with something? I might have to go to the nurse's office and call my mom to come pick me up, I wondered, as I took another step closer to the bus door.

I had only been to the high school once before, with my mom, to pick up my class schedule and show proof of my immunizations. At the time, I had overheard other freshman talking about how we weren't allowed in "Senior Park", and something about buying tickets for an elevator.

How am I supposed to find the elevator?

Once I took the last step off the bus onto the sidewalk, I felt vulnerable. Being in the open that way, it was like being a prey animal just waiting to be picked off. So I followed along behind the herd, with my head down, as they quickly made their way across the front lawn.

I held the crinkled list of my classes, tightly in my sweaty hand, as I continued following the mob into an interior quad. There, people began to scatter into their perspective cliques to sit at outdoor lunch tables or cement benches lining the perimeter. I kept praying I would see a friend so I could seek comfort in their presence, but I didn't see any of my close friends.

I had the campus map out to show me where the lockers were, and tried desperately to plan the quickest route from the lockers to my first class. In my frantic state of mind, worrying so much about being late, I bypassed the quad and the lockers altogether, and headed straight to the classroom.

The hallways were crowded with hundreds of strangers. Being a short girl, the majority of what I saw were guys' backpacks as they bumped into my head from every direction, and girls' faces in a blur as they passed by.

Was she staring at me? Is there something wrong with the way I put my make-up on? It's the outfit. I should have picked the other one, I worried to myself.

Finding the first class had me bordering on a panic attack. I had no idea what I would have done if the bell had rung.

Did you get put in detention for being tardy those first few days being a freshman?

I had hoped they would have mercy knowing we were new, and how big and confusing the school was.

"Gwen! Gwen!"

I heard my name being called, which broke me free from the potential of a mental meltdown. I stopped and turned full circle, scanning the sea of faces trying to find one I recognized. Finally a familiar smile came into full view.

"Gwen! Oh my god, I've been chasing you ever since you got off the bus. Didn't you hear me?" Cat asked, out of breath.

"No," I replied, "not until just right now. I've been looking for my first class, and was worried I wouldn't be able to find it." I held up my crinkled schedule. She tilted her head as she leaned in, trying to read it better.

"Well, you are in luck. It's right behind you, silly." She pointed to the room across from her, and then said, "I'm just down the hall over there."

"Ha, it's right there. I feel so stupid." I breathed out a huge sigh of relief. "Your outfit looks great, by the way. I'm glad you decided on the plum button-up blouse."

"Ugh," she complained, pulling at the front hem to line the buttons up straight. "I'm probably going to change into a t-shirt after P.E."

"No! You look great."

"Shush. You're just being nice. I better go... meet me here after the bell and we'll walk to Art class together," she said.

"Okay, I will meet you right here. Bye," I called out, watching her elbow her way down the hall.

I'll have to remember to ask her if she knows about the elevator, and if Mike gets to go to the "Senior Park" this year, I thought to myself.

The bell rang. My first period class teacher swung open the door until it was against the wall, and then he put down the door stop.

"Welcome to Algebra guys. Come on in, and find a seat," Mr. Thatcher greeted. He seemed nice enough.

However, it didn't take more than ten minutes after class started, for me to decide that this was the worst class ever - in all existence!

∾∾

When I made it home from school that day, dropping my overstuffed heavy book bag on the floor by the front door, my mom called out hello as she trotted out from the kitchen to greet me.

She had her long brown hair pulled back behind her head in a barrette, and was wearing one of dad's button-up white work shirts, with the sleeves rolled up, hanging loose over a pair of light blue cropped "pedal pushers", as she called them. In the background I could hear an old 50s album on the living room record player.

She was lost in the nostalgia of her high school days, I thought to myself.

"How was your first day?" she asked.

I could have shared with her that for the first half of the day I felt like I was alone and going to die from a panic attack. I could have answered that I slipped on a wet spot in the girl's bathroom by the sink, and had a dirt smudge on my pants for the rest of the day, which was horrifying. OR I could have told her that Chris avoided talking to me, which broke my heart.

"It was fine," I responded nonchalantly. "Is there anything to snack on?"

"Grab an apple. Did they assign you any homework?" she asked.

"Yes. Can you believe that?" I picked up an apple from the kitchen. "I'll be in my room if anyone calls," I said as I dragged my heavy book bag down the hall to my room. I shut the door behind me, put my back against it, and sighed deeply.

Day 1: Check, I thought to myself.

Mel Gibson's gorgeous blue eyes looked out at me from his picture across the room. It was hung with a thumbtack on a large framed corkboard that took up a huge section of the wall. I was allowed to decorate it however I wanted to because I wouldn't be messing the wall up with holes. I filled it with colorful whimsical drawings, and magazine cut outs of album covers or photos of a recent celebrity crush. Mel had maintained corkboard space the longest.

I walked over to my record collection on the floor, leaning against the corner wall next to my wood desk. I clicked on my fake Tiffany reading lamp with its beautiful colored glass so that I could see the records as I thumbed through them. The colors cast from the light offered a nice visual contrast to the lifeless white walls that ran throughout my room. I thought to myself that if I ever owned my own home I would paint every wall a different color, just because I could.

After a minute or two of running through my limited collection, I couldn't find anything that fit the mood. I went over to Chris' backpack tucked away in the closet, and rummaged through his cassettes until I found the tape, 4, by Foreigner. I put it into my boombox, fast forwarding until I found the right song, and then hit play. I let the melodic ballad of "I've Been Waiting for a Girl Like You" wash over me, as I sat on my bed remembering the one and only kiss that Chris and I shared.

I turned face first over into my quilted white satin comforter, feeling completely exhausted, as the stress of the day came flooding out of my body in a mess of hot tears. I really missed my old friend.

Chapter Two
Hanging' on the phone

Did you hear that Jennifer actually bought a ticket, and then spent half of lunch looking for it?" Cat asked, laughing to herself. "Sooo, my brother says there is no elevator! Apparently, all the upper classmen pull this scam on the incoming freshman."

"Glad I didn't buy a ticket then. I had a least three people offer to sell me one," I replied, as I lay on my beige carpeted floor with my bare feet up on the yellow butterfly sheets of my bed. The telephone cord was stretched out from the kitchen down the hall into my room under my closed door. As we chatted, I focused on the weird texture of the white ceiling and the sparkly flecks that refracted the light coming in from the window.

"All the teachers want me to buy book covers for my text books," Cat complained.

"Mine too," I responded.

"I can't afford to buy any more supplies, and no one is home to take me to the store," she grumbled. "I'm going to just do what I did in junior high and make them out of paper bags. That way I can draw on them in class."

"That's a good idea, but now that means I just have more stuff to do tonight."

"Oh, speaking of Art, did you notice the guy in the back of class today? The one with the spiked hair and silver studded dog collar around his neck?" Cat asked.

"Yes. It seems weird that a punk rocker would be in art class. I thought they were all angry and stuff," I replied.

"Perhaps he will draw really aggressively, and use only dark colors?" Cat speculated.

"It would make more sense if he was in a wood or metal shop class with blow torches and power saws!" I chuckled.

"I think Mike knows him. I'll have to ask about him when he gets home from work."

"Do you think he's cute? Are you going to try to talk to him?" I asked.

"Maybe, I dunno. Anyways, Mike is going to bring home pizza when he gets off his shift tonight at Straw Hat..."

"Hey, don't change the subject."

"So I'll bring a couple slices for us for lunch tomorrow," she continued, ignoring me.

"Mmm, that sounds good! We should find a table out in the quad instead of sitting inside the cafeteria," I suggested. "I heard that at the student store they sell candy bars, chips and fountain soda. I also heard you can leave campus and that there is a gas station just down the street that has arcade games and frozen burritos. We should try that one day. I want to play *Centipede*!"

"The hard rockers hang out down there, and smoke. I don't know if we should leave campus just yet," Cat cautioned.

"Since you didn't answer my question about the art class guy, does that mean that you and Kevin are going to keep seeing each other, or was that just a summer thing?" I asked. "I didn't even see him around today, did you?"

"We don't have any classes together, so no, and I'm not really sure what our status is," she replied. "I *had* been worried he was ignoring me, until I found out where he was spending his free time last month. Can't be mad about that, right?"

"Right!" I exclaimed. "Uncovering that gravesite, was above and beyond!"

"He's pretty damn awesome, that's for sure," she responded.

Reflecting back for a moment I said, "We wouldn't even have an investigation going on if it hadn't been for him."

"I know," she agreed. "How do you think that's going?"

"I wish I knew. Oh, by the way, Chris wasn't at the bus stop this morning," I said, changing the subject. It was a subject ever present in the back of my mind. "I saw him later and tried to talk to him. He wouldn't even stop! He just sort of mumbled 'hello' and walked away. What the heck is going on?"

"I don't know. I guess you will have to ask Kevin."

"Hmm, okay," I responded. "I also wanted to ask Kevin about the marble."

"What about it?"

"He gave me back the watch, but the marble was buried right below it. Did he leave it there?" I asked.

"That's a good question. I think he probably did," she concluded.

A feeling of guilt rushed over me, "I promised we'd be back for him, and that we'd get him to his mother. I don't know what I was thinking... how could I have promised that?"

"We can only hope that by discovering the bones and who they belonged to, puts them all to rest," Cat offered.

"Yeah, I hope so. By the way, where did you end up hiding the puzzle box?" I asked.

"Under my bed. I couldn't think of a better place to keep it," she replied. "It's not like anyone knows anything about it. The keys are safe - that's all that matters."

"I don't know. I've been thinking about that. We kept the keys so no one could open any of the boxes at the house, to not disturb the ghosts. But the ghosts are already awake, so I'm not sure what good it does," I mused. "I guess just as long as no one else goes in there, right?"

"Right," Cat exclaimed. She went quiet for a few seconds, and then nervously said, "I've been having some weird dreams."

I pulled my feet down, and sat up, completely intrigued. "Really? Me too! What are yours about?" I asked.

"I keep dreaming about that *horrid* doll," she whispered, afraid that if by saying it out loud it would suddenly appear. I heard a quiver in her voice as she said, "I **hate** that doll!"

"Yes, it was totally creepy that it looked so much like the little girl."

"Do you ever wonder what those noises were? The ones we heard when we were in the cellar," she asked.

"Of course I do! But it's not like we were going back up there to check it out," I said, laughing lightly. "We weren't that crazy!"

"I think about it every day," Cat continued, still very serious.

"Well, we locked up everything, and put the trunk back under the stairs... I know we closed the bookcase to hide the room," I assured her.

"Right, so what could have made those noises? Didn't it sound like something was scratching at the walls or something was being dragged across the floor?" Cat asked.

"Yeah," I replied as I twirled the cord around my finger over and over again thinking back on it. "I wonder about that, too."

"Probably that damn little girl," she grumbled.

"Do you think she and her mother are just lingering around in the house now, messing with stuff?" I asked. "Maybe your dad would know?"

"I've reached out to him a couple times," she replied. "To be honest, something is different. Ever since I got back from that house, it just doesn't feel the same. It used to be comforting, connecting whenever I needed him, now it just feels... creepy."

"Why?" I asked, but then suddenly realized something. "What if someone from the house is trying to come through when you talk to him?"

"You're just being paranoid," she scoffed. "This isn't like *Poltergeist* or *Amityville Horror*."

"Well, we didn't know what we were walking into that day, and we have no idea what we're dealing with now," I countered. "He warned us that there were others in the house. He warned us that the girl was awake and dangerous. What if when you made a connection to him there, someone else took advantage of it?"

Sounding concerned, Cat replied, "Now I am really going to have nightmares."

"I didn't mean to upset you, but I'm worried. Let me be with you next time you try to talk to him."

"Yeah, I'll wait. That's a better idea," she said, yawning. "I'm getting tired. I'll talk to you tomorrow, okay?"

"Okay," I said, and then I heard her hang up. Before the line disconnected and the annoying dial tone screamed in my ear, I heard the faint sound of other voices.

Chapter Three
Day Two

A ndrea and I had one class together, so we were able to catch up. We talked a little before the bell, passed a few notes in class, and continued talking a little on the way to our next classes.

It turns out she spent the last couple weeks of summer in cheerleading camp, and had made the team. She spent the weekends hanging out with her new friends from the squad. She told me about the hot guys on the football team, and how one had already asked her out. She talked about how busy she was now with practice, but that she was also thinking of running for student body council.

I realized quickly that the days of slumber parties and hanging out after school were quickly coming to an end. The more we talked, the more I began to mourn who we used to be before high school came along and changed everything.

Erin's behavior was harder to explain away. She had been nothing but rude since school started. She was hanging out with a new gang of girls that I didn't recognize. She probably met them during cheerleading tryouts. I was pretty disgusted with how easily she dumped her old friends, even Andrea, to be with this group of 'cool kids', as a means to climb up some unseen social ladder. It was fine if she didn't want to be friends with me anymore, but it was a whole other issue that she was deliberately saying bad things about me around school.

The first time the "bitch clique" passed me by in the hall, I tried to engage Erin, to ask why she was acting towards me in that way. I could feel the negative energy oozing off of her like the plague, infecting all those around her.

"You saw the same things I did that day," I reasoned with her, trying to keep a calm tone in my voice, "so I don't understand why you're telling people it was just me."

"Stop lying, Gwen," she said. She looked around at her friends for encouragement, feeding off their need for drama. "You'll do anything to get attention, won't you? Sooo totally pathetic."

I felt a darkness filling my chest, and I tried to push it away. I was dismayed by her blatant lies, and hurt by the ugly way she glared at me as she spoke.

How could she deny seeing Cat's father in the mirror? We all saw him! I know she did. She acknowledged as much when it was happening. I asked myself. *How could she deny seeing Joseph on the tracks... or had she? She pretended like she didn't understand why we were "wasting" our time... maybe she didn't see him? The grown-ups on the train hadn't seen him when I could.*

I wondered, *Maybe it was like that for Erin, or maybe she was lying to herself and her friends because it had actually scared her so much that it was easier to pretend it didn't happen? Did she feel trapped after she got scared, like she didn't have control of the situation? I know that not having control was something she wasn't used to. She was, after all, in her own mind, the center of the universe, and all those within her orbit were to obey her laws of gravity.*

"Nothing to say for yourself?" Erin challenged with contempt. She looked around to make sure everyone agreed with her, and then spat out, "See? Totally pathetic!"

"Totally!" one of her friends agreed, and then rolled her eyes as she walked past me, "Psycho!"

"Yeah, what a freak," one of them whispered.

"She tried to convince everyone that she could talk to ghosts," the third girl whispered back, and giggled.

Erin purposefully bumped into my shoulder as she walked by, "Bitch, watch where you are walking!"

The group cackled like a murder of crows, and then fell into lockstep formation with Erin down the hall.

The encounter left me feeling sick inside, like she had infected me with her darkness. It lingered on, long after she'd gone, threatening to eat me alive.

~

When the bell rang for freshman lunch, thankfully Erin and her new social circle were nowhere to be seen. Cat and I met up in the outside quad and were able to grab a table.

We arranged it that only one of us would go to the student store at a time, that way no one would steal the table from us. When I came back with fountain sodas, there were several other girls at the table with Cat.

"Hey," I said speculatively as I found an end of the bench seat to squeeze in to.

"Gwen, you remember Kelly, and Jennifer," Cat said. I hadn't known Kelly or Jennifer all that well from 8th grade. They lived near Cat and took her bus route, so she had always been closer to them than I had.

"Yeah, how've you two been?" I asked, smiling. They responded with the usual vague pleasantries.

"Guys, this is Liz, she's new," Cat announced. "She used to live in Sacramento."

"Hi! Nice to meet you," Liz responded. "Cat and I have a class together, and she asked if I wanted to join you for lunch. I hope you don't mind."

We all nodded, shrugged and smiled at the newcomer. It was always awkward making small talk when trying to make someone feel welcome, especially when you yourself felt alien to the whole high school experience. I suppose it was worse for her not knowing anyone, and being unsure how to behave around us.

"Gwen! Cat!" Kevin shouted as he walked over from the student store to join us.

"Kevin!" I shouted back. "I am so glad you found us."

He walked over to Cat and nudged her gently to get her to scoot over. Her cheeks flushed, and she grinned happily to herself as she munched on the leftover cold pizza slice.

"Hi," she said sheepishly. He pushed his shoulder into hers, slowly nudging her again, and getting her to giggle.

Leaning over, so that only they could hear me, I said, "Thank you again for getting my watch back. Dude, that was totally amazing."

"No problem," he replied shyly.

"Did you leave the marble there? Or did you grab it?" I whispered.

"I left it there for Joseph... you know, until the bones could be found," he answered a little too loud, and then leaned over and took a bite of the pizza Cat held in her hand. She giggled again.

Okay, I guess they are back on, I thought to myself.

"What bones?" Kelly asked.

"Yeah, Kevin, what the heck are you talking about?" Jennifer asked.

"It's nothing," I replied, trying to wave off the subject as I sat back on my side of the table. Turning back to Kevin, I tried to change the subject by asking him one more question. It was the one that had been weighing the heaviest on my mind, "What happened with Chris?"

"Well you know that he got community service, and after that was over, he spent the rest of the summer packing," he responded.

Surprised at this news, I asked, "Why?"

He looked uncomfortable, but obliged me by responding, "Well, his parents are getting a divorce, or something, so he and his mother moved out of the house."

That helped explain why his father said he wasn't there to take my calls, and also why he was no longer on my bus route. Still I was concerned, and I hated not being in the loop.

"Do you know how he's doing? I mean, is he okay?" I asked.

"I think it is safe to say he's been better," Kevin stated bluntly.

"Yeah, I know," I sighed sadly.

"Who cares about Chris," Jennifer suddenly blurted out, "do the bones have something to do with that day you guys all got in trouble?"

"Yeah, tell us about that," Kelly leaned forward anxious to hear the story.

"You tell them," I looked to Cat for help. "They might believe it if it came from you. I've already been called a psycho."

"Erin's gang?" Cat asked. "They called me names too."

"What?"Kevin asked protectively. "How could she do that? What a skank!"

This got appreciative smiles of agreement from Cat and I. It was a relief to know I was in good company, even if that meant we were all freaks.

When the bell rang signaling that lunch was over, Cat had caught everyone up. By the looks on the girls' faces, they were in a state of awe.

"Dude..." was all Kelly had to add, shaking her head in amazement.

Chapter Four
Sleep Over

That Friday night my parents allowed me to stay over at Cat's. They were slowly beginning to trust me more, and allow me back my old freedoms.

After school, I filled my book bag up with overnight things, mounted my silver 3-speed Schwinn bicycle, and cruised down the driveway onto Azalea Street. I had to fight with the bag to keep it centered on my back as I turned right down Briarwood Avenue, trying not to lose my balance. I maneuvered the weight again as I took another right onto Kildeer lane.

Within a couple minutes, her single-story brick house with white painted accents came into view. I pulled up into the drive-way, jumped off, and leaned my bike against the white garage door. When I was on her brick front porch, I rang the doorbell. Loud music was blaring within, so I knocked hard on the thick door a few times. Finally I heard the pounding of someone's footsteps as they ran towards the front of the house.

"Got it," I heard Cat yell over the loud distortion of the electric guitar and screaming vocals of "Six Pack" by Black

Flag. She opened the door, and the music was even more overpowering.

"Come on in," she said loudly, as she swung in the door. She was wearing a dark blue velour sweat suit and white socks. The main room of the house was 1970's chic, complete with a wood-paneled accent wall, a floor-to-ceiling rock fireplace and orange shag carpeting throughout.

She led me from the front door to a hall on the left that led to her bedroom. In between his loud punk rock songs, I could overhear Mike and a couple of his friends laughing heartily. His bedroom was down the hall from hers, separated by a shared bathroom.

She brought out a sleeping bag for me and laid it out across a folded comforter on the floor. I had my back to the door when the music finally stopped, and I heard the guys coming down the hall.

"Whoo hoo… pajama party! Why weren't we invited?" one of them asked loudly, and I turned to see a guy poke his head into the door frame. He had closely shaved blonde hair and blue eyes, and had the swagger of someone who thought all the girls found him irresistible.

"You wish!" Cat answered back, without bothering to look. She had gone over to her record player to put on her own music.

"No, *you* wish!" he jeered, and then turned to wink at me.

"Shut up, Erik," the other one said, which caused Erik to pull himself back into the hallway.

26

"What did you say to me?" he asked, pretending to challenge his friend.

Mike chided Erik as well, "Dude, not cool, that's my sister," he paused, and then stuck his head in the bedroom door frame, "Cat?"

In annoyance, Cat answered, "Yes? What do you want?"

I saw a tall guy, with wavy reddish-brown hair, pass by that I'd never met before. For a brief second he caught my eye, and I experienced a wave of déjà vu. *Why does he seem so familiar?* I wondered to myself.

"Stay out of my room," Mike commanded before he turned and continued on behind his friends toward the front door.

"Who was that with him?" I asked casually, as I heard them leave the house.

"The perv who wanted the pajama party was Erik. The other one was probably Russell. He's only been hanging around since this summer."

"Are they both seniors at our school?"

"Yeah, why? Did you think he's cute?" she asked, with a smirk on her face.

"Which one?" I asked slyly.

"Don't pretend I didn't notice. You two looked at each other for a *very* long second."

"Huh? I hadn't noticed," I lied, embarrassed that it might have seemed obvious to him as well. "Anyway, why is the only thing your brother is concerned about is his room?"

"He doesn't want me to touch any of his music, or steal his shirts anymore. I can't be seen in them now that we both go to the same school," she complained, as she pulled out an album from its jacket cover. Putting the vinyl carefully down on her record player, she then gently placed the arm down, lining up the needle at the beginning of the first song. Immediately the distinct voice of Adam Ant came crooning out, followed by jungle drums. She started dancing around the room to the rhythm of "Kings of the Wild Frontier".

"We'll have to find a place to buy you your own t-shirts just like his... then we can do horrible things to them," I began to dance around the room as well, spinning, and kicking my feet in rhythm of the drum beat, "like sew on sequins or something, and he will totally spaz out!"

"That would be totally awesome to witness," Cat exclaimed.

After the song ended, we both flopped back on the bed out of breath. Feeling sweaty from dancing, and wanting to get comfortable for the evening, I slipped out of my top into an oversized nightshirt. "Did you manage to get your mom to rent us any movies tonight?" I asked, as I exchanged my jeans for a pair of forest-green sweatpants.

Her mom was never actually around when I came by. As a single mom, she worked two jobs, one of which had her doing night shifts a couple times each week.

"She got us a couple black and white monster movies!"

"Alright! Jiffy Pop, too?"

28

"Of course. This is date night after all," she teased, all out of breath as the second song ended.

"It's pretty pathetic that we are here on a Friday night, alone, excited about Jiffy Pop. Where are Mike and his friends going?"

"Some party out in a field somewhere. He says there's an abandoned farm house, and that it's totally trashed with graffiti everywhere. They have bonfires and stuff."

"That actually sounds pretty bitchin. Would he ever take us?"

"Are you kidding me? He'd rather die than be seen with his little sister at a cool upper classman party," she said as she rolled her eyes.

"When does your mom get home tonight?" I asked. "Will she think it's weird if she hears us talking to your dad?"

"No. She's used to hearing me talk to myself at night. I've told her before that I'm talking to dad. She thinks it's a metaphor - like praying to God, or something obscure."

"So she's never seen him, like we have?" I asked.

"Not that I am aware of. I just don't think she's capable of it. Mike hasn't seen him either, so I don't talk about it with them. I was surprised you guys were able to see him when we were at the house. Maybe dad only chooses to show himself when he wants to? I don't know how it works."

"Did you tell Mike everything that happened in the house?"

"A little, at first, then he started making fun of us and laughing. It just pissed me off, so I stopped."

"What did he say?" I asked, the curiosity getting the better of me.

"Do you really want to know?" Cat asked, as if telling me would unravel the universe or something. I nodded. "He asked if we were trying to be like the *Scooby Doo* gang, and he then wanted to know which one was the dog."

"What a jerk!" I exclaimed, and then started to giggle, "Erin."

Cat busted up. "Ruh roh, I slipped on the hill. Oh, Raggy, this is too hard, carry me."

"Does that mean that Chris is Shaggy?" I asked laughing. "Oh my god, that means you and Kevin are Daphne and Fred?" I fell over with tears streaming down my face.

"No, I'm Velma. She's the smart one," Cat insisted.

"Well I am NOT Daphne. Maybe they have cousins, so we can be *different* characters," I pondered.

"The one cartoon called *Speed Buggy...* the girl looks just like Daphne but with a different hair color, and the guy looks just like Fred but with dark hair. The driver is basically Shaggy, but his name is Tinker, and they drive an orange dune buggy that is alive - like the Love Bug."

"How do you even remember that stuff?" I asked in amazement.

"Well they did a cross-over episode in *Scooby Doo*, so that's why I remembered it. You said cousins, and I used to think they were cousins because they looked identical,"

Cat responded, lost in the memory. "Anyways, you see why I don't share anything with Mike. He won't take any of this seriously."

"Okay, yeah. Did he believe you when you told him that we were the ones that discovered where the grave was that day, and that it was Kevin that dug it open for the authorities to find?"

"Yes. He didn't scoff at that, but he didn't believe that we saw actual ghosts and talked with them."

"I haven't been able to tell my parents anything. It's been really hard with them thinking I just make all this stuff up. I hate it," I complained. "At least we have each other to talk to."

"That's right," she said as she jumped up and ran over to the record player. She lifted the arm and moved it carefully to its cradle. "Do you want to go watch a monster movie now? I think there might be some TV dinners in the freezer. I'm starving," she declared and then darted out of her room, and ran down the hall into the kitchen.

"Jeesh! Wait up!" I called out after her.

~~

Hours later we both lay on our backs staring at the posters she had plastered across her ceiling above her bed: Sid Vicious; Adam Ant; a Union Jack flag, and a giant **X**.

"So how can you concentrate, when trying to contact your dad, with Adam Ant staring back at you?" I teased, as I fluffed up a pillow, and tried to get comfortable lying on the floor.

She lit a candle on her night stand, and then crossed the room to turn off the lights. "I close my eyes, and just listen in my head," she answered as she jumped on her bed, and got comfortable under the blankets.

"What does that mean exactly, listening in your head? Do you hear his voice, or your own voice?"

"I hear his voice, like he's in the room with me, just talking quietly," she replied. "I learned that if I just stare into the candle flame for a while, it helps me focus on 'the other side'."

She went completely quiet, and I found it absolutely painful to just lay there in silence. I couldn't get my mind to go quiet - there were images and voices coming in from all over the place. I was reminded of the phone line and how there was a ghosting of other people's conversations coming through.

"Do *you* hear him?" Cat asked.

"No. My head is really busy. It's like a bunch of people talking over each other," I complained. "I hear myself thinking, mostly."

"Focus on the flame of the candle, slowly inhale, hold it for a couple seconds, and then exhale slowly. Do this a couple time, it will help. When you are just focusing on your breathing it can quiet your mind," she explained calmly in a soothing quiet voice.

That's easy for you to say, I thought to myself. I started to feel anxious, and said loudly, "I can't calm myself. There are too many voices talking all at once."

"Find one voice, and just focus on it and what it is saying, even if it doesn't make any sense."

I felt really silly, but after a few minutes I was able to make something faint out. I focused all my attention on just that voice. I couldn't make anything out at first, but then I made out the words, "Help us."

I realized I was holding my breath, and exhaled, reminding myself to relax. Then I heard, "We're trapped, please help us."

"Holy crap," I said out loud, my voice cutting through the quiet like a knife. I was shocked that it had worked.

"What is it?" Cat asked, startled.

"Someone is saying that they are trapped and need help."

"My dad just said that the other spirits found him to use as a gateway to get their message through. So you were right."

"Did he say it was the children?" I asked.

"No, these aren't the children. I don't know who they are, but they are trying desperately to reach out to anyone that will listen and help them find peace. I can only talk with my dad, so you are going to have to communicate with them. Find the one voice that is the loudest. Focus on it and respond."

I lay back down, closed my eyes, and tried to slow my breathing. My heart was still pounding really loud. I could hear so many voices, and I slowly realized they had always been there - like white noise. I had gotten used to tuning it out over time. I always thought it was my own random

33

thoughts, never knowing that it could be spirits trying to communicate with me. I did my best to focus.

What can I do to help you? I asked. There was no reply for a while, until…

"Alright that's it!" I yelled, bolting upright. "Turn on the lights. That's enough." I ran across the room and turned on the light. Cat squinted at the brightness, and sat up confused.

"What happened?" she asked.

"Someone just yelled at me that we need to bring back the keys and let the girl have her DOLL." I shook my hands off, and paced the room, trying to rid myself of the awful sensation that was clinging to me like tar. "Someone else yelled that Mother is angry because there are people messing with her house!"

"Oh, damn!" Cat was alert now, coming back to her senses.

"That was really freaky! They all sound so desperate!"

"We have to bring the keys back? Why?" she asked.

"Good question," I replied, still rattled and shaking.

Cat and I looked at each other, when she asked, "Wait… who is messing with the house?"

Chapter Five
The Library

The noises from the kitchen woke me, followed by the distinct heavenly aroma of cooking bacon. I tried to sit up but my neck protested. It took me several minutes of rolling my head around from shoulder to shoulder to get the kink out. Cat was still snoring so I shook the mattress to wake her.

"Huh?" she asked groggily, rubbing her eyes.

"Good morning, sleeping beauty," I replied.

"Yeah, 'morning," she responded in a haze. "Sleep well?"

"Probably not as well as you. I should have put down a few more blankets."

"I did offer," she reminded me.

"I know," I conceded. "Is that your mom in the kitchen?"

"Yeah… it's Saturday, right?"

I laughed at her sleepy brain fog, "Yes, why?"

"That means there are pancakes and scrambled eggs to go with that bacon," Cat responded with a new clarity, and threw off her covers as she got out of bed.

"You are very food-motivated, aren't you? Don't answer! I already know," I teased, as I tried to lift my stiff body up off the floor. "I think your floor beat me up."

"You must have done something to tick it off," she jested, as she came around to offer me a hand up.

I grumbled as I stood up and could not feel my left leg.

"Come on," she gestured towards the hallway, as she exited her bedroom. I hobbled after her as she made her way across the house to the kitchen.

"Good morning, girls!" Cat's mom greeted, cheerfully. She was wearing an old pink terry cloth robe and matching slippers. Her thick dark brown hair was a mess of curls, and they hung over her wide glasses as she leaned over the stove.

"Good morning, Janice," I replied.

Cat walked over to her and gave her a warm hug, "Good morning, mom. How was your shift last night?"

"Long. Did you enjoy the movies?" she asked.

"Yes. Thank you. The breakfast looks delicious, by the way," I complimented her as I made myself at home and sat down at the table. I took in the large variety of breakfast foods spread out in front of us, as Cat came over and sat down. "This isn't all for us is it?" I asked.

"No, Mike's friends are crashed out on the couch," Janice informed us. "We'll have to keep our voices down."

"You're kidding, right?" Cat scoffed, laughing as she piled scrambled eggs on to her plate. "A herd of elephants could come stampeding through here and they wouldn't stir."

"I take it this happens a lot," I asked.

"This summer...yeah. We've turned into a flop house of gross snoring teenage *boys*," Cat replied.

"Don't let Mike hear you call him that," her mom warned.

"What, gross?" Cat asked innocently, biting into a slice of bacon.

I almost shot orange juice out my nose, as I laughed mid-swallow.

~~

After breakfast we took turns in the shower, and got dressed. We decided to head downtown to hit the library.

While I had been grounded, Cat had attempted to track down information on the Victorian house, but didn't have much luck. We figured, with some of the new insights we'd gained since then, we would give the library another go.

When it was time to go, Cat quickly referred to the bus schedule, and then we grabbed our stuff and headed back through the house. As we passed by the living room, I heard two sets of competing snores coming from the other side of the couch, and heard Cat giggling as she made her way to the front door.

"Don't worry, they'll be gone by the time we get back," Cat said looking back while she held the door open.

"They really can sleep through anything," I replied in amazement.

Once we were out on her front porch, she slammed the door behind her, just to make a point, and laughed as she walked out towards the driveway.

~~

The bus dropped us off on Alder Street right in front of the Library. There was a long rectangular wood sign out front just off the sidewalk that read *Douglas Public Library*, and in smaller letters below that was written, *Alder Branch*.

We made our way up the cement ramp with the cold metal handrails, climbed the few steps to our right and then crossed the long entry under the front overhang of the main entrance. Two large glass doors greeted us within the sheltered nook. The building was painted a beige putty color, which made the dark tiled roof and gutters that surrounded it stand out. The windows were tinted so you couldn't see inside very well unless you smashed your face against the glass and cupped your hands over your eyes. We could see our mirrored reflections as we approached the double doors, and pushed on the black handles. It didn't budge. Cat laughed at me because it clearly said PULL.

"It's a good thing we're going to the library today. You need to learn how to read."

Rolling my eyes at her, I responded with the perfect come back, "Hardy, har, har."

Cat pulled the left door open, and I pulled the right door open, and together we entered into the red octagon-shaped tiled main foyer. From there it opened up into an expansive building, with wood furnishings and multicolored Berber carpeting. The bays of banana-yellow metal bookcases lined up in rows before us.

"I haven't been here in so long," I remarked as I looked around, noting the changes that had occurred since being there as a child.

To the left of the foyer was the librarian's desk facing out into the heart of the building. In an office chair, with its back to the exterior wall, sat a middle-aged woman. She had plain features and with grey streaked black hair. It was held up on each side of her head with red barrettes, and a pair of glasses dangled from her neck on rainbow- color beaded strings. The beads clashed with the plaid pattern of her ruffled blouse that she had buttoned up to her neck. She wore too much blue eye shadow, and the lipstick shade looked unnatural. It was hard not to stare at her and marvel at her fashion choices, that day.

"Good morning," she greeted. I noticed that her name tag read, *Judy*. "You two girls are off to an early start today, aren't you? I just opened the doors." She spoke more to herself, not really expecting an answer.

"Good morning, Judy, do you remember me?" Cat asked. "I was here this summer trying to find out some information on a property from the 1800s. I went through some of the old newspapers on microfilm, but it was an impossible task not knowing exactly what I was looking for or an exact date."

Judy looked directly at her this time, and recognition crossed her face, "Oh, yes. I do."

"You told me that I might have luck in the County Tax Assessment Archives or with deeds at the Douglas County Courthouse. But they are only open during the week, and with buses and school schedule, it just hasn't been an option."

"Yes, I can see how that would be a problem," Judy responded.

"Well, we thought we might have some luck with going through the history of Douglas County, and looking at an old map to see if maybe the property might be on it."

"I can help you with that," Judy replied, clearly happy to have something to do. "I don't think you ever told me which property in specific you were researching. I might be able to help you more if I knew. Is it a historical landmark?" she asked.

"I don't know. It's the old Victorian house by the zoo," I answered.

"Oh?" she responded, looking at me curiously. She stood up from behind her desk, staring at me as if lost in thought. "Ah, the reference section," she stated suddenly, and then proceeded to lead us down an aisle that passed by an area for children's books.

I was immediately transported back in time, as I gazed down at the colorful worn area rug. Each letter of the alphabet was written inside a primary colored book. The books were spaced out around the outer edge of the rug, and in the center were two giant red apples. A worm came out of each apple, smiling at each other.

Bays of light colored wood bookcases, no taller than my waist, created a border along the children's rug. The ones lined up along the exterior wall beneath the windows were shorter, with red plastic upholstery on the top to serve as extra seating.

The Sneetches, James and the Giant Peach, The Phantom Tollbooth, and *The Lion, The Witch and The Wardrobe* were all standing upright on individual display stands across top of the closest bookcase.

It was bringing back so many fond memories of my visits there as a child. I remembered how the decorations changed with each season, just like in elementary classrooms. My favorite time of year was Halloween, when books with pictures of giant pumpkins, ghosts floating in white sheets above eerie cemeteries, or haunted houses with vividly illustrated pages filled with hidden images, were on prominent display. My dad did an exceptionally good job of reading these aloud to me, and made sure to tickle me, and say BOO, when he could tell I was hanging on his every word. That was a special time.

"Earth to Gwen," I heard Cat call out to me. She and Judy were all the way at the end of the row.

"Sorry, I'm coming," I replied, as I tried to bring myself back from being lost in nostalgia. I was aware that I was smiling as I made my way towards the back of the library, inhaling deeply the perfume of old books that permeated the air. I'd forgotten how much I loved that library.

"Okay, here is the shelf where we keep all of the books related to subjects relevant to Oregon, the county, and the history of the town. You are right about what you said earlier though; anything more specific would be found in county records. I hope this helps," she added, still looking at us inquisitively.

I had caught up by the time she was finished, and responded, "I think this will help a lot. Thank you."

"I hope so," Cat replied, seemingly doubtful. I could tell she was still frustrated from the last time she was there. "Is there like a club or something that specializes in keeping town history, local legends or anything? You know, in case we can't find what we need?"

"I'll look into it," she said. She then turned quickly around in her comfortable loafers, thick support stockings, and twirling wide grey skirt. Then she swiftly walked back towards the front desk.

I noticed colored light on the bookcase nearest me, followed it back up to a stained glass window on the far wall, and gasped in astonishment. "That is the same pattern of glass as at *the* house, Cat," I said pointing up to it.

In the center of the stained glass was an arrangement of red flowers and purple Irises with green and yellow leaves inside a blue vase with orange handles. Around the vase was a border of colored patterns – circles, diamonds, and triangles - sectioned off with red glass dividers.

"I'll bet it was from one of the boarded-up windows on the first floor," Cat responded, looking at me as if her mind had just imploded.

"How did they get their hands on it?" I wondered.

"Does that mean that all the other things missing from the first floor might also have been salvaged and preserved?" Cat asked.

"I sure hope so," I answered. "It's a weird coincidence, huh?"

Chapter Six
Reference Section

We started by taking each book down from the shelf, and skimming through the table of contents to see if anything jumped out at us.

"I am so glad you made copies of the papers from the house before you handed them off to the journalist. Maybe we can match them up with something today?" I offered hopefully.

"I would imagine with the connections Claire Beaumont has she's already gone through the county records, so I guess we don't need to worry about that so much," Cat responded.

"Nope... all we need to worry about is *who* the other people are that are stuck there, and *why*," I sighed.

"No problem," she replied sarcastically.

After finding a couple of books that looked promising, we each settled into a hardback chair of a privacy cubby used for studying. I settled into a book with old county maps and brief histories of the townships in it.

I read that in 1843 the first European settler of Douglas was Angus MacLean, a Scottish immigrant. He filed a 640 acre land claim with Oregon's Provisional Government.

The land encompassed his clearing for a homestead, the waterfront of the river, and the surrounding timberland. He finished building his log cabin in 1844 along the river, which he said was dark and mysterious. When the town was incorporated in 1850, he officially named it Douglas, which means *dark stream* in Gaelic.

There was an old black and white photo showing a total of four establishments in a row, dated 1853: a Wells Fargo Bank, a jail, a hotel, and a mercantile. The mercantile, in the foreground of the photo with four gentlemen in tall hats, was the *only* two story building. A big sign on its upper story read: *Dry Goods Groceries / Boots Shoes Liquors.*

"Are you having any luck, Cat?" I whispered loudly over the partition between us.

Judy came up on us, just then, startling me. "I think this book will be the most promising," she said, handing it over to Cat. "It's the history of the Douglas Zoo."

"The zoo?" she asked. "Okay, thank you." Taking the book, she immediately opened it up to investigate. Judy nodded her head in satisfaction, and scurried quickly out of view.

I opened up the folder of our copies of the documents, and poured back over them to see if anything lined up with the town's history.

A few minutes later, I heard a recognizable voice. "Gwen!" Andrea said, walking up behind me. "Hey!"

I turned, in response to her voice. "Hi," I replied, and got up to hug her.

She was dressed in a conservative light-blue sun dress with a white cardigan on to cover her arms, white stockings, and low heel pumps. "Why are you all dressed up?"I asked.

"There was a Ladies Luncheon across the street at my Church," she answered. "Are you doing research for homework? That's why I'm here. I have to check something out for an essay that's due on Monday. I have to be quick about it though, my mom will be back out front in just a couple minutes to pick me up." She spoke in her usual million-mile-an-hour pacing.

"Just looking up some history on the..."

Cat quickly interrupted, "On when the first federal building was erected. It's for Social Studies class."

"Cat. Oh, I didn't see you hiding in there," she commented with less enthusiasm. "So are you here together? Were you guys doing something fun last night, and I wasn't invited?" She pretended to be teasing, but I noted a hint of jealousy, and perhaps a little envy.

"Nothing exciting," I assured her, "just Jiffy Pop and a monster movie."

She pretended to not be interested, "Well, listen I have to get my book and get back out front. I'll see ya later."

"Later," I responded, waving as she sped off down a row of books. When she was out of earshot I asked Cat, "What was that about?"

"I just got the feeling it would be best to keep her out of the loop."

"She'd be cool. She didn't freak out nearly as bad as Erin."

"Would she, though? I've overheard her talking about that day," Cat reasoned, "and she pretends like we didn't see anything. She talks about how scary the house was, and that is was 'so cool', and how we almost got caught by the security guard, and how sad it is that Chris got in trouble…"

"Yeah, that all happened."

"But it's how she tells it, like it wasn't the big deal it actually was. Stuff that she calls 'scary', seems more like an exaggeration on her part to excite her friends. That way it isn't real. It's just a story. The whole thing with Joseph on the tracks…"

"What about it? Surely she mentions that we actually all saw him."

"Nope. I really think she means well, but she doesn't want to made fun of, like Erin and her little gaggle are doing to us. She and her family have a reputation to protect. That's why we just need to keep this between us."

"Okay, that makes sense," I resigned. It saddened me that even Andrea was in denial, although it made sense with her conservative and religious upbringing. Her parents wouldn't have believed her if she'd told them about seeing ghosts, and it also would have been hard to process when hearing a different version of reality coming from the pulpit each Sunday. The two things might be difficult to reconcile.

"By the way, I think I found a lead," she stated, as she held out the book, and pointed to the paragraph she wanted me to see. "It says that the land, where the Victorian house now stands, was a county "poor farm" until in the 1880s a wild fire swept through and destroyed all the surrounding forest, farmland, and buildings."

"What is a 'poor farm'?" I wondered out loud.

"I don't know, but we have something to go on now," she answered. "It goes on to say that the new owners, The Briggs, bought the land for a steal from the county with the financial offer as incentive to continue the program. As well as working the crops used for personal sustenance and income, the working poor tended stock and took care of what would become an extensive orchard, in exchange for room and board. The county extended it beyond a "poor farm" though, and made it into a sanatorium for people with diseases and mental illness."

"Oh, wow!" I exclaimed.

"I know, right?" Cat agreed.

"Can I read that," I asked. She handed me the book and I read out loud, "The Briggs' Family Farm had a reputation of lax and corrupt supervision, and living conditions that were considered unforgiveable. But before it could be officially shut down it was found deserted by the owners and staff. The surviving inmates and patients were moved to a new facility across town. Then the county deeded the whole thing to the city to develop into protected land and a public park, where eventually they built a zoo."

"It explains so much," Cat said with a satisfied smile on her face.

Learning what the farm had actually been used for was indeed news to me. The visions I had been shown of thin haggard people working alongside the children began to make sense. I realized that the people I heard in my head must be those people that worked the farm. I had no idea though, why they were trapped, or what I could possibly do to help free them.

She leaned over and quietly said, "Considering it says people with mental illness, it makes you wonder if maybe the little girl had something like that. How else can you explain the horrible things she did?"

"Either that or she was just evil," I whispered back.

Out of nowhere, Judy walked up, pushed her glasses up her nose, and said, "Girls, I hope you found what you were looking for?" She handed me a card with a strange name on it. "You should visit this shop next. Ask for Brighid (she pronounced it Bri-geed), she's the owner. I have a feeling you'll find answers to many a thing there." She then turned quickly, like a practiced ballerina, her skirt twirling around, and sped back towards the front desk.

"What does it say?" Cat asked, looking over my shoulder down at the card.

"Shanachie," I replied, trying to sound out the word. "There is an address. Oh, it's practically just across the street in the shopping center. We should go."

"Judy said she'd send us to someone who would know a lot about the town's history, so I guess it is worth a shot."

Cat gathered up the books to put them back on the shelves, while I put our copies of the documents back into my shoulder bag.

Chapter Seven
Secrets of the Shop

On our way out of the library, we passed by the front desk. Judy stood up from her chair, and reached over to hand me a flyer and mentioned, "We have a meeting here once a month in the evenings. You should join us sometime."

"Ummm... thank you," I replied awkwardly. I wasn't sure what kind of meeting we would be interested in with Judy, the fashion nightmare librarian, or the people she associated with. I didn't bother to look at the flyer before I shoved it into the opening of my shoulder bag, and said good-bye.

When we were out front walking down to the sidewalk to head over to the main intersection, I mentioned, "She was definitely giving off some strange vibes. Hopefully we won't regret going to this shop."

"I thought she was intriguing," Cat responded with an amused look on her face.

Once we'd managed to navigate all the crosswalks in the busy intersection of Ash and Alder, we walked across the parking lot of the Kilncroft Terrace Shopping Center.

51

The shops lined up in a row, under a continuous wood awning that stretched all the way down the sloped parking lot that ended at the Douglas Cinema 2 Theater. On the marquee it read that *E.T.* was still showing, as well as the newest release, *An Officer and a Gentleman*.

We cruised past the shop fronts looking for the right name to pop out at us. Having only ever parked down in front of the theater, or been dropped off there, I hadn't paid much attention to the names of the small stores before. After all, a day of shopping to me and my friends meant a day at the mall with a food court and an arcade nearby.

I smelled a hint of incense first, and then heard the faint sound of chimes. In the window there were dozens of hanging crystals and dream catchers. On the glass was the store name:

⁊ shanachie ⁊
where all tales can be told

As the door swung inward, a Tibetan bell attached to the knob rang out. Immediately a wave of déjà vu came over me. *How is even possible to remember coming in here, when I know I've never been here before?* I wondered.

It was always unsettling when it happened, and it had been happening a lot more frequently than it ever used to, sometimes to the point where I knew what was coming next.

After the initial shock of the déjà vu eased up, I was able to focus on the details of the shop. Along the left wall were narrow shelves with small watercolor paintings perched on tiny stands. Each canvas was a different scene from around Douglas, depicting it as an idyllic quaint small town.

A display card was written in a beautiful Celtic calligraphy script that read: This Week's Local Artist, Ewan Blackwood.

"Blackwood," I mentioned, "I wonder if that is the same Blackwood as where Kevin lives."

"I'm sure it is a common name."

"Does Kevin know why his cul-de-sac is named Blackwood Estates?"

"I don't think it's ever come up," Cat replied off-hand.

The next set of narrow shelves had paintings in different mediums, painted by different hands, but each with a similar theme. These were landscapes, with a focus on the sky at night and different phases of the moon.

Looking closely at each canvas they also shared small nocturnal creatures hiding behind bushes and rocks, or camouflaged within the texture of trees. If you looked even closer still, there were strange symbols carved into the rocks and trees, or drawn in the dirt. Spirals could also be found throughout all.

In the center of the retail space was a table display with a strange combination of books:

The Female Eunuch by Germaine Greer

Fear of Flying by Erica Jong

Roots by Alex Haley
Woman on the Edge of Time by Marge Piercy
Sophie's Choice by William Styron

The only name I recognized was *Roots*, because there had been a mini-series on television a few years earlier.

Along the wall to the right was a display of leather journals, each one featuring a different Celtic symbol burned into the cover. Walking over to them, I ran my hand along the etchings, and inhaled the smell of the leather, and again was overwhelmed with the sense of remembering.

Cat had come up alongside me, to look at the accompanying accessories. "Oh, I wish I had saved my allowance! Look at all these supplies."

There was a wicker basket full of different-sized metal nibs, next to another basket filled with a variety of straight dip calligraphy pens. Adjacent to that were empty glass ink wells, and jars filled with colored powder to mix your own ink.

Next to these, on the wall, were slanted holders filled with clear packages of paper aged to look like medieval parchment.

"We need to add this entire section to our Christmas wish list," I sighed enviously.

Cat picked up a book laying nearby that showed techniques for writing in calligraphy. "I know," she responded, equally greedy to have it all.

Tucked into the corners were more of the usual book store knick-knacks like spinner racks with greeting cards and book markers. I stopped to browse through some of the quotes on the book markers:

"*A good tale never tires in the telling.*"

"*Peace is the well from which the stream of joy runs.*"

"*There isn't a flood which will not subside.*"

"*When wine sinks, words swim.*"

"Ma fave tis, 'If you want to live a life that is long, don't get between she who is red-haired and a rock'," the store owner said in a sing-song accent, as she came up to greet us. We laughed when we saw that she herself was a red-haired woman.

She was very beautiful, with a radiant smile, flawless pale skin, and brilliant green eyes. Dressed sort of like the hippies I'd seen on TV at Woodstock, she wore a long flowing, multicolored skirt with leather sandals, a loose white gauze blouse, a wrist full of jangling silver bangles, and ring-adorned fingers. A couple of long chain crystal pendant necklaces hung from around her neck.

"Wylcome tae Shanachie," she said, pronouncing it shan-uh-khee. "Ma name's Brighid. Hou's aw wi ye?"

"Hi," I responded hesitantly, not quite sure what she had just asked.

"Hi," Cat responded. "We were sent here from the library by Judy."

Brighid kept extended eye contact with me, before she broke away to acknowledge Cat. "Aye, right! An whit were ye hopin tae find?" she asked.

"We are doing some research about the old Victorian house near the zoo," I responded. "Judy said she knew someone who would know the history of the town, and sent us to you."

"Is that all?" she asked, raising an eyebrow at me, as if I were playing a joke on her.

"Yes, that's all," Cat responded, slightly confused. "Oh, and we also saw that piece of stained glass built into the library. It's the same stained glass from the house, right? We were wondering if other pieces from the house were around town."

"That is a fair muckle o' questions. An hoo, if ye dinnae mind me askin, did ye ken whaur the' stained glass came fae? Hae ye been up thaur yerrselves?" she asked, grinning, because she already knew the answer. "Dinna fash yersel. A've got naw yin tae tell."

Cat and I exchanged confused grins before I replied, "I'm sorry, I didn't understand. Can you repeat that?"

"Hae ye been up tae the hoose?" she asked slowly.

"Oh, yes!" I answered, laughing lightly in embarrassment for having not understood her English through the thickness of the Scottish accent. "We were there one day this summer. That is why we are trying to learn more about it."

"Fur research..." she trailed off, while holding my eyes locked in hers. I felt her trying to pry the truth from my mind, and suddenly began remembering Joseph as he smiled, reaching out for the marble in my hands.

She smiled then, and nodded at me as if she were validating something I'd just said. "Gwen, is it?" she asked, turning around and walking deeper into the store.

"Yes... but how did you know that?" I asked in bewilderment. *Had Cat said my name out loud since we entered the store?*

I looked over towards Cat for an answer, but she was looking back, equally confused. "How did she know your name?" she whispered.

I shrugged in response.

As we walked past the checkout counter with the incense burning, I noticed the back half of the store took on a different thematic quality. There was a floor-to-ceiling apothecary, just like the travel-size one we'd seen in the steamer trunk, with hundreds of tiny drawers each with equally tiny porcelain knobs. Every one of them had an identification card written in beautiful calligraphy. There were oils, teas, herbs and plants. The fusion of smells was more than my brain could interpret.

In passing the wall of drawers, one name stood out to me: Frankincense. I had only ever heard of Frankincense in relation to the story about the Three Wise Men, but I had no idea what it actually consisted of.

A rectangular table was set against the opposite wall topped with wicker baskets of polished stones and displays of jewelry. Above that were shelves lined with Tarot and Oracle Card decks.

Brighid walked further still, through a doorway with a cobalt blue beaded curtain. Hanging from the ceiling were moon and star pendants. There was a poster on the wall which read *Moon Glyphs* that had strange symbols above pictures of the different phases of the moon. The room also held a wall full of candles, small pull-out drawers filled with crystals, a table of crystal balls, polished abalone shells, and ornate metal bowls. Hanging from the ceiling in the far corner were wood dowsing rods, and dried batches of vegetation wrapped in thin rope.

Then there was one wall dedicated to an entirely different classification of books:

Carmina Gadelica: Hymns and Incantations by Alexander Carmichael

Book of Shadows and *Witchcraft Today* by Gerald Gardner

The Witch-Cult in Western Europe: A Study in Anthropology, and *Ancient Egyptian Legends* by Margaret Murray

A Pocket Guide to the Supernatural and *Witchcraft Ancient and Modern* and *Practical Candle Burning Rituals* by Raymond Buckland

The Book of the Law by Aleister Crowley

"What kind of store is this exactly?" Cat asked.

Without answering, Brighid reached down and opened up a small box tucked away in a corner, turned to me and said, "Ah think ye wull need this." She held out a silver ring with a large black stone set in between two smaller orange-red stones.

"What's this?" I asked, as she motioned for me to take it.

"Tis Black Onyx, a braw stane tae wear tae protect ya fae harmful spirits wha wull try tae drain ya of yer psychic energy. The Carnelian stanes hae spiritually protective powers as well. The combination sud aid ye against onie black magic, an fend onie spells cast against ye."

"I'm sorry... *what*?"

"Tis a protection ring," she insisted, still holding it out for me.

"Oh, no, I couldn't, really," I protested. "Besides, I can't afford that."

"Please, tak the ring as a gift frae me tae ye. Ah want ye tae hae it."

Confused as to why I would need a protection ring against black magic, I picked the ring up from her pale hand. As I did, my fingers lightly touched her skin, and an image of the house came into my mind, memories of the mother and daughter staring at me from the mirror in the attic.

I jolted back, but she grabbed my hand before I could pull away. "Ye will need this, Gwen. Ye are up agin some dark forces in yon hoose. Ah wull send ye hame wi a book on the occult an spiritualism o' the Victorian times... ye can see whit Mrs. Briggs wiz up tae."

"Do you say something about a book?" Cat asked, looking on inquisitively, trying to figure out what was going on between the two of us.

Brighid turned back to the wall of books, sifted through several volumes, and pulled one down. "Haur, tak this. Nah charge. Bring it back tae me afore ye decide tae gang off and dae oniething daft. Thaur are some things ah can teach ye."

"Oh, cool. Thank you!" Cat said as she took the book.

"Yes, thank you so much," I responded.

"Nae problem." She turned and walked back towards the front where she grabbed a pen from the counter and scribbled something down. "Haur. Ye kin ring me at this nummer," she said as she handed me yet another card.

We followed her to the counter where the incense was still burning, and I noticed a variety of polished thick sticks lying on velvet-lined shelving on the wall behind the register. Cat didn't notice, as she was too busy thumbing through the book while making her way back towards the front door of the shop.

"What are these?" I asked, resisting the desire to stroke the smooth surface and hold one in my hand.

Brighid smiled slightly, as if somehow satisfied with a question that had been pestering her. "Yon are wands, my hen."

I laughed slightly and then asked, "Wands, as in witches?"

Brighid just smiled back, not even bothering to respond to my jest. "Gwen, ye hae tae come back tae see me," she said, laying her hand atop mine. "An if ye cannae get haur, ye need tae call me. Dinnae be skair. Ah dinnae want ye gaun back tae the hoose fenceless."

Briefly I saw an image of a room with candles being lit on every table and shelf, and as each one grew in brightness, shadows retreated into the corners. I had no idea what the image was supposed to represent.

"Okay," I answered with uncertainty, trying to shake off the images.

I noticed she was smiling at me. *"Da shealladh,"* she said, pronouncing the words daa halugh. "Ye hae the gift tae see." Then she reached out and brought me into a hug, as if I were a long lost daughter.

The sensation of heat radiating off of her body was off-putting at first. However, my entire body suddenly sighed in acceptance of her energy, like receiving a deep drink of water after a long walk in the desert. It was as if my body knew something about this strange woman that my mind didn't.

"Gwen, come on! We can just make the next bus!" Cat called out from the door, as she held it ajar.

I had no words to explain the connection I felt with Brighid, and could only just look at her quietly as I backed away, before turning towards the front door.

"Haste ye back!" she called out, waving good-bye. The Tibetan bell continued to ring out as Cat bounced against the glass door in impatience.

"Coming! Jeez, hold your horses," I complained as we made our way out of the shop and back into a world that made sense.

Chapter Eight
September Changes

Two weeks had passed since the beginning of school. One weekday afternoon, I sat at the dining room table with my blue Trapper Keeper open as I went through the colored folders in class order. Red was first, because it was Algebra. Red was the color of war in my mind, not love. It was war with a teacher that failed to explain math to me in a way that made sense. Letters equal numbers? It was so frustrating it made my head hurt. The '*Useful* Information: Multiplication Table' on the inside of the folder was not, nor were the Conversion Tables.

The heat of summer was finally wearing off, so the kitchen window was open to let in the fresh air. Every so often the wind would shift just right and a brisk breeze would pass through the window. In that moment I could taste, smell and feel the shift in the natural world.

I closed my eyes and inhaled deeply, feeling everything the wind had to share wash through me. The moments of sensing the seasons had been intensifying more and more the last couple years. Autumn was always the strongest, though.

At first it was an exhilarating high in anticipation of the inevitable changes to come, that was then dampened by a melancholy I could not understand. It could only be described as missing someone or someplace, combined with a longing for something that had yet to transpire.

Why did this always happen? What did it mean? I wondered, as I stared wistfully out the window.

I had, at least, managed to fall into a steady routine at school. I was no longer panicked about finding my classes in time, and no longer crippled with insecurity over every little thing.

The continual aggressive and hurtful behavior of Erin and her gang as they passed me by every morning was draining. I refused to allow her to bait me. My best defense was ignoring her and acting as if it didn't affect me. She had succeeded, though, at making my life miserable, and making me dread that part of the day. So eventually I found a new route to just avoid her altogether. Ironically, I saw Chris on this new path.

I was so surprised and happy the first time I saw him. I greeted him and turned with him as he walked by, putting my hand on his arm to get him to stop and talk to me. Immediately a vision began...

I saw Chris' mom and dad fighting, I saw a glimpse of his empty room where we used to listen to albums, play Battleship, eat Otter Pops, and set up incredible Hot Wheels jumps. I felt his sadness looking at the empty wall where his KISS poster used to hang. I saw our initials carved into the baseboard where the

63

record player used to be. I felt him missing the children we once were, but those happy memories were smothered in a cloud of confusion, anger, and resentment.

He fumbled a greeting back, surprised by the contact, then gently broke free of my hand, and said, "Sorry, but I gotta get to class." He continued on and didn't look back.

I had stood there, watching him walk away, flooded with his emotions, and shaken by the fact that I had just shared his memories.

After that, when we passed each other, he wouldn't make eye contact at all. No matter how I tried to rationalize it, I just couldn't. Something had changed. Was it his parents or being forced to do community service over the summer? Did he resent me?

I remembered the first time we'd talked on the phone, after I had some restriction lifted from being grounded, and he told me he didn't blame me for getting caught. He accepted my apology, and told me it was okay. We never discussed the kiss, but his tone at the time seemed friendly, and I still felt like we were as close as we'd ever been. That was until the last phone call, where it didn't seem okay anymore, and I never understood why.

While I stared at the contents of my folder, reflecting on these events, not really paying attention to my homework, I could faintly hear the television coming from the living room. My mother had it on to keep her company while she prepared dinner in the kitchen.

Our television was set inside a large wooden cabinet that sat on the floor centered on our living room wall. Above it hung a poorly painted landscape my mom bought. It held some sort of significance to her, family history or something, but I could never understand why dad agreed to let her hang it up in the house. It was depressing to look at, with its gray and brown tones depicting a cottage on a cliff overlooking a dreary coastal storm.

Everything about the living room was depressing. The drapes were always drawn in the afternoon because the sun would hit the horizon at an angle that bathed our house in a blinding glare. The tall lamp in the corner gave off barely any light through its beige lampshade. It stood next to our beige cushioned couch, which sat on a coffee-stained beige carpet. The wooden coffee table sat in front of the couch, which faced the television cabinet. The table had circular coffee cup stains despite my mother's attempts to get my dad to use weird tile coasters that had green and red mushrooms on them. This hideous design carried on into the kitchen where she had a matching tea set.

There was just no life in the room, and yet it was called the living room. Maybe it was called that because it is where the television was, and that was the only life to be found.

I absently heard the news broadcast come on, and as its words made their way to the forefront of my brain, I realized they were talking about the house. I immediately felt my pulse quicken and pushed away from the table to run into the living room and stare at the television. On the screen were images of the Victorian house with men in hardhats carrying around clipboards surveying the exterior.

"The Briggs' house, up on the summit at Douglas Park, is scheduled to finally resume renovations after five years of delay. Over the decades, there have been multiple attempts to restore the old Victorian, but each attempt has failed. Rumors began to spread that the house was cursed, due to the numerous accidents that befell members of construction crews. It got so bad that no one would take the job. As a result windows were left boarded up or broken, and we've been told that several rooms had been left untouched, or unfinished in clean-up attempts. The security guards at Douglas Park have done their best over the years to keep people out, and prevent any vandalism.

In the late 1800s "the old Victorian house", as it's become to be known, was once the main home on the Briggs' Family Farm. Their property encompassed most of the land in the surrounding area, including where the Douglas Zoo stands today. Recent events, specifically the discovery of a mass grave with children's bones, have brought more focus to the history of this area.

The farm was abandoned for unknown reasons decades ago, and the house left in a state of ruin. Douglas County took possession of the land and commissioned the construction of the zoo. By 1960 a mile-long circuit of track was laid for the zoo train. Over the last five years the remaining land has been developed into a park as well as walking trails for all the public to enjoy.

We'll be following this story as it develops to bring you updates on the progress of the renovations and skeletal excavations. The county hopes to restore the Victorian home to its once grand state and use it as a museum to share this area's rich history for generations to come."

I immediately ran into the kitchen to call Cat, but her phone line was busy. I tried again several times before dinner, and after, until eventually I gave up trying. I tried to call Andrea, but she was at cheerleading practice. I then tried Kevin, but his phone was also busy, which meant he was most likely to talking with Cat.

I finally gave up and went to my room to finish my homework. I wished I could have called Chris, but I didn't have his new number, and doubted he'd accept my call even if I had.

I started scrounging through the mess at the bottom of my book bag looking for a pencil sharpener when I came up with the flyer from the library. I'd totally forgotten about it. I straightened out the flyer it read:

Join Us
THE CIRCLE OF THE DARK STREAM
And the High Priestess
 BRIGHID
Each Lunar Cycle
DRAWING DOWN THE MOON
Contact Judith
For this month's location

What the heck is that supposed to mean? Wait, Brighid is a High Priestess? Who is the Circle of the Dark Stream? I asked myself.

I moved all the assorted things that had gathered at the bottom of my bag until I found the card she had given me. It was different than the store card Judy had handed us. This was a personal card, with a phone number. It reminded me that Cat had taken the book from the store. She had told me I could read it when she was done, and I was still waiting.

Lying down on the bed, I took a long look at my new ring. I found myself rubbing it a lot throughout the day when I was anxious. It soothed me, made me feel more in control, as if touching it created a protective bubble from the troubles of the world. Whether it was because Brighid told me it would work, or because it actually did, I felt better.

I took the ring off and placed it on my night stand, and did my best to quiet the noise in my head by singing quietly to myself. Slowly I could feel sleep wanting to take over...

I was back in the old Victorian house. I was alone in an enclosed space. I could barely make out the shape of a door, by the dim light coming from the keyhole of an old brass lock. I looked down at my hand, and realized I held one of the old skeleton keys from the puzzle box. I looked around hoping to see my friends, because I really didn't want to go through the door alone.

Where had everyone gone? *I wondered.*

Thud! Scraaaaape... Thud! Scraaaaape...

I jumped at the noise. It seemed to be coming from behind the door, but it also sounded like it was in the room with me because the sounds were exaggerated and echoed off the walls in an unnatural way.

***Thud!** Scraaaaape... **Thud!** Scraaaaape...*

I watched in a disconnected way as my hand, with the skeleton key held between my thumb and forefinger, put the key into the lock and turned it. I heard a click as the locking mechanism disengaged, and the door visibly loosened in the frame. My opposite hand came up of its own accord and wrapped around the aged porcelain door handle. I did not want to go in, yet I watched helplessly as my hand turned the knob and pushed at the door.

Thud! Scraaaaape... Thud! Scraaaaape...

The sound was louder now, and I knew it was coming from behind the door within the room.

"NO!" I heard myself scream. But the sound was only inside my head.

I watched helplessly as my hand pushed the door inward into the dim and dusty space, slowly revealing a pile of bricks stacked up in the corner against the far wall.

There was an outline of a person in the shadows, just to the left of the brick pile, hunched down near the floor, facing the wall.

Thud! *The shadowy figure placed something heavy down in front of it.*

*It then brought its shadowy right arm across, dragging something back horizontally. **Scraaaaape...***

As I crossed through the threshold, I felt like a spectator, a prisoner within my own body. Even as I willed myself to stop, to turn around and leave, my body defied me.

"STOP!" I yelled out loud at my dream form. I heard the word echo back at me from within the room in a distorted vocalization. Still, my body continued forward, and I couldn't tell if I was actually taking steps, or just floating.

The sound of my voice caused the shadowy figure to cease its repetitive movements, and turn towards me. There were no features, no distinctive characteristics, but its form was distinctly human.

Instantly, I was in the center of the room, and the figure slowly straightened up, its height not much more than my own. It stepped forward, still enshrouded in darkness. Each step brought the form into clearer view, revealing another layer of its identity.

70

It was covered in a black lace funeral veil that flowed over its head down to its ankles. As it inched closer, I could make out a female face between the knit of the lace. I saw her arm slowly come up with a spade in her hand, covered in a wet muddy sludge.

I tried to scream, but no sound escaped into the room.

She continued to come towards me with her arm raised. I turned my head away and brought up my arms to protect myself, trying to scream again.

This time I began to feel a strange sensation in my throat. My terrestrial self became more aware as I acknowledged the tingling sensation.

Suddenly she lurched towards me, clearing the distance between us in a flash. Her features distorted in a mask of rage!

I jolted awake, as if I had just jumped back into my body, swatting at a non-existent attacker. I heard the last gasp of a deeply garbled scream escape my throat, as I the sleep paralysis left me and I was able to sit up.

I tried to focus on the concept of breathing oxygen, and bringing my heart beat back to a natural rhythm.

What the hell was that?

Chapter Nine
Homecoming

Friday night, my dad dropped me off outside the Douglas College stadium. When I walked inside I was in awe at how large it was. We didn't have a stadium on our high school campus, only a P.E. field where the teams practiced. It was the first time I had to use my student I.D. for anything, and it felt so... official. High school was no longer this far off in the future; it was reality, and I was at a Homecoming football game.

I recognized some of the scrawny little boys I knew from junior high on the sidelines, decked out in their freshman football jerseys. They were supporting the varsity team, as they bash heads with our rivals out on the field. Most had grown a foot taller over the summer and replaced their baby fat with muscles. It was a bit surreal.

Walking along with the wave of other students, the smell of clove cigarettes and 'skunk' weed hung heavy in the air. Some kids were staggering around, smelling strongly of the vodka and orange juice hidden in their soda cups. I noted with surprise that these were the honor student/ teacher's pet/student body council types.

Looking down at the many rows of cement benches within the stadium I could see that the same trend from the quad at lunch was true in the stadium - the cliques sat together. It made sense, safety in numbers. I scanned the crowd looking for my group of misfits, and glanced again down at the football players standing on the sidelines. I am not sure why, but I was looking for Ryan and Jonathan.

I wondered how Andrea had handled seeing Jonathan at football practice all summer. I know it would have been hard for me seeing Ryan every day, after the cowardly way they had broken it off with us. But it seemed like forever ago at that point, even if he had been my first "love".

As I continued to scan the stands, I saw Mike and his friends standing in a large group. The taller guy, Russell, was looking straight at me as I started down the stairs. We made eye contact for a moment. I felt a strange little flutter, and immediately got self-conscious so I looked away. I continued to scan the crowd pretending to have a purpose, until my gaze settled on Erin sitting among her gaggle of girls who were all filled with extreme school spirit.

They looked like they had bought out the entire student store of its mascot-themed merchandise. Some of them had the number of a football player painted on their cheek in hopes that they would be dating the stud someday. They cheered loudly back at the actual cheerleaders on the field. It seemed a bit much, really trying too hard, probably because Erin didn't make the cut for the actual squad.

Looking elsewhere in the stadium, I was able to see Kevin's tall form standing over a group of girls. Kevin saw me and waved me over. Cat and the gang were all there. Cat had on a billowy pirate shirt with a large black belt worn loose around her hips, over black pants. When I came to sit down, I nodded at her with approval.

"Nice," I said, playing with the feathery earring just in one ear. She had a white handkerchief tied around her forehead holding back her bobbed dark hair.

I noticed a group of oddballs to our right: three boys wearing t-shirts from a high school we weren't even playing, shouting cheers that made absolutely no sense.

"We want a home run!"- *"Tackle the goalie!"*- *"Kick 'em in de fence!"*

I leaned over and whispered to Cat, "Do they even go to our school?"

"Yep. Blonde 'Flock of Seagulls' hair is Craig; dark hair and glasses is Drew; and, brown hair and denim jacket is Brian."

Craig overheard us talking about them, and leaned over, "So we are going to ditch this place and hit the Dairy Queen at half-time if you ladies want to join us." He winked, like he had been rehearsing the line all summer. His friends all laughed and patted him on the back. Maybe it was the first time he'd spoken to a girl.

I overheard Jennifer, who was sitting on the other side of Cat, whisper… *"Weirdos."* Liz and Kelly, sitting next to Jennifer started to snicker.

"Aren't we all, Jennifer?" I reminded her. Everyone nodded and giggled, because they knew it was true.

She was dressed up like her favorite band, the Stray Cats, and had a '50's throwback, Rockabilly look going on. Her brown hair was tied up in a ponytail with a blue handkerchief, an oversized white button-down work shirt with its sleeves rolled up hanging loose over jeans rolled up above her ankles with white socks and white sneakers. Liz, on the other hand, had her dark hair teased up with hairspray, wearing white powder make-up, tons of dark dramatic eyeliner, and dressed mostly in black. She had been listening to a lot of Siouxie and the Banshees.

Shopping at second hand stores had become the new thing, peppering every ensemble with some vintage flair. Kelly, a diehard Duran-Duran fan, wasn't as outspoken with her outfits. She wore a long classic trench coat with dozens of band pins all over the front. We were each very different from the other that way; our musical tastes, our fashions, and our hobbies. No one was quite sure how to classify us as far as cliques went, which made it even better.

Kevin nudged me with his elbow, and reached out his hand, "I'm gonna meet up with Chris soon, so can I get the backpack now?"

Kevin had approached me the day before, to tell me that Chris had asked him to ask me to bring his backpack to the game... yeah... ridiculous. Why couldn't he just ask me himself?

I hesitated letting the pack go. Silly, I know, but I felt it was all I had left of him. I implored Kevin, "Please ask him to talk to me."

"I'll ask," he responded, not making eye contact. "I know. It sucks, Gwen. It doesn't seem fair. He has been through a lot of shit though, and it's not just that. It's just... well, it's just that... it might be best to let it go."

"What do you mean, let IT go? We've been friends since we were little kids. He was my best friend... how do you just let that go?"

"Gwen, calm down. Come sit," Cat suggested as she put her hand on my arm, and nodded for Kevin to take the pack and go while he had the chance. I couldn't shake the feeling that there was something else going on.

"Hey, if it doesn't work out with that guy, you can come with us to Dairy Queen!" Craig yelled out.

Brian took off Drew's glasses and handed them to me saying, "You can keep these if you come with us." He bowed as he presented them to me. Drew jumped up on his back trying to grab them back. Brian kept them just an arm's length out of reach teasing him.

"Dudes! Get a life!" Jennifer yelled back. Liz and Kelly busted up, which encouraged the boys to continue doing stupid things to get attention. The weirdo magic worked, and the girls were completely entertained by their back and forth banter.

~~

Just minutes before half-time, Erin and her puppets came up the stairs to where we were all sitting. With her hands on her hips she addressed me, "What are you doing here, freak?"

I was taken aback for a second by her hatred and brazen behavior. "Doing great, thanks for asking," I responded sarcastically, ignoring her name calling, as usual. "So what do you mean by, 'what am I doing here'?"

"You heard me, psycho! You aren't welcome," Erin barked as she flipped her hair back, and looked at her cronies like she was going to give a signal to brawl.

"It *is* homecoming, remember?"

"You have a lot of nerve showing up," Erin countered back.

"I go to this school, and I have as much right to be here as you do!" I responded angrily. Looking at Jennifer, Cat, Liz and Kelly, I asked, "I *am* welcome at my own homecoming aren't I?"

"Yep, you sure are!" Cat responded standing up, making direct eye contact with Erin.

"The only ones not welcome here right now, are you and your goons," Kelly spat angrily.

"Oh, I am sooo sure!" she responded, completely insulted. Looking Kelly up and down she responded, "Nice shoes, by the way. Did you get those at K-mart?"

"Good come back, Erin," Jennifer commented flippantly. "Why? Was your mom working the register?"

I couldn't help myself and began to giggle.

"Gwen, you are such a bitch!" Erin spewed, returning her attention towards me.

"Awww! Coming from *you,* that's quite the compliment!" I mocked in a sticky- sweet voice.

"You better not be at the dance. That's all I have to say about that," she fumed, and then turned and stormed off. Her little spirit squad turned awkwardly and followed after her.

"Erin, what exactly is your problem?" I called out after her, not sure if I wanted to scream or laugh at the ridiculousness of her behavior.

Was it all because she got grounded for two weeks over the summer? She was certainly doing a good job of playing the victim, making it all my fault, and taking no responsibility for her own decisions.

Why tell people that I set out to scare her though, pretend to talk to ghosts, *and* to purposely get Chris in trouble? Why lie about that? I would never have wanted Chris to get in trouble, *and* risk losing life-long friendships.

"That's all I have to say about that!" Kelly mocked, then shook her head in disbelief.

"It's not too late for you guys!" Liz called out to the girls. "You can escape at any time from Erin's vortex of suck!"

"I think that went quite well," Jennifer said, watching them leave.

"I feel like that dance is calling my name now louder than ever. Don't you hear it?" I asked.

"I hear it!" Liz yelled, laughing gleefully.

"I hear my name too! I never felt more like dancing!" Kelly said.

"I seriously don't know what crawled up that girl's butt," Cat blurted, loud enough for everyone to hear. We all burst out laughing, especially the weirdo boys who had subtly scooted closer to us.

"I heard you mention a Chris, earlier. Would that be the Chris Larsen that she is going out with?" Drew asked. "What did you do to piss her off?"

"That's an interesting question," I responded, looking over at Cat in disbelief. She returned my shocked expression. It felt like a gut punch. My blood began to boil and I wanted to break things. I *knew* there had been more going on than what Kevin was telling me.

"That ice cream is sounding pretty good, right?" Cat stated, trying to divert my attention. She looked around at the rest of the group, "What do you say? We'll be back, before the end of the second half, for our ride."

"Let's go. I don't think I can take another minute of being here," I growled. "But nothing is going to stop me from going to the dance!"

"Hell, yeah!" Jennifer yelled, and the other girls all cheered.

"Oh, and I've got some weed," Craig chimed in, about to pull something out of his pants pocket. Brian and Drew looked at him with daggers in their eyes.

"Dude! You just don't say that out loud! Look around at where we are," Drew warned him.

"You will have to forgive him," Brian started, "We only let him out in public for special occasions."

Chapter Ten
High School Gym

When the game ended, I grabbed a ride to the dance with Cat and her older brother in his 1975 blue Oldsmobile *Starfire*. He had his friends get into the backseat, and I was forced to squeeze between them because Cat called 'shotgun'. The car, as usual, reeked of cigarettes, but at least the dirty carpeted flooring was free of empty beer cans.

As we drove, Erik, who sat to my right, slurred something about how he thought I had beautiful eyes... I think he said 'eyes'. He was so drunk he could hardly hold his head up straight, let alone focus on my eyes. Russell, behaving far better than his counterpart, sat to my left, and seemed to be sober.

Mike took every corner way too fast, each of us flopping from one side of the car to the other. Russell apologized each time his weight fell against me. Being stuck in the middle, I had no idea where to put my hands. I apologized each time I had to hold onto his knee to keep myself upright, until the car straightened out again.

I noticed in the reflection from the rear view mirror, Mike grinning on several occasions. It really seemed like he enjoyed making us uncomfortable and was doing it on purpose.

When we finally pulled into the parking lot of the high school gymnasium, I was relieved just to get out of the car. I felt a sense of dread course through me, however, when I noticed dozens of teens milling around out front. My first high school dance!

I checked my watch to see how long it was until my dad would be there to pick me up. Time was either going to fly by because I'd be having so much fun, or I'd be staring at the gym clock watching the minutes tick by, praying for the night to end.

Cat exited the car first, after we parked, and pulled the front seat forward. Erik didn't budge, so I was forced to crawl over the top of him. I was horrified to think my butt was practically in his face as I made my way out. Thankfully, I had on my black jeans instead of the mini skirt I was going to wear.

Cat and I began to walk away, when I heard Erik slur, as he was trying to exit out of the low back seat, "Hey... where you going?"

I turned to answer, but stopped when I saw Russell standing on the other side of the car watching us. He waved and smiled. I waved back, feeling slightly embarrassed by the mutual acknowledgment of each other's existence outside of the backseat. I turned back to see that the rest of our group was waiting for us at the front door, so Cat and I hurried our way across the parking lot.

Once we were up alongside everyone, I noticed someone was missing. "Is Kevin meeting us here?" I asked Cat.

"I thought so, but we don't need to wait," Cat responded. "He can find us inside."

"You ready to get your groove on?" Kelly asked.

"Totally!" Jennifer answered. Each person in the group nodded in varying degrees of confidence.

When we entered the gym it was warm from collective body heat. Our senses were accosted by a potpourri of teenage smells. I think the Brut Cologne was the most pungent smell to cut through. A small group of girls had gathered in the direct center of the gym, all facing each other, copying each other's rockabilly dance moves to "Rock this Town" by the Stray Cats. Everyone else hung back against the walls staring on in a mixture of fear and fascination. It was obvious that we freshman were the first to arrive.

Among the wall clingers were our new friends Brian, Drew and Craig. Liz and Kelly raised their hands and waved. The boys looked at each other in disbelief and then excitedly responded by racing over to join us.

I looked around the gym and noticed that Mike and his friends had not come in behind us. There might have been an unwritten code that the freshmen weren't aware of, about the proper time to show up to a dance. I also noted that the football players and cheerleaders weren't there either.

"Well, are we going to just stand here looking stupid, or are we going to show those skanks how to dance?" Liz asked.

"Are they actual skanks?" Craig asked in astonishment, suddenly intrigued.

"They're actually really nice," Drew responded in a matter of fact tone. "I have a couple of classes with them."

"Dude, she was just kidding," Brian said as he shook his head in embarrassment.

Liz walked over to Brian, grabbed his hand, and towed him out on to the floor next to the circle of girls. With a little prodding she got him somewhat moving to the beat of the music, but it looked more like he was having some sort of out of body experience. Liz kept coaching him along, forcing his arms to mirror hers. By the end of the song, we agreed that we could call what he accomplished a form of dancing, sort of.

In any case, his bravery emboldened Drew and Craig and they rushed out when the next song came on, "Once in a Lifetime" by Talking Heads. We ran up alongside them, and, as a group, started imitating the awkward dance from the video. The circle of girls also started dancing in the same way, and pretty soon we were of hive-mind, embodying David Byrne's dance style.

The next song, "What I like About You" by the Romantics, brought even more of the wall clingers to the floor. The more it filled up, the less self conscious we all became about how we were dancing. It was liberating.

Even as sweat drenched as my body was, I stopped noticing the heat, and could no longer distinguish one odor from another. A state of euphoria washed over me as one hit song after another came on.

Cheers would erupt over the older ones that were familiar to all of us, especially when the song, made famous from the movie *Animal House,* came on. Everyone immediately gathered, jumping up in the air to yell "Shout" and doing the twist. Then when it said "...*softer now*", we would mimic the scene from the movie, getting quieter with each verse, as we twisted down lower and lower to the floor, until some kids just flopped onto their backs and wiggled around. Then we'd twist our way back up and jump up and down again with our hands in the air.

After that explosion of energy, we took a break at the water fountain before rushing back out when "Kids in America" by Kim Wilde came on. I was singing along, swinging my arms side to side, and kicking my feet out, when I felt a push on my shoulder.

At first I thought I had accidently bumped into someone, so as I was still keeping time to the music I turned to apologize, only to come face to face with Erin.

I had forgotten, for a couple of blissful hours, all about her crazy drama at half-time. Her angry face brought it all back into focus, though, and I stopped dancing, completely exasperated. "What now?" I asked angrily.

"I thought I told you not to show up," she said loudly over the music.

I was so over it that before I could even stop myself, I stood my ground and wagged my middle finger in her face as I yelled, "Screeeew yoooou!"

Cat, dancing next to me, turned just in time to hear what I said, and her mouth dropped. Then she looked at Erin and started to laugh out loud. The look on Erin's face was priceless, and for one second I felt empowered. I said what I felt, no longer worried about confrontation or hurting her feelings.

The moment passed and she stepped forward and pushed me backwards, causing me to reach out to grab hold of her arm so I wouldn't fall.

In that brief moment of contact I was overcome with her memories...

She was back in the Victorian house with us, watching as Chris and I came out of the room under the stairs. I was blushing, and our hands were touching. Chris was looking happy with himself as he stepped aside to let Cat look into the room. I could feel this well of jealousy rising within Erin and a pain like a knife twisting in her gut as she watched Chris lean over and whisper in my ear.

Leading up to that day she had expected that she would be the one getting Chris' attention, and getting him to like her as much as she liked him. She saw how he noticed her in her tank top at the mall. She could tell he was into her, so she was confused. How could Chris be attracted to me? How could he kiss me? She was filled with hurt and jealousy. She was the one that Chris was supposed to kiss. All she wanted to do was hurt me...

I let go of her arm, having found steady footing, still trying to recover from having the vision, and the shock of realizing that someone that I had called a friend wanted to hurt me. My mind reeled from the insight of what was behind it all.

"Hey, that is not cool!" Cat yelled at her over the music.

"What the hell is wrong with you, Erin?" Kelly yelled.

I looked around to see that my dance crew had all stopped and had circled around me, staring her down. It was a great feeling, to know that others had my back.

Instead of fighting though, I responded in a way I don't think she could have anticipated. I stood up straight, took a deep breath, and found myself touching the Black Onyx stone of my ring. It settled my nerves, helped me focus past the anger, to say what I thought she needed to hear - something to cut through the pain that was driving her aggression.

"I'm sorry, Erin," I said slowly, emphasizing each word so she would hear me. I couldn't believe I was apologizing to my bully, and my friends seemed stunned as well.

The strategy worked, because she looked confused. I was sincere about the apology, which is probably what was so powerful about the moment. I didn't give her what she wanted, which was an excuse to escalate the situation. I felt her need to feed off the anger... and it was a sickening feeling.

"I'm truly sorry for what happened this summer, I didn't know how you felt," I continued, holding my arms out at my sides to show that I was not a threat. "You won though, didn't you? You got Chris, he's all yours."

She blinked twice, now even more confused. "Damn right, he's mine. So stop trying to get in between us!" she replied aggressively. I could tell she had absolutely no idea how I could have known what she was thinking, and she was wrestling with a lot of emotions.

"I'm not trying to. You've succeeded at making it so we aren't even friends anymore," I said sadly. "You have nothing to worry about. You won. Just let whatever *this is...* go."

She looked around at the crowd who had stopped dancing, all looking at her. She clearly was embarrassed, and could not collect herself. So she turned around, pushed her way past the people who were standing around her and stomped off. I watched as she made her way across the gym and approached Chris just as he walked in. He reached out as she dramatically threw herself into his arms, acting like the victim again.

Conveniently, he had missed his girlfriend push me and try to start a fight. I made eye contact with him, and for the first time in weeks, felt a cold steeliness build up inside me. I shook my head at him in disappointment, completely letting go of months of my own pain and confusion surrounding what might have been. He looked away before I could tell if anything had registered or not.

As I turned back to our little group to try to find that dance euphoria zone again, I caught sight of Andrea across the gym, watching the drama unfold. She waved and then flipped her hand over, palms up, miming, *"What the hell was that?"*

I shrugged and waved back trying to get her to read my lips as I made the universal thumb and pinky gesture meaning, *"I'll call you later"*.

Her attention shifted though when a guy walked up beside her and put his arm around her waist. It was my ex, Ryan.

He was chatting with Jonathan, and Jacob, Erin's old boyfriend. Andrea glanced nervously back at me just as Ryan leaned over to kiss her. She looked mortified to know I was watching, but she still returned the kiss.

Wow, the hits just keep coming, I thought to myself. *What's one more dagger to the heart, right?*

Chapter Eleven
First Dance

The fast tempo of "Good-bye, Good-bye" by Oingo Boingo came on. It couldn't have been a more perfect song to help drive away my angst and help me purge the 'old love' demons from my heart.

I closed my eyes, pushed my body hard to the pace of the song as the sweat flowed freely. I let the whole world outside of that song fall away.

When the tune ended, it fluidly morphed into the beginning of "Should I Stay or Should I Go" by the Clash, which helped keep the meter revved.

Unfortunately the momentum slowed a bit when "Heat of the Moment" by Asia came on, so we all took the opportunity to cool down and make our way through the crowd to an open set of doors looking out on the back parking lot. "Jack and Diane" by John Cougar played after that, and then it really slowed down for "Up Where we Belong" from the movie *Officer and a Gentleman*.

Most of the dance floor had emptied at that point, except for the couples. To be honest, I didn't want to see who the couples were, so I just stared out into the night sky, trying to find the stars above yellow street lights, and breathed in the autumn air.

Behind me, I heard Mike and his friends' voices from across the gym. Erik was making a scene, heckling the couples dancing. I turned towards them and saw that a whole new group had filtered in; all the seniors making a late appearance after partying somewhere else.

"Where has your brother been this whole time?" I asked Cat.

"God, I don't want to know. But at least he's here now so I can get a ride back home with him," Cat answered.

"Well, my dad can always drop you off if all else fails," I offered, as I saw Mike catch sight of us and make his way over.

"What's happening?" Mike asked as he walked up beside Cat, and nudged her. His friends hung back behind him, checking out the crowd.

"Are you going to be able to drive me home?" Cat asked, looking at Mike suspiciously, and sniffing at the air. I noticed it then too, the definite smell of weed.

"What? Stop that. I'm fine," Mike swatted her away from sniffing at him.

"Hi guys!" Kevin interjected, as he strolled up. "Sorry I'm late."

"Kevin!" Cat and I cheered in unison. "What took you so long?" She asked as she ran up to hug him. It caught him off guard, but then he relaxed and kept his arms around her. She was beaming from ear to ear, which was great to see. I then became aware of an ugly jealous twist in my heart, and fought to keep away any sad emotions from intruding.

"Hey, dude! Get your dirty hands off my sister!" Mike jested, and punched him playfully on the shoulder.

"Mike, cut it out!" Cat protested pushing him away.

"You gonna let this pipsqueak fight your battles for you?" he laughed, as he swatted his sister away like she was a fly.

"She knows where to kick when it matters," Kevin laughed watching the two siblings go at it.

Another slow song started in the background. I groaned out loud, and turned my back away from the dance floor, breathing in the autumn night. I checked my watch, and told myself, *it's almost over! I can make it! Just keep breathing.*

I was startled by a tap on my shoulder and immediately thought *Please no, not Erin again.*

I didn't turn around right away. I took in a deep breath instead, trying to find a calm center in the storm of emotions that were threatening to rise.

"Um, Gwen? Hey," an unfamiliar voice said, followed by another tap on my shoulder. "Hi."

I turned around then. "Oh... hi," I replied, recognizing Russell's cute face.

"You want to dance?" he asked awkwardly, as he held out his hand. Erik made some slurred inappropriate comment, while Mike heckled the gesture. I heard Cat smack Mike and tell him to shut up.

"Yes," I found myself answering without hesitation. I hadn't noticed what song was playing until I found myself being led out into the small crowd of couples: "Save a Prayer" by Duran Duran.

I was hyperaware of how his hand felt in mine, his skin soft and his grasp firm. Although he led with confidence, he was gentle, and kept looking back at me to see that I was okay following him through the crowd.

He stopped when he found a place in the middle of everyone that was conveniently out of the view of his friends standing against the wall. He turned towards me and put one hand on my waist. I put my arms up on his shoulders and realized just how tall he was. His arms were long enough that he didn't have to stoop to place his arms at my waist, but I definitely felt that I had to stretch.

My whole body felt awkward as if I suddenly forgot how to exist in my own skin. I hated that feeling. I didn't want to look around the room and accidently see Erin and Chris, or Andrea and Ryan… I just wanted to hide.

"So, I heard there was some drama," he said leaning over towards my ear so I could hear him.

"Wow! Rumors spread fast," I responded, trying to hide my embarrassment.

"Everything is okay now, though?"

"Yeah, I guess. She just ruined what could have been a perfectly good night."

"Well… the night isn't over yet," he whispered loudly in my ear before he pulled his face back, and I took a really good look at him for the first time.

92

Although the lights were dim, I could make out that he had hazel colored eyes, more green than brown, as they gazed down at me from underneath a mid-length mop of slightly wavy reddish-brown hair. Maybe, on a subconscious level, I'd noted their color from sitting next to him in the car. He also had some freckles across his nose, had a little stubble along his jaw line, and I could make out a couple nicks on his neck from shaving.

Sure I had noticed he was "cute" before, but he was actually *really* attractive. He didn't smell of the cheap drug store cologne that the other boys wore, it was much better than that - something kind of exotic combined with a smell uniquely his own.

I felt my body start to relax, and my defenses started to lower. I realized then that I had a death grip on his shoulders before. "I am so sorry. I didn't realize I was squeezing so tight."

"It's okay. Payback for smashing you in the car," he smiled and then maneuvered his hand a little bit further back along my hip to slyly inch me closer to him.

Something about him made me feel completely at ease. "I think we should blame Mike for that," I replied, smiling back. I continued to take in his face, as we swayed back and forth in each other's arms. I am not sure how much time passed before I realized he was staring back at me in the same way, just taking in my features, trying to see the person behind the eyes.

"Maybe I should thank Mike. It wasn't so bad," he grinned, a hint of mischief in his eyes.

An emotion washed over me, something completely foreign. The best I could describe it was that I was exactly where I was supposed to be. Unlike when I touched Erin, I wasn't seeing Russell's memories, but I realized I was experiencing his emotions... was it, contentment?

What the hell is going on with me tonight? I wondered. *First it was Erin. I touched her and then I felt her emotions as well as saw in my mind what she remembered. How is it even possible? It did happen though, and she confirmed it, without realizing it, that I basically had read her thoughts. The same thing had happened with Chris. Is that what is going on with Russell? Does he actually feel this happy just to be dancing with me?*

I was brought back to the moment when I felt his hand slide up my back a little, while the other hand left my waist and also came around to my back. This movement brought me in even closer. We had found a nice rhythm together just as the song was ending, but the DJ smoothly transitioned the song into an arpeggio from a synthesizer indicating the beginning of the next song.

"Last chance to kiss your sweetie before the lights come on, so make it count," the DJ crooned in a smooth velvety voice.

"Well that isn't awkward or anything," Russell remarked, chuckling nervously. "Care for another dance?" he asked, even though we were still in each other's arms, swaying.

"Sure," I answered, feeling the blush on my face. The sultry tones of Alison Moyet's voice from Yaz washed over the room, singing "Only You".

Russell and I continued to move back and forth in unison, shifting our weight hip to hip. When we turned in a circle, I saw Cat and Kevin dancing not too far away, with their lips locked.

Just then I felt an intense tingle throughout my body as I felt his fingers lightly stroke down my lower spine. He continued to look into my eyes, and said, "Erik was right, you do have very pretty green eyes."

"He was drunk," I replied quietly, as I blushed and turned away. He must have noticed my eyes from earlier as well.

"Maybe so... but he was still right!" he whispered, his lips right next to my ear. Then he pulled his head back to look me in the eyes again.

The intensity of the moment increased as I became keenly aware that I was locked into emotions coming off of him, and I could not tell where my feelings ended and his began. Swaying together, the music enveloped us in a cocoon, and it was like we were standing there alone. The last time I felt that intense a connection with anyone was when I got lost in the ghosts' memories - a sort of merging of the souls.

I felt his body shift as he lowered his head towards mine, and knew with every cell in my body what he wanted. I was fighting back against the waves of images of him touching me, breathing on me, whispering to me… it was making me feel faint.

He leaned in towards my lips, and it took every ounce of will power to turn my head away at the last second. I felt his lips graze my cheek. "I don't even know you," I whispered as I felt myself nuzzle my cheek against his lips. I breathed in his delicious scent. I felt myself almost give in and turn towards him.

"I'd like to change that," he whispered into my skin.

He pulled his head up, and only then did I turn to look at him. He could not hide the disappointment that his kiss went unrequited, but he still smiled and I felt the genuine warmth behind it.

I smiled back as warmly. "I think I would like that too."

We continued to sway in time to the music just looking into each other's eyes and not saying a word. Alison Moyet finished singing, as the arpeggio of the synthesizer repeated on for several more bars, fading out.

CLICK! Then the gym lights came up.

There were groans of disappointment, and people shielding their eyes from the onslaught of light, like vampires. Suddenly vulnerable and exposed, everyone started to scurry for the exits.

Chapter Twelve
In Confidence

When I got up Saturday morning, my first instinct was to call Cat. We hadn't had time to talk when leaving the gym. I basically had to rush out because I knew my father was waiting out front. He ended up being very annoyed, after having to sit in the car ten minutes longer than he'd expected to.

I thought better of calling before 10 a.m., and decided to wait until it was closer to noon. I figured, by then, she would have eaten a huge Saturday morning breakfast and had time to be thoroughly alert for a conversation.

Turns out she got up a lot sooner than I expected, and called me first.

"So, um, you and *Russell*?" she implied more than questioned. "What's up with that?"

"It was just a dance," I deflected glad she couldn't see how much I was blushing. "Hey, listen I'm glad you called, I wanted to talk to you about something."

"No, no, no. Don't change the subject. It looked like the two of you were *also* getting up close and personal."

"He tried to, yeah. But no," I replied in a neutral tone, as if it were no big deal. The truth was that it was all that I'd been thinking about.

"He tried to? You mean you didn't kiss him back? What's the deal?"

"Cat! I don't even know him! Listen, what I wanted to talk to you about…"

"Yes… but… there was *clearly* some serious chemistry happening between the two of you," she continued on, talking over me.

"Ugh! Okay," I resigned, sighing heavily, "Yes! There *really* was."

"I knew it! So why didn't you kiss him? The music and the lighting… it was perfect!"

"It was, wasn't it?" I sighed longingly, regretful that I let the moment pass me by. "I think I was overwhelmed by everything that had happened that night. I was confused."

"What was there to be confused about? He's into you.

"But he's a senior, and hot. He could have anyone, why me?"

"Why not *you*? Have you seen you lately?"

"Well, okay, and… maybe it was because I was still trying to process what happened with Erin," I admitted.

"Erin! Oooh I just wanted to *punch* her in the face," Cat grumbled.

"Okay, now can I tell you something, and you promise you won't think I'm crazy?"

She chuckled as she answered, "Well I already think you're crazy, so shoot!"

"Stop it," I pleaded. "It's not funny. Seriously, something weird has been happening."

"Okay, seriously," she responded, sounding more earnest. "You've got my attention."

"You know that thing you have with your dad, how the two of you can communicate?"

"Of course," she responded.

"And remember the visions I had when we were back at the house?"

"Yes…"

"At first I thought it was just something to do with the ghosts or the haunted objects from the house. But ever since school started," I continued, "I've been having those sorts of things happen more and more. *This* time it's with real people."

"What do you mean with real people?"

"I mean, I've seen Erin's and Chris' memories just by touching them. I also had a *really* strong déjà vu when we went to Shanachie, and *then* had a vision when I touched Brighid. She even seemed to realize it, and told me, 'I had the gift to see'."

"The gift to see? Like, to see into people's minds? As in E.S.P.?"

"I think so… and when I was dancing with Russell," I started.

"Did you read his mind also?" she interjected.

"No, but I *felt* his emotions. Or at least I think I did. And, oh my god, it was *so* intense. Like I said, it was really overwhelming."

"And this has been going on for weeks, and you're *only* just telling me now?" Cat scolded, and then asked, "Wait! Have you been able to do it on *purpose*?"

"Uhh, I hadn't thought about that," I answered, pausing as I reflected back trying to remember. "So far... no, it just sort of *happens*. Then I'm left thinking I'm going crazy."

"I don't think you're going crazy, but I do think it's pretty awesome!" she exclaimed. "Let me know when you can start to predict the future though, I have a few things I'd like to know!"

Laughing I responded, "me too."

Chapter Thirteen
Manic Monday

The following Monday, waiting for the first bell before school, our group gathered around what had become our lunch table in the inner quad. Kevin walked up behind Cat, and leaned down to kiss her head.

"Aww! Kev, who knew you were such a romantic?" I teased.

"Well, I knew," Cat replied, and leaned in to his embrace.

"You guys are too cute," Jennifer cooed.

"Ew, gross," Liz teased.

"Hey, I saw you slow dancing with that dude. What's up with that?" Kevin asked in a protective tone like the brother I never had.

"I don't know. What IS up with that?" I laughed, feeling the heat of a blush rise to my face. "I guess you'll have to do some investigating to let me know if he's a nice guy."

"He better be, or I'll have to do some very bad things to his pretty face," he said as he punched his fist in an overdramatic way. It looked so unnatural and awkward that we all laughed.

"You'll have to take a turn, because if he isn't nice to her, I get to be the first one to kick him in the nuts," Cat stated as she attempted some sort of karate kick.

"Nice to know you two have my back," I replied, rolling my eyes, "I love you too!" I leaned across the bench to hug them both, making Kevin squirm to get out of the way.

"Is someone giving away free hugs this morning?" Craig shouted out from across the quad, as he, Drew, and Brian closed in. They tried to come around to our side of the table to get in on the action, but Kevin blocked their way.

"Hey, these are MY women," Kevin said, as he thumped his puffed-up chest.

"Ugh, me Jane," Cat quipped, as everyone joined in the joviality at the table. Cat stopped laughing suddenly when something caught her attention. "Ohhhh... Gwen," she elbowed me, and pointed toward the lockers, "there *he* is."

"Cat, don't point," I said as I hid behind her and turned away, completely embarrassed. "Did he see you?"

"He's coming over," Cat whispered, giggling, clearly enjoying my torment. I sat up, trying to compose myself, and act completely normal.

"Hi, Cat. Hi, Gwen," Russell greeted as he meandered up to the group.

"Oh, hi," I replied, trying to act casual. Inside I felt like I was going to pass out from how fast my heart was racing.

"Hi," Cat responded. "Russell, these are our friends. This is Kevin. These three are Craig, Drew, and Brian.

Those girls over there pretending to not know us are Jennifer, Liz, and Kelly."

"Hey guys," he said, tossing his head towards the group with a nod. "Um, hey... So, Gwen, can I talk to you for a second?" he asked. "Over there." He pointed towards the lockers out of earshot from the group.

"Sure. Can you watch my stuff, Cat? I'll be right back." I got up, and walked behind Russell towards the lockers. He led me to the back of the far right row, and then turned towards me, clearly nervous.

"You ran off so quickly after the dance, we didn't get a chance to talk or anything," he started. It was clear he was struggling with small talk, because there was something bigger on his mind.

"Yeah, I know. My dad was waiting out front," I replied lamely.

"Okay, well, I am going to just blurt this out before I lose my nerve. I have been working on it all weekend," he started. "Okay, so, um, here goes... I haven't been able to stop thinking about you!" He stopped, and just stood there looking vulnerable. His cool façade was suddenly down, and there was a less secure young man on display trying to speak his heart.

"I really like you, and want the chance for us to get to know each other better. I'd like there to be another dance like that... I mean, another moment like that... with you." He stopped again, and waited, looking at me to say something in response.

103

"Oh... wow," is all that came out. I had not expected that. I hadn't been able to stop thinking about him all weekend either. I fumbled for words. "Um, yes, me too. All the things you just said," I responded, sounding completely stupid. The balls of energy building up inside of me were about to burst out like a million exploding suns.

"Awesome! Good!" he said clearly relieved, a wide smile on his face. It was as if a huge weight had been lifted from his shoulders. He was just about to say more, when the bell rang.

"Um, okay then..." he whispered to himself awkwardly, clapping his hands together as if he had succeeded at some monumental task.

"Okay," I responded, unsure what else to do or say. Then I remembered something. "Oh my god, I have to get my stuff from Cat!" I turned to run the other direction, when I stopped, and asked, "So how will we get in touch with each other?"

"I'll find you," he said, encouraging me to hurry on. "Go, go. Don't worry."

I ran from the lockers across the quad to the table where Cat was waiting impatiently. Her face changed when she saw my face glowing.

"What just happened?" she asked, as we ran together down the hallway to first period.

"I think Russell just sort of asked me out," I responded gleefully as I turned in to my class and Cat continued to hurry down the hall to hers. I made it inside just before the tardy bell went off.

∾

After third period I went by my locker and discovered a note had been wedged inside the slot. I pulled it out once I had the door open. Inside the note were a few scribbled lines in nearly illegible handwriting. I was able to make out a phone number, followed by a name, Russell.

How did he know which locker was mine? I wondered, smiling, and looked around to see if anyone was watching. Then I tucked the note into my book bag.

I made my way back across the inner quad to go to my fourth period class, the last class before the freshman lunch period. I heard my name, and turned to see Russell running across the quad towards me, waving for me to stop.

"Hello," he said, as he came to a stop out of breath. "This is my lunch by the way. Did you get my note?"

"Yes," I said, feeling my face flush, and hating that it always did that. He seemed to like it though, because he was grinning. "I guess that means that you would like me to call you?"

"Definitely," he said as he walked up along side of me. "Can I walk you to class?" He gestured towards the doors leading into the hallway of the building.

"Sure," I replied, trying to sound casual about it, when inside I was feeling all those pesky butterflies again. My hands were full of books, so he opened the building's doors for me.

Is this guy for real? I asked myself. We walked side by side as I navigated us through the crowd towards my classroom.

"Okay, well this is my class," I said, standing awkwardly in front of the closed classroom door. He opened this door for me also. As I walked into the room I realized that the students inside were staring, whispering and giggling.

"Call me later, okay?" he said smiling, which caused more murmurings throughout the classroom.

"Okay, I will. Bye," I smiled back, and headed to my seat.

Let them whisper, I thought to myself. I was feeling too giddy to care what anyone said. I stared up at the round white clock above the chalkboard at the front of the room - it was only 10:45 a.m. It was going to be a long day.

Chapter Fourteen
Coincidences

When Cat and I were on the phone that evening she mentioned, "I finished the book Brighid loaned us. I was going to tell you at lunch, but I forgot."

"That's okay. When can I get it from you?" I asked.

"I put it in your bag."

"You did?" I asked laughing. "I'm totally surprised I didn't notice. I guess it's already so heavy. Did you learn anything useful?"

"No. It was just as I suspected from seeing the other books that were up in the attic - she was definitely trying to contact someone who died," she stated. "Did you know that séances, or Ouija board parties, only feed the unhappy spirits and make them more active?"

"No, I didn't know that. I guess I'll have to read the book tonight and get caught up."

"So, did you call him yet?" she asked impatiently.

"Not yet," I answered in exasperation. "Am I crazy? Can he really be that sweet?"

"Well, he's not a creep like Erik, I know that much. He's the quiet one of the three," she responded.

"I haven't been able to stop thinking about him since the dance," I said as I twirled the extension cord through my fingers as usual. In my comfortable sweatpants and white t-shirt I lay on my back with my feet up on the bed, staring at the ceiling.

"Well, *are* you going to call him at some point?" she asked impatiently.

"Yes! I called you first, because I was nervous," I responded. "I'm having a hard time processing everything that's been happening," I explained, feeling like I was in some crazy hormone-fueled tornado. "First I find out that Chris and Erin are dating. Then Erin tries to start a fight. Then I see Ryan kiss Andrea."

"Yeah," she teased, "and *then* you have this cute senior suddenly trying to make the moves on you during a slow dance, and he wants to, you know, 'get to know you better'."

"Okay, okay! I get it. I guess I should just get this over with and see what happens, right?"

"Right. Just hang up right now with me and dial, before you chicken out," Cat insisted. Then the line went dead. I stared at the phone for a second, realizing that she just hung up on me, and wasn't going to let me get out of calling him.

I ran back down the hall from my room bringing up the loose extension cord as I went along. I hung the receiver up, and looked at the note in my hand, memorizing the number. I was startled when the phone rang.

"Hello?" I asked.

"Is Gwen there?" A polite male voice asked.

"This is her," I replied.

"Hi, it's Russell."

"Oh! Hi!" I replied enthusiastically, grinning from ear to ear.

"I got your number from Mike. I hope you don't mind me calling."

"No, it's fine! I was going to call you just now, I swear! You just beat me to it," I laughed nervously. I took the phone and headed back down the hall to my room again, stretching out the cord to fit under my door, and then shut myself in to talk privately.

"So how did the rest of the day go? Are your classes easy?" he asked casually.

"Well, I like my Art and English classes. I really don't like my first period Algebra class. I feel like it shouldn't be so confusing, and the teacher is awful."

"I can help you with math. Algebra isn't so hard if you learn the tricks," he boasted.

"Thank you, I might take you up on that. How was the rest of your day?" I had found my usual position on the floor, and elevated my feet up onto my bed as I stared at the ceiling.

"Boring and long. I was very distracted."

"Why is that?" I asked, even though I knew our distractions were related.

"Oh, I don't know, just looking forward to a phone call with a certain someone," he said coyly.

"Okay, so besides talking on the phone with strange girls, what do you usually do after school?" I asked.

"I don't have a lot going on after school, except tons of homework. You think you have a lot of work, just wait until you're a senior. I also work some Saturdays for my mom's shop downtown. What about you?"

"I don't have a job or anything, just school. What kind of shop does your mom have?"

"She sells specialty books, candles and other odds and ends from around the world."

"Oh, that sounds like a neat store. Maybe I'll go check it out sometime. What's it called?"

"Shanachie," he said. "It's a word from Scotland which means a bearer of old lore...like a story teller."

"I know that place!" I announced in shock sitting up. "Your mother is Brighid?"

"Yes," he answered just as shocked. "How did you know?"

"Cat and I went there a couple weekends ago! We were looking for some history about... a place we're research-ing," I mentioned, treading cautiously. "It was really difficult to understand her, but I loved her accent!"

"You'd think after being here for over twenty years it wouldn't be so bad, but believe it or not, it's nothing in comparison to when she gets around the family."

"So are *you* from Scotland?"

"No... just my mom. My older sisters and I were born here in the States."

"How many sisters do you have?" I asked.

"Three of them... the oldest is Ciara (he pronounced it Keer-ah), it means 'the dark one', because she has dark hair and eyes. The middle one is Aileen, it means 'rays of sunshine', because her hair was blonde, and the younger one is Roisen (he pronounced it Ro-sheen), which means 'rose'. Can you guess why she was named that?"

"Well, I've met your mother... does she have the same red hair?"

"Exactly!"

"That is a lot of girls in one house. Do you ever get a turn in the bathroom?" I asked.

"There are enough bathrooms, so occasionally I get a turn," he laughed.

"Does the name Russell mean anything?"

"Yes, it means the 'red-haired one'. I had my mom's red hair when I was born. Did you know that *your* name also has a meaning?" he asked.

"I hardly think Gwen has any significance," I scoffed.

"Gwen is short for Gwenevere, isn't it?"

"Yes... how did you know that?"

"My dad is a Literature Professor... you share the same name as King Author's wife."

"But how did you know Gwen was short for Gwenevere?"

"Just a hunch. The name is Welsh... it means 'the fair one'."

"Wow. I guess that makes sense, though. My father's parents are from Wales – our last name is Evans," I responded. "Do you know what Iona means?"

111

"That's your middle name, I assume," he said.

"Yes… apparently a name from my mother's side. But she doesn't tell me much about her family."

"That's a pretty powerful name. My mother would find it very interesting."

"Oh, speaking of your mom, I got this flyer from the librarian before we went to the shop. It says that your mom is the High Priestess of a group called The Circle of the Dark Stream," I said, as I heard him gasp. "What is that about?"

"You got an invitation?"

"It's a flyer, I thought it was like a public get together or something for weird librarians," I said, laughing at the memory of Judith, her strange fashion choices and behavior.

"No, it was an invitation for a very private ritual," he said, pausing for a second, "I'm actually surprised she gave that to you."

"You know Judith?"

"She's my mother's cousin, so I guess that makes her my second cousin, or something."

"So… is this some sort of witches' coven?" I asked half joking. "I mean, all that stuff in the back of the store…" I trailed off, leaving him an opening to fill in the blanks for me.

"She let you back there?" he asked, sounding even more shocked than before.

"Yes, she loaned us a book she wanted us to read. And she gave me a ring!" I answered, looking down at it, running my finger across the dark smooth surface of the stone. It never seemed to get warm no matter how long I touched it.

He was quiet for a long time, as if he were deep in thought. "So, Iona," he began, seemingly changing the subject, "is an island off of Scotland."

"An island?"

"It is said to be a destination for spiritual journeys, in relation to a goddess."

"Wow, and here I thought it was just a stupid name that I heard only when I'm in trouble," I replied. "So, I wonder if that means that my mother's family is from Scotland as well."

"You don't know anything about your mother's side? Nothing?" he asked in astonishment.

"No," I answered, saddened by how very little I knew of our family history. It never seemed important before. "So what sort of goddess?"

"Oh okay, changing the subject I see," he teased, perhaps realizing I was uncomfortable. "Well, she is considered, by some, to be a triple deity. United as one being with her two sisters; a weaving together of all their powerful energies. She's the goddess of poets, a woman of wisdom, and the daughter of the chief of gods, The Dagda. She's associated with healing, midwifery, herbalism, and can offer protection. Her name is Brighid, which means 'the exalted one'; the ancient mother of Scotland."

"No way!" I exclaimed, and then I looked down at my ring and remembered the mention about protection.

"Way!" he responded, laughing.

"So Iona is the island that worshipers of the goddess Brighid would go to?"

"Pretty much," he responded. "I was curious, did my mom know about the flyer when you met her?"

"I didn't mention it, because I hadn't read what it said yet, so, no," I answered.

"But she wants you to come back to see her?"

"She wanted to give me some advice about something I'm dealing with..." I trailed off, feeling overly cautious about sharing the strange things that had been happening to me over the last few months. Hearing the nasty names being flung at me in the halls echoed in my head. The last thing I wanted was Russell to think those things too.

"Does the phrase *daa halugh* mean anything to you?" I said trying to sound out the word the way I heard her say it.

"It's Gaelic for "two sights". It means that someone has the ability to see the ordinary world and the spirit world. Why?"

"It's nothing," I replied off-handedly, as if it were of no importance.

"Hmmm? Okay then, if you don't want to tell me, I won't pry. But I do have *one* question you have to answer."

"And what is that?"

"What are you doing this weekend?"

"Hmmm, let me check my social calendar," I teased. "Looks like I am all booked up with *tons* of fun stuff!" I knew where this was headed, but found it deliciously satisfying to play the game.

"Oh, that *is* too bad," he replied sadly, "I guess another time then..."

"No! Wait, I was just kidding!" I blurted out, thinking he was going to hang up. I heard him snicker on the other end. "Ohhhh! You're good! You had me there," I said.

"I have sisters, remember?" he asked. "I know how you girls think. By the way, you didn't answer my question."

"What was the question?" I teased. "I don't remember a question."

"Damn. You are killing me... okay... Gwen, would you like to go out with me?"

"*This* weekend..." I asked, clarifying the question. I had a mischievous smirk on my face that I am glad he couldn't see, but I am sure he heard it in my voice.

"Well, yes and no," he sighed. "I want to know if you would go out... with me?" He emphasized the last two words in such a way that I knew that it was much more than a request for just one date.

"Oh!" I finally managed to respond.

"Oh?" he questioned. "Am I rushing things too much? Sorry, it just doesn't feel like that for me. I've liked you for such a long time!"

I was totally surprised by this admission. "You don't have to be sorry, I just had no idea," I responded.

How long has that been? I wondered. Then I thought back to the moment he caught my eye when I entered the stadium - how flustered it made me feel. I remembered the moment his delicious scent overwhelmed me as we danced, and how magical it felt when his lips brushed against my cheek.

"Yes," I answered.

"Really? You aren't messing with me again?" he asked, a bit impatiently yet hopeful.

"Yes," I said a bit louder, but only loud enough for just him to hear.

"Cool. You said yes," he whispered, more to himself than to me.

"I did." I sat there quietly, letting the reality wash over me. I just became Russell's girlfriend.

"Will you meet me before school tomorrow, by the lockers, so I can walk you to class?"

"Of course," I said. "Oh, hold on…" I heard my name being called from across the house. "WHAT?" I yelled.

"Is that your mom?" he asked, laughing at my outburst.

"Yes, I really should go," I said as I got up from the floor and started to make my way out of the bedroom. "Sorry if I yelled in your ear. I guess I'll see you tomorrow?"

"Definitely," he said. I could tell he was hesitant to hang up.

I made my way into the kitchen and stood there. "Okay, I need to hang up now," I said, unwilling to be the first to disengage. "Bye."

"Bye," he responded after a pause, and then the line went dead. I was so disappointed that he was no longer there, while at the same time giddy with the thought of him. I didn't know what to do with myself. Then I remembered that Cat had stuck the book in my bag for me to read.

"Gwen, are you off the phone now?"

"Yes!"

"Okay, remember to empty the dishwasher."

"Mom, I need to do something first…"

"No, dishes first then the something else…"

"Dude!"

"Don't 'dude' me… dishes!"

Chapter Fifteen
Tabitha Briggs

Once back in my room, I found the book tucked in my bag between two well-doodled paper covered text books. I read the title as I lifted it towards me, *Startling Facts in Modern Spiritualism* by N.B. Wolfe, 1883.

As I skimmed through the pages, not really knowing what I was looking for, I came to understand that people in the Victorian era were attracted to the paranormal and occult, and the idea of mesmerism, clairvoyance, reading minds, and Spiritualism. This was a religious movement that rebelled against traditional religious authority, and emphasized individualism. It was the sole religion of its time that saw women as equals. They believed that the spirits of the dead existed, and that the spirit world was not a static place, but a place where spirits continued to evolve and even had an inclination to communicate with the living.

A formal communication session with the spirits was called a séance. These sessions were led by people with clairvoyance, a medium, who could receive information about the afterlife from the spirits themselves or through a spirit guide – a specific spirit contacted who was relied upon for spiritual guidance.

Oh, like Cat and her father, I thought.

While I continued reading, I saw a flash of the mother, Tabitha, holding the very same book. For a second, her sadness washed over me.

Brighid had said I'd see what Tabitha was up to. Is this what she meant?

I was all but consumed in a black cloud of grief. I felt as though I was suffocating in her darkness when her memories began to flood my mind…

In her grief she'd left the care of the orphans to the maid and kitchen help, including the first child, Jane Elizabeth, who had become a disruptive nuisance.

She'd left the property and its inhabitants in the care of the Farm Supervisors; she had no interest in managing over it like her husband had. She just couldn't handle the stress of it all - it was too much to bear alone.

The men came around often to check on her. Their presence made her uncomfortable, and disturbing her in a time of mourning was disrespectful and inappropriate. The county and city government officials also came by to check on the state of things, and she despised the intrusion. In addition, they were due for an inspection of the living conditions of the workers. She feared the program would be shut down, and that they would no longer receive funding.

She believed with all her heart that her husband still existed in the spirit world, but was unable to communicate with her. She

119

often dreamt about him at night, visiting her bedside, trying to tell her something important. She had to speak with her husband again. She yearned for his guidance.

Desperate for contact, she gathered some friends from town, who, like her, believed in Spiritualism, to try the Ouija board. She'd heard that her husband might be able to speak to her through the device. She missed him. Having left her own family behind to migrate to the West Coast, her husband was all she had.

It had been his idea to help the county with the overflow of vagrants and the infirm. In exchange for this they received some funding, and a means to help work the farm. He took care of all the details while she tended to the home and helped with the orphans. With him gone though it was running away from her, and she could not trust those charged to manage the inmates and workers. She was in fear of her safety and their family possessions. Children were dying mysteriously, and field hands had gone missing.

Despite inviting all spirits that might be present to join her and assuring them that they were welcome in her home, to speak with and to guide her, she received no communication from anyone, let alone her beloved Samuel, no matter how many times or ways in which she tried.

She read about clairvoyants who could speak to the dead through spirit guides, or by channeling the spirits directly and allowing them to use their bodies to speak through. She wondered if this is what was missing.

One night she and two other like-minded townsfolk gathered with a medium for a séance. The medium had Tabitha spread objects that had been important to Samuel in his life around the table to entice him into the space where they could speak with him. Then they were told to join hands, and not let go during the session for fear of breaking the circle of energy.

Throughout the room lit candles cast quivering shadows along the surrounding walls. The medium then closed her eyes and tilted her head back, speaking out into the room.

She asked Samuel to join them, and then she asked for anyone in the spirit world who had a message for Tabitha to make themselves known...

Chapter Sixteen
Autumn Leaves

The next morning was chilly, the quad covered with fallen leaves. It was a beautiful display of nature's colors. Everyone was wrapped up in warm sweaters. I could see their breath coming out in quickly evaporating clouds as I walked across the quad. Russell was waiting by the lockers when I got there. He smiled warmly and greeted me. "Good morning."

"Good morning to you too," I responded, suppressing a yawn. "You look so… chipper."

"I'm in a good mood. And you look… tired," he noted. "Did you not sleep well?"

"Not really. It's been going on for a while, so I think it's finally starting to catch up with me."

"Well, we could get a hot chocolate from the student store to perk you up?" he offered.

"Sure that sounds great." I looked over at my usual table of friends. They were all staring at me, smiling and whispering to each other. I shot them a glance telling them to cut it out. This just made them start laughing. I did my best to maintain some sort of lady-like composure, and not just flip them off.

Russell slung his backpack across his left shoulder as he offered me his free right hand. My heart fluttered slightly as I took it. The warmth of his large hand enveloping mine was a welcome relief to the cold.

"Brrr," he commented, "I guess it's officially *pawkie* season."

I laughed at the word. "What the heck is a pawkie?"

"It's what my mom calls mittens or gloves. You know, because your hand is so cold."

He led me across the crowded quad to stand in line at the student store. It reminded me of how he had led me across the crowded dance floor - constantly looking back to make sure I was okay. No one had ever treated me that way before, as if I were truly precious to them.

After standing hand-in-hand in line waiting for our hot chocolate, we received our white Styrofoam cups, and he then led me away from the tables to a cement bench that bordered a raised garden bed, where we sat down.

"Can I ask you something?" I inquired as I blew cool air into my cup.

"Sure, anything," he replied while trying to take a sip but finding it too hot.

"Yesterday on the phone you said you've liked me for a long time. I've been having a hard time understanding that."

"What do you want to know? Why I like you? Or how it is that I've liked you longer than you were aware of?"

"Both?" I shrugged. I was trying to figure out why he seemed so sure about how he felt about me, and how he seemed to be more familiar with me than I was with him.

"Well, I saw you around with Cat at Mike's ever since earlier in the summer, you just never noticed me." He put his cup down on the cement bench and took my free hand in between his as he spoke. "I saw you at school way before homecoming, and you still didn't notice me. So when you agreed to dance with me, and then you said you'd go out with me, well I wondered to myself, 'how did I get so lucky'? So maybe I should ask you, why did you say yes?"

"Oh, wow," I replied, looking back into his earnest face. "That's a lot." I felt a tug on my heart like a door opening. He was looking deep into my eyes, as if he were trying to read my mind, the whole while stroking my hand with his fingers. I could feel a connection happening with him that was beyond anything I'd experienced.

I saw him move his hand up towards my face, where he then proceeded to brush the hair away from my face, and tuck it behind my ear.

"I love the color of your hair, by the way," he whispered, as he brought his fingers down the line of my face. "The streaks of blonde from the summer sun weave in and out of the reddish brown strands beautifully."

"Thank you." I felt heat blush my cheeks, and suddenly became aware that we were in full view of everyone. But he held me in his eyes, daring me to not look away, to not let the outside world intrude on this private moment between the two of us.

"Ever since the dance all I have wanted to do was kiss you," he said as he leaned his face towards me.

With each heartbeat he closed the distance between us, gauging my response. I didn't pull away, and I held his gaze, accepting his silent dare.

I could feel the heat from his breath and smell the sweet scent of chocolate as our lips were about to touch. I closed my eyes, seeing a kaleidoscope of colors swim around in my eyelids, feeling almost faint... when the bell rang.

I opened my eyes as I felt him pull away. I heard him grumble under his breath, "Wow, that's a total bummer."

"Yeah," I sighed, trying to clear my head.

We stood up awkwardly, looking around self-consciously, suddenly aware of our surroundings again. After we retrieved the hot chocolates from the cement bench, we challenged each other to drink them in one gulp.

"Nice mustache," I smiled, as he pulled his cup away from his mouth.

"Like that? It's my new look," he teased.

I reached up and wiped the chocolate off his lip with my finger. He grinned, and I knew that he was thinking about biting it. So I pulled my hand away quickly before he could - grinning back at him.

He took my hand, squeezed it tight two times in a row. "Shall we?" he asked as he indicated the direction we should walk to head to first period.

"Indeed," I responded, giggling at my failed attempt to sound proper.

The sound of decaying leaves crunched beneath our shoes as we walked slowly together, not wanting our brief time together to end.

Chapter Seventeen
Under the Porch Light

Wednesday morning we weren't able to meet up, and we barely had any time to talk at the beginning of his lunch period. To make the day worse, my parents said they wouldn't let me go to the movies with Russell Friday night until they had a chance to get to know him.

After dinner I went into the kitchen to call Russell and tell him the bad news. As I reached for the receiver the phone rang. I knew it was him.

"Hi," I said before he had the chance to say anything.

"Hi? How did you know it was me? Or, wait… you didn't know it was me, you thought it was someone else!" he said, pretending to be offended.

"No, just you, silly. I have some bad news about Friday night."

"Oh, and what is that?" he asked skeptically.

"My parents insist on having you over for dinner before they'll agree to let me go out alone with you," I said, just spilling it all out. I didn't mention their concern over him being so much older as well. I was beside myself with frustration, and worried that, by having to cancel, the connection between us would simply evaporate.

127

"Would you like me to come over and meet them?" he asked, completely serious.

"Well, I guess we have no choice if we're ever to see each other outside of school," I replied, feeling somewhat embarrassed that I was too young to share the same freedoms as he did.

"What are you doing right now?" he asked suddenly.

"Talking to you, and then after that I have to finish up some school work that is due tomorrow," I replied flatly.

"Answer the door in ten minutes. Bye." He hung up the phone, and left me standing there.

Ten minutes? Wait, what? He's coming over here!

I panicked and raced down the hall to the bathroom to check my make-up and brush my hair. Then I thought I should brush my teeth. Then I realized I had to pee. I was just about to run to my room to change, when the doorbell rang. I heard my mom heading to the front door.

"I'll get it!" I yelled, sprinting down the hall hoping to intercept her before she got there.

"Hi. Is Gwen here?" I heard Russell ask my mom, who stood there, doorknob in hand, staring at the stranger on our doorstep.

"Mom, it's fine. I got it." I ran up to the door. "Hi!" I turned to greet him. He changed from what he'd worn to school, and was dressed in a loose button-up light blue Oxford shirt, the cuffs rolled up to his elbows, over a pair of jeans. I thought he looked handsome. "You got here fast!"

"And who is your new friend, Gwen?" my mom asked.

"Who's at the door?" my dad yelled from the living room.

"A friend of Gwen's!" she yelled back.

"Oh my god, Mom, stop yelling. *This* is Russell," I said, and then I pointed at my mom. "Russell, this is my mom."

"Elizabeth," she responded smiling warmly, as she held out her hand. "Hi, it is nice to finally meet you."

"Hi Elizabeth, it's nice to meet you too," he responded as he took her hand to shake it.

I heard the pounding of my dad's feet walking towards the door, and couldn't help feel slightly nauseated from the anxiety of my father scrutinizing my would-be suitor.

"Hi..." he said as he held out his hand, "Robert."

"Russell... nice to meet you, sir," he replied politely returning the hand shake. It all seemed to be going along quite well.

"So, *you* want to take my daughter out to the movies, huh?" he asked, looking Russell up and down.

I felt myself die a little inside as I squirmed uncomfortably at the front door in embarrassment.

"Yes, sir," Russell replied. I was shocked at the second use of the word *sir* and how respectful he was being. All the other boys I had known had been, well, I guess, *boys*. This was an entirely new experience. I was witnessing a young man trying to impress upon my father that he was a decent guy and could be trusted.

"Do you drive, Russell?" my dad asked, as he continued to size him up.

"Yes, that is my father's old car right there on the street - the silver Volvo. It is still in good working condition and has never broken down. My father and I like to work on it together."

"I see, and what does your father do for a living?"

"He is a professor at Douglas University. He teaches Literature," Russell replied, his one hand still behind his back, and the other one now in his front pocket.

"Do you work?"

"Yes, part time at my mother's shop, downtown."

"You seem like a nice young man. I'm sure you can understand our concern with our only daughter going out on a date with a complete stranger."

"Yes, sir, I can. That is why I thought I would come over and introduce myself." I was so proud of how he was holding his own with my father. I felt my heart flutter a little more each time he spoke.

"Well, I appreciate that. Come in, would you like a beer?" my father asked, no longer puffing up his chest in overprotectiveness.

"No thank you, I'm not 21 yet," he responded without batting an eye. I think he knew it was a trap.

My dad turned to me and winked before he smiled and responded, "Right answer!"

"Anyway, I can't stay," Russell continued, suppressing a grin. "I just thought I would stop by for a moment."

"Okay then. It was nice to meet you. I'm going to go back to the news. Why don't you come over for dinner on Friday?" He turned to move back down the hall towards the living room, but not without smiling at me first and giving me another little wink.

"That would be very nice," Russell answered.

I scooted my mother aside, and walked out onto the doorstep, trying to close the door behind me as I did.

"I'll be inside in a minute, mom," I said, finally closing the door behind myself.

I stood under the porch light, as twilight crept across the neighborhood. The street lamps followed the creeping darkness, popping on one by one, pushing against the coming night, and casting everything in shadows.

The briskness of the air hit me, and I pulled my arms around myself for warmth.

Russell pulled his arm from behind his back and handed me a sickly orange-tinted flower. "This was the last blooming rose of the season from my mom's garden," he explained.

"Oh, it's lovely!" I put it up to my nose and inhaled its sweet delicate aroma. "I think that went pretty well," I offered. "My dad may actually like you!"

He reached his hands out to my one free hand and I let him take it. He glanced down to see that I was barefoot, and asked, "Where are your shoes?"

"I didn't have much notice to dress appropriately," I answered.

"Are you cold? You're shivering."

"No, I am good! Really, really good," I responded, gazing up into his eyes. "How did you get here so fast anyways? Wait… and how did you know where I lived? Did Mike tell you?"

"Is that okay?"

"Yeah, that's fine," I said as I held the fragile last rose of the season up so that I could smell it again, and looked down at my other hand that he was holding. "It's all better than okay. It's actually pretty great."

Before I knew it, his lips were lightly pressing against mine. Startled at first, I pulled back, until I could see his face. Then I couldn't help myself. I reached up and threw my arms around his neck, pressing my lips firmly against his. He responded by wrapping his arms tightly around my lower back and lifting me up.

Our kiss went deeper and deeper as we pulled our bodies together in a tight needy embrace. Under the looming night, and beneath the cover of the front porch, we lost ourselves in one another.

Every few seconds we would frantically come up for air while trying desperately not to disconnect. I felt the whole of his arm drop down from my back, his hand sliding down across my right butt check, squeezing gently, pulling me closer to him.

My whole body ignited. It was unlike any sensation I had felt before. My chest hummed in response, which made him hold me even tighter. I knew, in that moment, that our passion had transported us into an entirely different realm, a dangerous territory filled with mysterious unknowns.

I heard the soft sound of footsteps approaching the front door and began to disengage from our lip lock. Just then the door knob rattled behind me, and we immediately jumped apart. Russell nearly toppled off the step, but caught himself, recovering quickly, just as my mom opened the door and peaked out.

"Um, sorry to interrupt," she said and then looked at me with a glint of acknowledgement, "but your dad wants you in now. So say goodnight. It was nice to meet you by the way, Russell. Hopefully we'll see you on Friday."

She looked back and forth at the two of us, and smiled as she pulled her head back inside and closed the door.

"Oh, my god... I am mortified," I whispered, as I composed myself. I was trying to slow my breathing, and tamp down the fire coursing through my blood. I noticed him standing off to the side awkwardly.

"You?" he asked in an amused tone. "I don't know how I am going to make it back home without crashing the car!" He stumbled like he was intoxicated, which made me laugh. I knew what he meant.

"I guess I better go," he said sadly, as he walked over and kissed me again briefly. I used every ounce of will power I had to push him gently away, and turn around to go back inside.

"Okay, well... bye, then," I said sadly, not wanting him to leave.

"I'll see you tomorrow at the lockers," he said smiling, and then turned and walked back to his father's car.

I grinned as I watched him wave good-bye before getting in the car and driving away. I ran back inside the house, high on hormones, and intoxicated with infatuation. I didn't know how I would concentrate on homework, let alone make it until the next morning without my heart bursting out of my body in anticipation of seeing him again.

~~

Thursday morning I opened my locker, and inside was a poem written in a familiar near illegible handwriting:

> *Why me? She asked with sun kissed cheeks*
> *Her eyes like deep still water.*
> *And when we kissed my knees went weak*
> *I've known since I first saw her.*
> *Why me? She asked when in my arms*
> *Her colors were pure beauty.*
> *Love's whispers spoken without words*
> *You are everything to me.*

"Should I be concerned?" I heard Russell say, as he walked up behind me, making me jump.

"Oh!" I startled, turning around. "Don't sneak up me like that!"

"I see that someone has left you a love poem in your locker," he teased, and leaned in to lightly kiss me on the lips.

"Yes," I answered flustered from reading his words and receiving the kiss. "I need to find this secret admirer and tell him how beautiful this is!"

He rested his hands on either side of my jaw line, cupped my face and brought it up to meet his. It was such a simple kiss, but it was sweeter than any kiss deserved to be. It felt genuine and heartfelt, which I think was more effective in making my knees buckle.

"Did you really write this?" I asked, as I recovered.

"Yes," he answered, looking at me lovingly. He brought his hands down and held both of mine in his as we stood face to face.

"You aren't a hallucination or anything right?"

"Not that I am aware of," he smiled, breathing in the scent of my hair. "Are you? You clearly have me under a spell."

"No, if anything it's you bewitching me!" I accused him playfully.

Chapter Eighteen
Another Grave

That night, after I got off the phone with Russell, I was settling down at my desk, to attempt Social Studies homework. I had put the poem up on my cork board in a place of honor, right next to the picture of Mel. Staring at it, I was daydreaming, until I was interrupted by the sound of my dad yelling from the living room, "Elizabeth! Hey, come here! Listen to this!"

"What is it, Bob? I am trying to get the dishes cleaned up," she yelled back.

"They found more bodies! Can you believe that? There was a second mass grave!" he yelled.

I pushed my chair back, and got up from my desk quickly to run to the living room. On the screen was a news anchor talking about the newest finds along the hillside near the Douglas Zoo. He briefly cut away to a video of people bringing tarps to a section of the woods, near where we found Joseph's grave. He reported that with winter closing in, and the beginning of the rainy season, they had to finish recovering the bodies quickly before evidence could get washed away.

I went into the kitchen, when the segment ended, picked up the receiver from the wall phone, and dialed Cat's number.

"Can I talk to Cat?" I kept the phone up to my ear as I walked down the hall into my room, shutting the door over the extension cord.

"Hello?" Cat said when she came to the phone.

"They found another mass grave site!" I blurted out.

"NO WAY!" she yelled. "When?"

"I just saw them talking about it on the news. They didn't give many details, only that they were trying to hurry in recovering the remains before it starts to rain."

"Wow! Where did they find it?" she asked.

"Along the same hillside where Joseph and the other children were buried," I replied.

"Was it more children?" she asked hesitantly, as if she really didn't want to hear the answer.

"I don't know, they didn't say. They just discovered it, so the news didn't have all the information yet."

"I wonder if the people they found were the 'others' that were trying to communicate with us."

"I don't know. Maybe they're no longer trapped now that the grave has been discovered," I wondered aloud. The memory of the eerie voices I heard calling out to me for help sent a shiver down my spine.

"I hope so!" Cat responded. "If that problem has been solved, we only have one more bit of unsettled business, right?"

"One more? You mean besides an angry ghost kid wanting her doll?" I asked.

"And besides a ghost mom angry at the people messing with her house?" she added.

"You're referring to the key situation."

"Yeah. I worry that the keys might be acting like a gateway with my father. I want to return them, but I don't want to have to go back to that house."

"Me either! I guess I assumed that by turning over the information we had, and Kevin opening up the grave under the tracks for them to find the children, we did what we needed to. I just wanted Joseph to be at rest."

"I hope he is now," she offered. "If we have to go back though, what happens then? How can we protect ourselves from the angry mom and the evil little girl?" she worried.

"I don't know," I replied. "Maybe we don't have to go back. I mean, would returning the keys actually solve the problem?"

"What do you mean?"

"If they're renovating the house, it wouldn't matter to the crew one way or another if they had a key to get into the rooms, right?"

"Right, they probably just bust them down or something."

"If they found the boxes up in the attic, I imagine they'd probably have to turn them over to the historical society or something. And maybe no one will even discover the room beneath the stairs!"

"Yeah, but the spirit that spoke to you seemed pretty insistent that we return the keys," Cat sighed. "There has to be more significance to them than we're aware of! Maybe it's just about the doll? So if we open the trunk and give the little girl that stupid doll, she'll just go away!"

"We should tell Russell's mom the whole story," I suggested, "and see if she has any advice."

"That's too weird that Brighid is Russell's mom, by the way. But yeah, we should. I don't want this creepy puzzle box of keys with me anymore," Cat confessed, "and I am tired of having nightmares."

"I didn't realize it was that bad. I am having a lot of trouble sleeping too."

"Please don't tell me what *your* nightmares are about, I don't think I could stand any more fuel for my imagination!"

"Oh, no, Cat, don't worry! I won't burden you with them," I sighed, thinking upon my nightly ritual of singing quietly to myself to silence the voices and hope for a dreamless sleep. I made a decision. "That's it. I guess we have to go back. There isn't any way to escape it. Damn! I am so sorry I dragged you into this in the first place."

"What are best friends for?" she offered.

"Well, this has been above and beyond the call of duty. You're the best."

"Awwww, shucks," she giggled. "Okay, so I guess we need to start working on a plan to return."

"Yep," I said quietly. "Let's not worry about that tonight though. Try to think of good things… like Kevin or

139

something. I'll catch up with you tomorrow after Art Class."

"Okay… sweet dreams about your new Prince Charming," she teased.

"Stop it!" I laughed. "But, okay, I will. But not because you told me to!"

"Ha! I definitely don't want to know what those dreams are going to be like. Gross," she said, busting up.

"Good bye, Cat. I am going to hang up on you now," I said as I walked from my room down the hall to the kitchen.

"You wouldn't dare!" she challenged. "I am going to hang up on you first."

"Ha!" I cried in triumph right before I clicked the button down with my finger, and placed the receiver back in its place. I walked back down the hall chuckling to myself. I closed my bedroom door behind me, and attempted to settle back down to finish up my Social Studies. It was hard not to look forward to sweet dreams of Russell…

…I heard a disgusting sound of something heavy being dropped in mud, followed by a disturbing scraping noise. I knew what the sounds were, because I had stood at this door many nights before. The familiar skeleton key was in my hand, and I knew I would have no power to stop myself from putting the key into the lock on the old door, and pushing it forward to expose the room.

Each time I found myself there I tried different ways to wake myself, all too aware I was dreaming. But each time I found myself completely at the mercy of a force I could not fight.

The door swung open, and the dim light allowed me to see the shadow in the far corner. I had tried to speak to her in my many visits to this dreamscape, but was never able to make a sound.

Something about the room this time had changed. I shifted around, trying to pinpoint the difference. Then I noticed it, another shadowy figure in the opposite corner. It stepped away from the wall and came into the dim light so I could make out its features. It was an older man, with a large dark mustache. He wore a black round hat with a small brim, a black suit jacket with a button-up vest and pocket watch over a white shirt, and a bow tie. I couldn't make out the bottom portion of his body - it was indistinct like wisps of smoke. He didn't seem to notice me because his attention was on the woman busy laying bricks within the exposed wall.

I saw her stand upright, as she did most nights, but this time instead of turning towards me in a fit of rage, she saw the man, and her demeanor changed. She began to weep and came towards him with her arms outstretched, seeking comfort... but just before she could touch him, he backed away in disapproval, and disappeared.

She lifted her head towards the ceiling and let out a horrifying scream of pure agony. I tried to back up quietly to exit the room, hoping this time she would not notice me. But I was frozen in place.

Once she had stopped screaming, she stood still, and then she turned her head towards me. The hatred and rage were worse than they had ever been, and I felt more terrified than I ever thought I could. I kept telling myself to wake up, that it was just a dream, that I had control, and that nothing bad could actually happen.

She stepped towards me, away from the shadows and into the dim light. I noticed she still had the trowel held tight in her fist. It was dripping with mortar.

"Please don't hurt me. I mean you no harm!"I knew I couldn't vocalize my words so I pushed these thoughts at her.

She stopped, and looked at me with curiosity. For the first time it occurred to me the black veil she wore, head-to-toe, was for mourning. I realized then that this was Tabitha, and the man I just witnessed was Samuel.

"I'm sorry you're grieving. What can I do to help you?" I asked. I felt empathy for her state, and wondered if this was where all her anger came from.

Her face softened for the first time. So I tried again to send my thoughts to her, "What can I do to help you?"

She stood aside and allowed me to see the hole she was bricking up in what used to be the nursery fireplace.

I gasped in horror at the sight, and started screaming.

The woman kept motioning towards her handy work, but I had stopped trying to understand.

I screamed and screamed, and willed my body to move. I put all the mental energy I could into making my body move.

WAKE UP! I yelled.

WAKE UP!

WAKE UP!

I jolted upright into a sitting position, suddenly back on my bed, the remnants of a scream dying in my throat and sliding back into my heaving chest.

I reached for the small lamp on my nightstand, and turned the knob. Glorious light flooded out over my bed, and I focused on the happy colorful printed butterflies flying around my yellow sheets.

I focused on my breathing, a deep inhale, hold, a slow exhale, and then repeat. This had become a nightly ritual.

I looked at the digital clock radio next to the lamp - the time was the same as it had been every night for weeks: 3:13 a.m.

Chapter Nineteen
Dinner with the Evanses

Russell arrived at our house that Friday night, and rang the bell. I watched from the edge of the kitchen as my father stomped to the door, putting on his best "intimidating father" look. He swung it open and just stood there with his hands on his hips. I heard my mom snickering from behind me. I didn't think it was funny at all - I was completely embarrassed by the entire display.

"Hi, Robert, sir... is Gwen here?" Russell asked politely. He was doing his best to maintain eye contact and not appear nervous.

Suddenly my dad broke character and visibly relaxed, a goofy grin forming on his stern face. "Hello, Russell. You can just call me Bob," my dad said as he stepped back and motioned him inside. "Come on in, she's in the kitchen."

"Hi," I said meekly, waving to him as I came around the corner and joined him in the entryway. He wore a beige plaid button up shirt under a casual brown corduroy blazer. The shirt was tucked into his jeans with a matching brown belt. I was taken back again by how handsome he looked.

"Do you want to sit down?" I asked as I led him into the living room. I did my best to not be embarrassed by the state of things. The couch looked so dingy, and I could see dust on the coffee table around the magazines that barely covered the coffee cup stains.

"Sure," he replied as he caught up with me in a single stride, and then whispered in my ear, "You look lovely."

"Thank you," I said, turning my head away as I felt my face flush. I was wearing a teal blouse tucked into a white skirt that came up just above the knee, with white pumps.

I went to the furthest end of the couch, and sat down. Russell eased down beside me making himself comfortable on the center cushion. "You look... um, very handsome as well," I whispered back. I was a mess of nerves.

My dad came in and sat in his dark brown recliner. He leaned forward and addressed Russell like it was a job interview, "So, how long has your family lived in Douglas?"

"A little over twenty years. My mom came over from Scotland, while my dad was working on the East Coast. They met when he was studying in Scotland, and she followed him to America after they got married. They decided to move here to raise a family," Russell replied politely. He didn't seem rattled by the interrogation, he seemed prepared.

"Do you come from a large family?"

"I have three older sisters. Baby of the family, you could say. But yes I have a lot of family back East and overseas."

"Douglas seems like an interesting choice to settle down in. Did he come here for work?"

"I'm not sure what initially motivated them to move here, but I've heard them say they liked that it was a Scottish town."

"Okay, everyone, dinner is ready," my mom called out, as she headed over to the dining room table in the small kitchen alcove.

My father got up first and motioned for us to go ahead of him. I had a feeling he didn't want to leave us alone. Russell got up next, and held out his hand to me as I got up. He winked, squeezed my hand two times, and smiled, saying without words, *we got this.* That simple thought made me completely relax. We then made our away across the living room into the dining area, with my dad close behind.

For dinner my mother had pulled out all her comfort food tricks. It was almost a feast worthy of Thanksgiving, except it was a roasted chicken instead of a large turkey. She had made a large bowl of mashed potatoes with gravy, a side salad and dinner rolls.

"This looks wonderful, Elie," my dad said, looking at her lovingly. I loved it when he called my mom that. He seemed to only reserve calling her by her nickname for special occasions. I never understood why he was so stingy with his affection towards her, but because it was so rare, she blushed at the sound of it.

"Yes, it looks delicious. Thank you again for inviting me," Russell said as he took a seat next to my father, who

146

was at the head of the table. I ended up sitting opposite my dad, and my mother took the last chair opposite Russell.

I was surprised at how comfortable the room felt. Initially I thought it was going to be horrible, and I wasn't going to be able to bear it. Instead I found myself smiling, laughing at my dad's bad jokes, and enjoying a good meal.

"Mr. Evans, how long has your family been in Douglas?" Russell asked midway through the meal.

"I moved here after I got out of high school, because they needed construction workers. Elie and I met soon after that."

"Evans? Is that Welsh?"

"Close, it's Cornish. My family emigrated to the U.S. in the late 1800's from Cornwall, England."

"So that is what you do for a living, construction?" Russell asked. It seemed he had become the interrogator. I liked how he had taken control of the conversation.

"I'm General Manager for a construction company. Nothing as exciting as being a professor, and studying overseas. No fancy schools or anything. I learned everything on the job. I've worked with my hands my entire life. It's honest work, and it pays the bills," he said proudly.

I had never thought anything less of my dad because of his job, and it was surprising but also comforting to realize how hard he worked to support our family.

"I think my father would envy you. Aside from a few interesting book discoveries, there is nothing exciting

147

about being a professor of literature," Russell replied. "He couldn't even make a table."

My father chuckled in response, clearly satisfied, and sat up straighter.

"What about you, Mrs. Evans? Where is your family from?" Russell asked. I suddenly realized what he was up to.

"Oh, please call me Elizabeth. I've been in Douglas my whole life, as was my mother. I don't know much about her family, and I never knew who my father was."

"Oh, I'm sorry. I don't mean to pry," he replied. The answer she had given him was nothing I hadn't heard before. I was disappointed he hadn't managed to elicit more information from her.

"Oh, no, you're fine," she said brushing it off.

"It's just that I thought you also might be Scottish, seeing as how Gwen was given the middle name of Iona. She said it was from your family."

My mom looked rattled at this revelation, as if it were a skeleton in the family closet, "Oh... well... that is a story for another time," she replied awkwardly. "Anyone need anything else to drink? Bob? Another beer?" She scooted away from the table and stood, waiting for requests. "Okay, going once... going twice."

"Okay, fine, I will have another beer," my dad laughed. "Break my arm, why don't you?"

"So, Russell, what movie were you taking our little girl to?" my dad asked.

"What?" I asked inadvertently. "Does that mean you'll let me go out tonight?" I was trying to not get my hopes up.

"Well," Russell paused, looking back and forth between the two of us. "I honestly didn't know if I would pass the test," he laughed.

"You have in my book," my mother said, smiling, as she brought a tray of brownies to the table along with another beer. She then proceeded to clear the dishes from the table.

"Brownies, Mom, you are spoiling us tonight!" I immediately reached over for one, and offered it to Russell. He nodded his head eagerly.

"So?" my dad asked.

"I didn't expect to go to a movie tonight," Russell admitted. "Maybe that wouldn't be as much fun..." he trailed off, looking at me curiously. "I'm wondering what you think about... skating?"

"Skating sounds fun," I responded.

Then he addressed my dad, "If Gwen is up to the challenge..."

"I know how to skate!" I balked.

Russell, grinning mischievously, continued, "I know a bunch of people who are meeting at the roller rink tonight." He swallowed the last of his brownie, and then asked, "Would that be okay if I took her there for a couple hours?"

"Sure, that sounds fine. But, I'd like you to have her home by 10:00 p.m. I don't want to stay up too late."

"Yes, sir! I'll have her back by 10:00 p.m., on the dot!"

"Yay!" I blurted out, and then I motioned to my clothes. "But I can't skate in these."

Giggling with excitement, I pushed my chair back and shot out of the room down the hall to go change into my favorite pleated jeans, and exchange my pumps for my white Keds.

When finished, I found Russell standing in front of the painting over the TV.

"I noticed this earlier. You'll be interested to know that *this* is your namesake..." he gestured towards the landscape, proud of himself for figuring it out.

"What is?" I asked, walking up to him.

"That is the Isle of Iona off the Isle of Mull in Scotland. Beautiful, isn't it?"

"That's Iona?" I asked as I gazed upon the dreary painting I had always hated.

My mom walked up to us with a strange look on her face. "I had no idea either," she commented. "It was originally my grandmother's, who gave it my mom, and then handed down to me. I never heard any stories attached to it."

Still looking at the painting, Russell added, "My father's family the MacIntyres are from near there, in Kintyre," he looked at my mother then and said, "Do you know the song by Paul McCartney?"

"Mull of Kintyre," she responded, nodding her head and humming it softly. "It's a beautiful song."

The moment was killed by father coughing from the recliner, and said, "Well I guess you better be off."

My mom gathered herself and walked us to the front door. She whispered to me in a conspiring tone, "Your dad's having a hard time with you starting to date, you know, because his baby girl is growing up."

"It's okay, mom, we're just going skating. Tell him I'll be fine. I'm in good hands." I turned on the front stoop, and gave her a hug. Russell was already walking down the driveway towards the street.

"Okay, well, have fun you two!" she said louder this time, so that Russell could hear. Then she closed the door.

I ran up behind him as we approached the car. He opened the passenger side door for me, explaining that it had a tricky handle.

"Lucky for me I guess. I get the princess treatment."

"I am your humble servant," he gushed, and bowed as I sat down, shutting the door behind me.

Inside the car I was struck with the smell of his exotic cologne again. The scent brought me back to our first dance, then to the front porch kiss that rocked my world. I was aware that my hands were sweating, and tried discreetly to dry them off on my knees before he managed to scoot into the driver's seat.

He turned to me and smiled, and my heart raced slightly. I tried to tamp down the butterflies in my stomach. He put the key in the ignition, got the engine going, and then pumped the gas pedal a couple times to rev it. He then pulled a knob on the front panel to turn on the headlights.

It was an older car with a minimalistic spacious and clean interior. There were two individual bouncy black leather seats with a long stick shift centered in the front. The giant black steering wheel had a silver airplane wing-like shape in its center, with the word *Volvo* written in a cursive silver metal inlay.

The sound of the car engine made me think of my dad, and I looked back towards the house. Sure enough he was peeking through the curtains at us, as we pulled away. Turning back around to look at Russell in the driver's seat, I felt like I was having an out of body experience. I had to keep reminding myself this wasn't a movie. I really was going on an actual date with an older boy - in a car!

Once out of the neighborhood, he turned to me and said, "I had fun at dinner. Your parents are very nice."

"I thought it was going to be awful, but yes, that was nice."

"I am so glad you said yes."

This caught me off guard, "You mean yes to this date?"

"Yes to dating *me*. For you know…all the dates." He grinned again. He took his hand off the gear shift for a moment to lay it on top of my hand. He interlaced his fingers in between mine, and gave a little squeeze.

"I'm glad you asked me," I replied as I turned my hand palm up, and re-entwined our fingers, squeezing back.

When he came to a stop light, he had to free his hand to shift, and apologized. But he took the moment to lean over and give me a quick kiss, before the light turned green.

I scooted over closer to the center, so that I could lay my hand on his right knee. I leaned my head against his right arm that flexed with each shift, and watched the street lights go past as we continued on through town. It felt like we owned the night and could go anywhere and do anything we wanted. The sense of freedom was wonderful.

Chapter Twenty
All Skate

We pulled into the crowded roller rink parking lot, and slowly drove up and down the rows until we found an open space. There were groups of teens milling around outside the entrance, as well as smaller groups hanging behind a car here and there. Some sat on the hoods of their cars, watching as we drove past.

I didn't recognize any faces, and began to feel insecure again. I wondered why I agreed to come there on a Friday night, knowing that teens from all over the county gathered here *en masse*. It had been one thing when I had come to skate with my friends, for a birthday party or something, but the Friday night crowd was something altogether different.

One group was made up of punkers wearing silver studded black leather jackets over ripped up black t-shirts, and they wore heavy black Doc Martin boots. A few of them had nose piercings and safety pins in their ears, and they wore a lot of chain jewelry. Some of them had partially shaved heads with giant Mohawks. They laughed obnoxiously, calling people *"poseurs"* as they walked by, and blasted music from their car radios. If anyone dared to make eye contact they tried to look menacing as they glared back, wound up and itching for a fight.

Across the parking lot was a different group – headbangers - rockers into heavy metal. They mostly had their hair teased up, not much different than the punkers except for the shaved head part. They also wore black leather jackets but with Iron Maiden or Scorpions t-shirts underneath, and had cigarettes hanging off their lips. Some of them had red bandanas tied around the legs of their torn jeans with ankle boots that had chains hanging from them. They glared back at the punks, also seemingly keyed up and hoping for some excuse to fight.

The tension in the air was palpable. I exited the car as Russell held the door open for me. When I stepped into the lot, I could feel the menace and hatred radiating off of each group. "Maybe we should have gone somewhere else?" I asked timidly.

"It'll be alright. Mike and Erik will be here too, and so are a few others from school. It'll be fun. Don't worry." He reached for my hand and held it tightly as we walked through the parking lot and up to the entrance.

There we had to push our way through another group of teens to get to the double glass doors and make our way inside.

"See, that wasn't so bad," he said.

Walking through the dimly lit lobby I was attracted to the colorful flashing lights over the rink. Skaters of all ages were doing their best to dance while not falling flat on their butts, while Olivia Newton-John sang "Xanadu" loudly through the overhead speakers.

When we made it up to the counter, the male clerk asked me, "What size do you need?"

"A 7 ½," I replied. I watched the young guy go back through rows of skates on wood shelves until he found my size. He came back bearing a ratty beige pair with dingy red shoe laces, and handed them to me.

"And you?" he asked Russell.

"A 12, thanks," he answered.

I walked over to a nearby bench, and started to take off my shoes, when I overheard my name in someone's conversation. I looked around to see where the voice had come from, and spotted Erin and Chris several benches away, lacing up their skates.

Oh, great. I thought to myself.

Just then Russell sidled up next to me, and asked, "What's wrong?"

I wasn't sure how he could have known anything was wrong, but maybe my face gave away more than I was aware of.

"See those two over there?" I asked, lacing up my first skate. "The girl with the tight rainbow t-shirt... you can't miss her," I said, not hiding my disgust.

"Yeah, I see her. That's the girl who bothered you at homecoming, isn't it?"

How in the hell did he know that? I wondered.

"Yes," I replied.

"Is she bothering you right now?" he asked with a protective tone.

"No, I just heard them talking about me," I complained, before gesturing and saying, "That's Chris."

"Ohh, yes, Chris," he said, sounding unimpressed.

"You know about him?" I asked, standing up slowly as not to roll away. I didn't remember ever discussing Chris. "Let me guess, Mike told you, didn't he?"

Russell hesitated before answering. "Yeah, he might have mentioned a few things about you guys, but only what Cat shared with him," he answered casually, trying to push his foot down into the narrow neck of the skate. He stopped to loosen up the laces, when he realized I was standing there staring at him with my hands on my hips. "I'm sorry. Did I say something wrong?"

"I guess it bothers me a little that you and Mike were talking about me," I replied trying to hide how much it actually hurt. My emotions seemed to be all over the place. It felt like there were just too many people, the music was too loud, and the lights were flashing too much. "You just seem to know a lot about me, and I don't know as much about you."

He finished tying his second skate, and stood towering over me. He put his hands down at my waist and leaned over, so I could hear him over the loud music. "Anything you want to know, just ask. I'm an open book." He moved his head closer to mine and kissed me gently. "Remember, I liked you for a long time before you

157

even knew I existed. I had time to ask questions about you."

"I guess," I mumbled, suddenly fragile. The sight of Erin and Chris together had sent me in to a tailspin that I couldn't control.

"Don't worry about those two. They've got nothing on us." He kissed my forehead gently, letting his lips linger, then he took my hand.

"You Dropped a Bomb on Me" by the Gap Band came on over the speakers. He pulled me out after him on to the smooth surface of the rink, waited until I got some momentum going, and then turned around so he could skate backwards while holding my hands.

"Show off!" I said loudly, doing my best to keep up. "You definitely can skate well."

"I have sisters, remember? They have me dragged down here more times than I can count. I have a confession…"

"Yeah, and what is that?"

"I kind of love this stuff, even disco… it's really fun to skate to."

"See?" I scolded, "I hardly know anything about you!"

"Okay, well if I'm confessing…" he admitted as he spun around so he was back at my side, "I also had to learn dance when I was a kid."

"Seriously? What sort of dancing?"

"Traditional Scottish dances mostly, but I also had to go to all my sisters practices for ballet, tap and jazz. So I picked up stuff there as well."

"Remind me to thank your sisters when I meet them," I replied.

Suddenly he got a glint of mischief in his eye and asked, "Do you trust me?"

"Umm, should I?" I asked warily.

"I'm going to take your other hand and spin you around, so be prepared to keep your weight centered." He then spun me around so that I was facing backwards. It freaked me out at first because I couldn't see where I was going. "Relax. I got you," he smiled.

From that vantage point, I realized that Erin and Chris were holding hands skating just a few people behind us. I did my best to avert my gaze and look up at Russell instead.

"Okay now, just match the rhythm of the song, lean your weight deeper into each push off of the wheels, and just trust that I'm going to guide you." I nodded back begrudgingly not at all confident I wasn't going to run someone over. "Trust me, and relax. Just focus on my movement, and stay in rhythm with that."

He pushed off with one foot, simultaneously pulling me towards him, and in one swift motion had his arm at my side and my arm up in his hand... in a dance position. I dropped my free hand to his waist, and we swayed side to side as he propelled us around the rink.

Earth, Wind and Fire's "September" came on, and it made me smile. "The words are perfect. Can you hear them?" I asked, laughing lightly. "They are asking if we remember our dance in September."

"How could I ever forget?" he asked. "Oh, look... we're about to lap your *friends*." He laughed, as we glided by Erin and Chris, still stumbling along. I heard Erin muttering as we passed, and I was shocked to find I no longer cared what she had to say.

"Now they are singing about it being December, and that our love is here to stay," he said, smiling as he continued to stare into my eyes.

Did he just say 'our love'?

"Hey Russ!" I heard a loud male voice yell in close proximity. Mike and Erik had skated up alongside us, doing a great job keeping up, but with far less grace.

Erik's flannel, tied around his waist, flapped behind him as he leaned forward in a race stance, arms swinging side to side. Mike, trying to look cool, kept both hands tucked in the pockets of his jeans. I think Russell heard me groan out loud in protest to their presence, because he flashed me a comically exaggerated frown.

"Sad you no longer have me all to yourself?" he asked, then broke out in a smile.

"Another One Bites the Dust" by Queen came over the loud speakers, and Erik yelled out, "Oh cool Mike, I'll race you!"

The two of them dashed out ahead of us, weaving in and out of the other skaters, racing each other around the rink.

Russell slowed down to a leisurely pace and let go of the dance hold to allow me to face forward again, "I'm sorry if you thought I was teasing you. I was actually thinking the same thing."

There he goes again, getting inside my head.

"Good," I responded. "I was getting worried. It's hard to compete with those two."

Russell laughed, "Oh, you have nothing to worry about. They aren't my type!"

After a few minutes of quiet I thought I'd dig a little deeper, "So did you and your sisters do anything else that was interesting?

"Interesting? We took music lessons together," he answered. "But I have interests of my own, you know?"

"Like what?" I asked, as I noticed we were coming up on Erin and Chris again. I tried to keep my head turned towards Russell so they wouldn't know I had seen them.

"Soccer. I played soccer my entire life, until this year."

"Oh? What made you stop?"

"I would have had to advance to the next level which meant traveling for games, and spending all my free time at practice."

"You were that good? Wow!" I responded. "But you just didn't want to invest that much of yourself anymore?"

GINGER G HOWARD

"Pretty much. Let's just say that during this summer something changed. I realized I had other things I wanted to focus on."

"Well, I'm glad you weren't traveling and practicing in all your free time! We might not have met," I said, smiling up at him.

"Exactly," he replied, smiling back.

In the corner of my eye, I could see that we were coming up even with Erin and Chris. Erin was glaring at me, and mouthing the word *bitch*. Chris was doing his best to pretend he didn't know I was there.

Russell followed my gaze over to the two of them, as if he almost had planned the timing of it. "So, Chris is it?" he asked, directing his question their way.

Chris looked over, and met my gaze. He seemed confused and hurt by it. Then he glared at Russell and said, "Yeah, what's it to you?"

"I just thought I would introduce myself to you. I'm Russell. Oh, and you must be Erin?" he asked, now making eye contact with her.

"Yeah. What are you slumming now, Russell? What happened with Megan Warner? Did she dump you?"

He ignored her, looked at Chris instead and asked, "Are *you* slumming? You passed up this," he said, motioning to me, "for... that? Tragic. But your loss is my gain!"

He looked over at me and squeezed my hand twice, our new unspoken code, reminding me, *we got this*. Then he gracefully pushed us off, leaving the two behind.

162

"Gwen," Erin yelled, "he's got girls lined up all over the place. You're nothing but a notch on a bedpost," Erin yelled as we skated away.

"She just doesn't know when to quit. Does she?" Russell asked, a darker edge creeping into his voice.

At that exact moment I heard a crash behind us, and I turned to see Erin sprawled out on the floor, blood coming from her nose. She must have face-planted.

I was shocked by the sight of it, and even more shocked at the satisfaction that it brought.

"Serves her right," I mumbled under my breath before changing the subject. "Hey, when we get to the other side, can we stop over at the food counter and get something to drink? I'm getting hot."

"Sure," Russell said, distracted by his obvious pleasure over the karmic retribution that just occurred.

We skated off the waxy wooden rink and out onto the carpet. The assault of sweat and stinky feet was more pungent than earlier. Together, we rolled over towards the counter.

"After we get something to drink, we could always leave, if you aren't having fun anymore?" he suggested.

I looked up at the clock to see that it was already 8:30 p.m. I had forgotten that we had a late start after eating dinner. It seemed like the time was flying by too fast.

"Where else would we go? It's too late for a movie or anything," I asked.

"We could get some frozen yogurt, and go for a walk or something?" he offered.

"Yeah, let's do that. I don't need a soda." I looked over to the rink, and saw that Chris was bringing Erin in. People were offering her things to get her nose to stop bleeding. They had turned on the lights, and asked everyone to skate off for a few minutes so that someone could go out and clean up the mess.

"Alright then, let's go."

"Hey, Russ!" It was Mike again. "Are you guys leaving already? Wanna go out to MacLean's field? There's gonna be a keg, and it's supposed to get *wild*!"

"Not tonight," he responded, trying to subtly motion his head towards me. "I'll catch up with you guys tomorrow."

"You can bring her with you. We don't bite," Erik said loudly as he came up alongside Mike, and then winked at me. I felt my insides cringe, and unconsciously scooted in closer to Russell.

"That's okay, we have plans. I'll catch you two later." He took my hand and led me back to the counter to exchange our skates for our shoes they held hostage. Once able to stand firmly on solid ground, we headed back out to his car.

The groups of punkers and metal heads were actually yelling at each other now from across the parking lot. Russell squeezed my hand harder as if to say he would protect me, and then guided us the long way around the groups to avoid being caught in the cross fire.

I heard bottles breaking, and saw shards of glass skitter across the asphalt in front of my feet which made me jump back in surprise. I tried desperately to fight of the panic rising out of my chest.

"Gwen, they aren't interested in us. Just keep moving. It'll be okay."

Once we made it down a few rows towards where we parked, I could hear police sirens approaching. When the two warring groups also noticed this, they jumped into their cars and took off.

I let out a huge sigh of relief, and eased up on the death grip I had on Russell's hand. "That was scary," I said as I waited for Russell to unlock the passenger door.

"There've been a few bad fights out here. The police were called just in time tonight, it seems. No one got hurt." He opened the door, allowing me to get in.

When he lowered himself into the driver seat and shut his door. He looked disappointed, as if sensed the shift in my mood.

"Do you want me to just take you home, or would you still like some frozen yogurt?"

"What about a walk? Is there somewhere we could go?" I asked. He suddenly perked up.

"Sure. On the way to your house is a park with a kids' jungle gym."

"No one is supposed to be there after dark. Won't we get in trouble?"

"Nah, we will be fine," he answered. "Besides, why install parking lot lights that come on automatically, if you didn't want people there?"

Chapter Twenty-One
After Dark

Russell parked beneath the only lamp in the empty lot next to the small park. In the center, the metal from the play area glinted in the light of the nearly full moon.

We found our way over and headed for the swing set nearby. The air was cool, with a clear, star-filled sky.

Choosing a seat we immediately began to see who could swing higher. The foul mood cast upon us from the parking lot at the roller rink dissipated with each pump of our legs.

"Are you going to tell me about this Megan person?" I finally asked. Erin knew I would, and I hated that I had. *God damn you, Erin*, I thought.

"Not much to tell. We dated for about six months last year. She was a sophomore," he replied without emotion, swinging back and forth gaining more height with each swing.

I began to slow my swing so I could turn myself in a circle, lost in thoughts that were making me feel insecure about my trust in anyone. I was so angry at Erin for seeding them; threatening to ruin a great first date.

"You do see what this is?" he asked, also slowing his swing, dragging his feet in the sand.

"Yes," I sighed, doing everything I could to not fall victim to jealousy and insecurity. I stopped winding the swing up, lifted my legs up, and let the momentum of the chains untwisting spin me dizzy.

"Why on earth did you even talk to them in the first place?" I finally asked.

"Because," he explained, "I felt like you've been allowing them to rule your emotions for too long. I did it to help free you of them. Are you angry?" he asked grabbing hold of my legs as the spin was about to stop.

"I don't know. It's weird how often you know exactly what I'm feeling. Then you say something or do something that is," I paused, "*exactly* right!" I paused again, analyzing how I felt. "It's unsettling. But don't get me wrong, I am happy you did," I admitted. "I do feel better."

"Good. That's all I wanted. I want you to be happy," he said, pulling my swing towards him, so that our legs were in between each other, and our hands were resting on top of each other's knees.

"You do get why I get caught off guard sometimes, you know, when you just know things about me that I had no idea you knew, right?"

"Yes," he confirmed. "I can see how that would be weird. Sorry." He pulled my hands up to his lips and kissed them.

A thought struck me, and before I could work IT through, it tumbled out, "Is it a *Circle of the Dark Stream* thing?" I asked.

The question hung in the air a bit too long before he finally answered, "How do you mean?"

"Nothing... never mind. I don't even know why I asked that." I shook my head, feeling stupid. But I couldn't help but think that, as the leader of a group of self-proclaimed witches, his mother might have the same abilities I was discovering in myself. It would just make sense that Russell would then have some sort of ability of his own, but he didn't seem willing to fess up to anything.

He was quiet, just looking at me, and again I had the sense he knew exactly what I was thinking.

"Why did you and Megan break up?" I asked suddenly, changing the subject and hoping to catch him off guard.

Casually he responded, not put out in the least, "She was the younger sister of my best friend from soccer. She was very pretty and always hanging out with us at practice. I assumed she was there because of her brother. I was too dense to realize she was into me. She asked me out," he said, laughing to himself at the memory.

"Erin reminds me a lot of Megan," he continued, and in the blue glow of the moonlight I saw his smile fade. "If I'm not mistaken, they're both manipulative and love drama. They aren't content unless they're the center of chaos. In Megan's case, it turns out I was just a trophy for her, like arm candy or something to show off to her friends. She wanted a lap dog. Someone she could treat badly."

"Did you love her?" I asked shyly, gazing down at our intertwined legs, our swings swaying back and forth.

He lifted his hand and brought it up to my face. He tilted my chin up to make eye contact then said, "No... I did not love *her*. I broke it off with her."

"Then why did Erin make it sound like it was such a big deal?" I asked frustrated with always feeling confused about why people behaved the way they did.

"To do *this* to you," he responded, with a sad smile on his face. He could feel the pain she caused me. "Megan tried to tank my reputation by spreading rumors about me sleeping around - payback for breaking up with her. Just like Erin has been trying to do to you." He used his other hand to pull our swings closer together, so he could wrap his arm around my back, and bring me in to his embrace.

"So is she why you quit soccer?" I asked, relaxing into his embrace, and staring into his face.

"No. We were over well before then." His face was now inches from mine, and he was staring at my lips. I was involuntarily lifting mine in anticipation of his kiss, as he whispered, "I'm not thinking about the past, I am already thinking about this December."

It took me a second, to register the lyrics, and responded, "And that our love is here to stay?"

"Yeah…" His lips finally came to rest on mine, as our arms wrapped tightly around each other.

He brought my legs up on top of his so that I was no longer on my own swing, but straddled his lap with my legs wrapped around him. A contented hum rumbled from this throat.

Between deep, hungry kisses, he would whisper something about keeping track of time, and how we couldn't stay long. I would whisper that I wouldn't be late, as his hands squeezed the outside of my thighs. I could feel a rise from my loins heating up my insides. I moaned unconsciously, and as soon as I became aware of it, I tried to gently push him away, gasping for air.

"Ohhh," I said, practically hyperventilating, "*Wow*." I tried to gather my thoughts, as I looked at my watch. I couldn't read it, despite it almost being the full moon. "What time is it?"

"9:40," he responded after glancing at the glowing numbers of his digital watch. "I guess we better go." Even as he said this, he continued to rub my thighs and I pulled him back in for another kiss.

He gave in for a moment then whispered, "Gwen, we really need to stop. I know, I don't want to stop kissing you either," he said, pulling away once more from wanting to dive deeper into the passion. "I need to get you home on time."

He slowly pushed me off his lap until I could get both feet back on the ground.

"I don't want you to have to go," I pouted playfully, trying to lull him back into an embrace.

He laughed as he pulled away, "If you ever want to be able to go on a second date, we need to get you back on time."

"Okay. Okay. You win!" I laughed, letting him stand up. Self-consciously he turned away slightly, straightening down his pants. I turned my head away quickly, as if I hadn't noticed. Then he took my hand and we walked back across the park to his car.

At the stroke of 10:00 p.m. we had successfully made it back to my front door. I opened it up to find my dad standing there waiting.

"You cut that close," he stated. "Thank you for getting my daughter home on time."

"No problem," he replied. "I'll talk to you tomorrow Gwen." He gave me a little wink that only I saw, making my heart skip a beat.

I waved goodbye from the safety of the well-lit foyer as my dad closed the door shut between me and the night.

Chapter Twenty-Two
Formulating a Plan

The following Sunday Cat and Kevin showed up on my doorstep after lunch. When I opened the door, the brisk early October wind blew dried leaves that had gathered outside the threshold into the entryway. It looked like it was threatening to rain.

"Come in guys," I insisted, hurrying them along with my hand. Before shutting the door I used my socked foot to push the leaves back outside, where they belonged.

They had come over to help plan our return to the old Victorian House. Knowing how little my parents would approve, we tucked ourselves away in my room, well out of earshot.

Cat sat crossed-legged on the floor, while Kevin stretched out across my white, quilted comforter. I sat on the floor, under my window, my back leaning against the wall. Skipping the usual pleasantries, we dove right in, formulating a plan.

"Well we know that the weather will keep the archeologists and investigators away. They said as much on the news," Kevin stated at one point.

"True. What about the renovations going on inside the house, though?" Cat asked.

"I think they called that off as well," I said. "So if we can just get a ride up there, the three of us could get inside. Maybe the back window we used last time will still open?"

"I doubt it. I'm sure they boarded it up after our visit. And even if it were still open, the floors in that back area were pretty dangerous," Kevin mentioned.

"Why don't we just walk in through the front door?" Cat suggested, laughing at the notion.

"Did either of you notice a way into the cellar from outside last time we were there?" I asked.

"Not that I can remember. Too bad we couldn't pick Chris's brain," Cat lamented. "He might remember."

"I'm through with him," I announced with finality.

"Wow," Kevin said under his breath.

"What? He's not the Chris I remember anymore. Whatever has changed in him over the last couple months has made him someone I don't even recognize, and Erin has just made it worse. I want nothing to do with either one of them!"

"I bet you really enjoyed watching her face plant at the rink," Kevin said, an undertone of disapproval in his voice.

"You heard about that?" I asked, in surprise. "I don't want people to get hurt, so no, I didn't enjoy that part of it. But did I feel a little vindicated in the moment? Yes! She was being a total bitch."

Cat giggled, "I wish I could have been there." Then she looked over at Kevin sheepishly, "Sorry, Kev, but she really *is* a bitch. Karma, baby!"

"Maybe…" he said quietly, still not hiding his disapproval.

"What? You haven't been on the receiving end. You've no idea how it's been for me, and hell, if Chris really cared about our friendship he wouldn't have shut me out, and he wouldn't have allowed her to bully me! Whatever he's been going through, he's made it pretty hard for me to sympathize."

"Yeah, I get it," he replied. "He's my friend though, you know? We hang out and stuff. This is making me feel like I have to pick a side or something, and I shouldn't have to."

"So don't," I said. "Look, it's not that I don't care, I do! But I'm also just done being hurt. If you want to ask him about the house, you can do that, and then just get back to us," I said, trying to ease the sudden tension.

"Okay, fair enough," Kevin relaxed. "So… how are we going to get there? Mike again?"

"No way!" Cat exclaimed. "He already thinks I'm nuts, and he'd probably snitch if he found out what we're planning. He got in trouble with mom last time."

"What about your new *boyfriend*, Gwen?" Kevin asked. "He's got a car."

"I haven't told him about any of this. I just… well, I don't want him to think I'm crazy. I'm surprised he hasn't asked, considering the shit Erin was saying about me at the beginning of school."

"Maybe he didn't hear about it. It's not like they run in the same circles or anything," Kevin offered.

"He seemed to know she had been bullying me, and he somehow knew that Chris had thrown our friendship away," I mentioned. Looking at Cat, I asked, "Have you ever mentioned any of this drama to Mike?"

"No! Ew! I don't talk about my friends with him," she said. "Besides he doesn't care about what's going on in my life."

This shocked me, because Russell kept saying he heard things from Mike. "Did you ever give Mike my phone number?" I asked.

"No. Why would I do that?" Cat asked, and then laughed at how silly that sounded.

"Could Mike have gotten my number and address from your room? Do you have it written down somewhere?"

"I have a small address book I keep in my desk drawer. So I guess it is possible, if he really needed to know. Why?" she asked.

"Hmmm... just curious," I mumbled, and shrugged it off, not wanting to admit my nagging suspicions Russell hadn't been entirely truthful, and I hated the idea. I was beginning to suspect there was another side to Russell, and so far, my hunches had been right.

"He might be our only chance of getting a ride up there. You're going to need to bring him into the loop if we're going to return those keys," Kevin suggested. "It's either that, or we wait until I get my license next summer."

"We can't wait that long," I sighed.

"I know I can't. My dreams are getting worse," Cat said in all seriousness.

"Mine too," I admitted. This brought Kevin to attention.

"Really? So, the both of you are having nightmares? It's not just me?"

"What?" I asked in surprise, completely shocked that Kevin had been affected in the same way Cat and I had. Did that mean that Chris, Erin and Andrea may have also have been affected?

"Oh, Kev! I had no idea. Why didn't you ever tell me?" Cat asked, getting up from the floor and joining him on the bed.

"It's been hard... I feel like I haven't slept in weeks," he admitted, and then he let Cat put her arms around him, pulling her into an embrace. "I didn't tell you because of how awful your dreams have been. I didn't want to share what I was seeing and make it worse for you."

He then looked at me and said, "I never told you guys, but while I was digging around in the embankment under the tracks, trying to find the grave, I started seeing things. Like brief shimmers within the shadows. The more I dug, the more frequent the shimmers would appear around me, and the brighter they became. It started to freak me out, especially when they took on the forms of full-grown men."

"What?" I asked. "This is big stuff, Kevin. How could you not tell us?"

"That would be terrifying!" Cat confirmed.

"It *was* pretty scary! I just wanted to put it behind me, ya know? I thought it was all done."

"Yeah, we know! I think we all wanted this to be behind us," I offered.

"The dreams started after that. The ghosts of those men were trying to get my attention, trying to talk to me, but they were angry and confused. They would chase after me, and I would run up out of the forest only to find myself back at the house. In the dreams I am always forced to either flee into the house to get away from the ghosts, or turn to face them. But I never get the chance to make a decision because I suddenly find myself upstairs in that back hallway. It's dark, and I am alone. I freak out when I see them in the hallway coming towards me. They just aren't right. Something's wrong with them. They start to surround me, and I wake up screaming."

"That's awful, Kevin," I offered.

"Poor baby," Cat replied, hugging him again, and planting his face with kisses.

"Okay," I coughed, "back to the plan."

Kevin, blushed, then pretended to be disgusted with her overzealous display of affection, and gently pushed her back. "The plan is you have to tell Russell the truth about what's going on," he said with certainty.

"I agree!" Cat nodded. "He'll find out eventually, Gwen. You can't keep this from him."

"What if he thinks I'm lying like my parents did? What if he breaks up with me because he thinks I'm crazy?"

"Gwen, he's obviously totally in love with you," Kevin said, as if this were something I should have known already.

"I think he'll surprise you," Cat offered.

"Do you know something I don't know?" I asked her, trying to read her face to see if she was just messing with me. "Did he say something to Mike?" I continued, as I got up off the floor and walked over to her. I casually put my hand on her arm, and asked again, "What do you know?"

"Ohhh nooo you don't!" she exclaimed pulling her arm away, and laughing. "You're not reading MY mind."

I laughed, and then sat beside them on the bed, "You have nothing to worry about. I still can't figure out how to do it on purpose!"

"Oh, that weird mumbo jumbo voodoo shit," Kevin remarked.

"Cat!" I exclaimed. "What happened to 'I promise I won't tell a soul'?" I knew perfectly well she'd confide in Kevin, but I had to give her a hard time anyways.

"I never said any such thing!" she declared.

"It was implied," I responded, trying to suppress a grin. "And now Kevin thinks I'm a complete lunatic!"

"I was there, remember? I saw what happened to you. We've all experienced some crazy shit lately. I believe what Cat told me. I pretty much believe anything at this point."

"That's a relief. I didn't want to have to use any of my mumbo jumbo voodoo magic on you."

178

"Gwen, you're stalling," Kevin chided.

"Oh. My. God!" I exclaimed dramatically. "You want me to call him *right* now?"

"Yeah, just get it over with," Cat responded.

"Yeah, and we'll be here for moral support," Kevin said, cuddling Cat in his arms, and nibbling at her ears.

"Stop it you two. Gross." I stood up from the edge of the bed and walked across the bedroom to the door. "I'll be back in one minute, so just cut that out." As I left the room I could hear them kissing, and Cat giggling.

I took the phone off the hook, and dialed Russell's number. I assumed he would be home, considering it was Sunday, but I had not heard from him yet that day.

"Hello?" A young female voice asked. It was the first time I had ever called his house when he wasn't the one to answer.

"Hi. I am looking for Russell, is he home?" I asked politely.

"Oh, you must be Gwen?" the voice asked, and I could hear her curiosity oozing through the phone line.

"Yes. Hi," I replied.

"This is Ciara," she said, "Russell's sister. Sorry, but he's at Shanachie."

"Oh, I thought he only worked there on Saturdays," I responded.

"He's helping out today. Did you want me to tell him you called?" she asked.

"Yes, please. Can you ask him to call me when he gets home. Will he be back late?"

"The store closes tonight at 7:00 p.m. don't you worry, Gwen. He'll be calling you as soon as he walks in the door," she said. "You're all he thinks about. Can't wait to see what all the fuss is about."

"Ha!" I laughed involuntarily. "I don't exactly know what all the fuss is about either." I couldn't tell if she was teasing me, or being genuine.

"Oh, you don't have to worry about me," she chirped. "I know you and I will get along wonderfully! I'll give him the message. Oh, and just like your friend said, I think he will surprise you. Ta!" The phone went dead.

I stood there staring at the receiver. *'Just like my friend said'? How could she have known what Cat said?*

After I hung up, I walked back to my room, making sure I was loud enough for Cat and Kevin to hear so I didn't walk in on anything embarrassing. I pushed open the door to see Cat sitting on the edge of bed, waiting for me. Kevin was back in his reclining position.

"We heard. Sorry we couldn't help ourselves," Cat admitted.

"So you weren't just back here getting naked?" I asked, grinning.

"I wish!" Kevin exclaimed. Cat turned around to hit him playfully.

"How much did you hear?" I asked.

"Well it's more like what we didn't hear - you asking Russell for a ride," Cat responded.

"He's at his mom's shop. His sister answered the phone. It was the strangest thing…"

"What was the name of her shop again?" Kevin asked, interrupting.

Cat smacked him again, and answered, "Shanachie."

"What the hell kind of store is that?" he laughed.

"It has books and candles and incense and, like, stuff about magic," Cat explained.

"Ah, voodoo mumbo jumbo!" Kevin quipped.

"Stop it," Cat replied, punching him lightly on the arm.

"I looked the name up after we were there. It basically means *storyteller*. In traditional times there would be a shanachie assigned to each Scottish clan. They were the keeper of traditions and ceremonies and serve as the historian and genealogist. I think it's a great name for a book shop, don't you?"

"Yeah, I guess it's cool," Kevin responded.

"He won't be home until after 7:00, so... I guess there isn't much more we can do today as far as planning goes," I sighed.

"We can go back over to my house and watch some movies?" Cat offered.

"Yeah, let's do that," I responded. "I don't want to sit around all day just waiting for him to get home."

"Okay!" Kevin jumped up off the bed, grabbed Cat by the hand and started for the door. Cat quickly grabbed my hand, tugging me along behind her.

I slipped on my shoes, and as we exited the house I yelled, "Bye mom, going over to Cat's!"

"Be back by dinner!" I heard her yell as I closed the door behind me.

"Okay, so about the strange thing that happened..." I began, as we walked to Cat's house.

Chapter Twenty-Three
Revelations

Picking up the phone on the first ring, I responded, "Hi, Russell."

"Oh, hey!" he replied in surprise. "Were you just waiting by the phone?" he teased.

"Yes, as a matter of fact I was," I answered, trying my best to not be a nervous wreck.

"Is everything alright? You sound off."

"Yes, everything is okay," I answered. I was amazed at how easily he could hear even the slightest shift in my tone. It was impossible to keep anything from him. "But I need to tell you a story," I continued as I held the phone up to my ear, holding on the extension cord as I made my way down to the bedroom.

"Okay..." he trailed off with a questioning tone to his voice. "It sounds heavy."

"It's sort of a big deal, so yeah," I replied, taking in deep breaths to calm my nerves, as I shut the bedroom door behind me. "Please don't think I'm crazy. I swear what I'm about to tell you is the truth." I went over to my bed, and lay down on my back. I wrapped the comforter around me, a literal security blanket.

"There's nothing you could say to me that would make me think you're crazy. Hold on… let me go down the hall to my room. My sisters are looking at me with stupid expressions on their faces, and I don't want to be distracted." I could hear girls giggling in the background and the sound of his footsteps as he walked down the hall, and then I heard the door shut. "Okay, it's just you and me now," he said sweetly.

"Maybe you should get comfortable."

"Alright, I'm walking over to my bed, and I'm lying down on my back. Okay, all comfy."

"Okay. It was my 10th birthday…" I began, and then laid out the whole story.

When I'd finished recounting everything prior to the summer's adventure, I waited to hear Russell's response.

"That'd be pretty scary for a little girl to process," he responded

A huge wave of relief washed over me. "Yes, that's it exactly!" I exclaimed, happy at his validating what I had experienced.

"I'm sorry you had to go through that," he replied.

"Thank you," I responded, feeling better now that I was sharing this part of myself with him, and also surprised at just how well he was handling it.

"Sooo… this isn't freaking you out?" I asked in complete astonishment.

"No, not at all," he said matter-of-factly. "Go on, finish the story."

"Okay, so I became obsessed with going back someday to prove to myself there was a ghost, that I wasn't nuts. Somewhere along the line, I got it into my head that the old Victorian House up there was somehow connected..." I paused, trying to gather my thoughts.

"Gwen, you still there?" he asked, concerned, as the pause stretched on. "It's okay. You can tell me anything. There's nothing to be afraid of."

"Well, that's the problem." I stammered. "There IS something to be afraid of. I took Chris, Erin, Andrea, Cat and Kevin with me last summer up to that house. I...we... in the house was..." I couldn't find the words.

I had tried really hard to suppress the memories of the visions I had when touching that awful doll, but suddenly they came flooding back. I became lost in the memory of the little girl menacingly glaring back at me from the mirror in the attic, and of what I had seen through her eyes, image after image. Then I started to remember the dream...

"You were saying, 'in the house', then what?" he asked. I could hear his voice through the phone but it seemed so far away, as I went deeper and deeper into remembering. "Can you hear me? Try to focus on the sound of my voice... follow my voice back from wherever you are. Gwen, come back to me."

"Yes," I said quietly. His soothing, hypnotic voice grabbed hold of something inside me, bringing me out of the trauma of that day. I saw his face, I could smell the scent of his skin, and I could actually feel his arms around me.

"You okay?" he asked. "I think I have a pretty good idea now about what happened up there."

I sat up, confused, "Did I black out, or something? I don't remember finishing…"

"No, you didn't," he replied quietly, hesitating. "Did my sister happen to know something about you today that couldn't have?"

"Yes, but…how…" I trailed off, losing track of the conversation, and completely bewildered.

"You asked me about it before," he said.

"Like ESP, right?" I asked.

"Yes! Exactly like that! It runs in our family. Remember that thing my mom said to you, *da shealladh*?"

"Yeah."

"She sensed it in you. It means two sights. You are like us," he admitted. "Like just now, when you were lost in your memories of what you saw in the house, well, I was sort of seeing it as well."

"So that's why I always get the feeling you know more about me than possible," I replied. Everything began to make sense.

"You're able to do the same thing, especially when you're able to touch people or objects," he offered. "The Scots call that *taibhsear* (he pronounced it tah-shar), the vision seer."

"Wow, this is so weird!"

186

"When did you first notice it? Has it always been like this for you?"

"No. At least I don't think so. It's been happening mostly since this summer, and happening more often. I've always experienced déjà vu, but that hits me a lot more now than it ever used to. Sometimes it not just visions from touching, it's just a sense of... knowing, or feeling."

"Yep, that's what it's like. It'll get easier once you understand the extent of the gift. Soon you'll be able to control it, instead of the other way around. It took a long time to get used to my sisters always reading my mind. I could never get away with anything. But they also helped me learn to harness the ability within myself. It's just a part of who we are. Accept it, and trust it."

"So then..."I was going to test his claim. "What was I planning to ask you?"

"Well, either... am I really in love with you, or will I drive you, Cat and Kevin back up to the house?" he asked, then laughed lightly to himself, as if he knew that my jaw had just hit the floor.

Chapter Twenty-Four
Twin Flame

After an awkward silence of being caught off guard, and trying to remember if the subject had even been brought up, I stuttered, "Wh wha what? Wait! Go back and repeat that first part."

"Of course, I'll definitely drive you guys up there," he answered, trying to mask the toying tone in his voice, and completely ignoring my request. "By the way," he continued, "my mom and I were discussing you today. She thinks I can help."

I waited a few moments before responding, my heart sinking. I was thinking to myself, *Maybe I'm reading too much into this. Maybe he wasn't implying that he actually loved me. He was just asking if that is what I wanted to know. Now he's not responding, so what does that mean?*

"Okay, thanks," I managed to respond, trying to swallow the lump in my throat. "Help with what, exactly? We just need to sneak in and return the box of keys to the steamer trunk."

"Hmmm. She believes there's another reason you need to return to the house."

"Well, Cat and I think that by returning the keys, the ghosts won't haunt our dreams anymore."

"What makes you think that the ghosts are attached to the keys?"

"Well, for starters, Cat can communicate with her father, even though he's been dead for quite a few years. When we were in the house, he acted like a guide. The other spirits talked through him. That's how we learned that they were trapped there."

"Oh, that I *didn't* know," he answered back, genuinely surprised.

"Finally something you don't already know," I teased.

"And the keys... did *he* tell her something about them?"

"No, the spirits communicated that to me. They were with her dad the night Cat and I contacted him. They must have realized he could communicate with us, and then sort of attached themselves to him, to get through to *us*. I don't know how it works on their end. All I know is that I heard men yelling at me, begging me to help - that they were trapped. They told us the mother was angry because people were trying to renovate her house, and that the little girl was angry because she wanted her doll. They told us to bring the keys back."

I briefly explained then who Tabitha and Jane Elizabeth Briggs were, and how they were haunting our dreams.

"I don't think the keys are the problem," he responded. "I do a lot of reading about this stuff at work, and one thing I remember is the theory that it isn't the objects themselves that are haunted."

"Then why did I get taken over by the people whose things I touched, like Joseph's marble, or Jane's doll?

"Psychometry," he answered.

"I'm sorry… what?"

"Some people, like you, have the ability to read someone through their belongings. The more someone handles their things, the more of them they leave behind, like psychic fingerprints."

"So you're saying I'm psychic?"

"Yes, but more than that, you're able to see inside someone's thoughts… and feel their emotions, which means you're also telepathic and empathic."

"Wow!" I responded. I finally had names for the things I had been experiencing. "Is that what *you* can do as well? Feel people's emotions and read their thoughts?"

"Yes," he answered, sounding relieved to have finally confessed the truth. "Does everything make more sense to you now?"

"It does," I sighed in relief.

"And since you're able to communicate with spirits, you're a *natural* medium. It's no wonder the house awakened when you started interacting with it, unfolding its secrets, touching the walls. Cat's connection with her dad was important, sure, but you were the spark that brought it back to life."

"So then, why are my friends also having nightmares?"

"Your energy and abilities to communicate with the spirits in the house drew them to you like a beacon of light in the darkness," he explained. "A little of you has rubbed off on those closest to you, just enough, to open a pathway through them, as well. The spirits communicate through your dreams, because that's when your subconscious opens up and you are more able to hear them. Clearly they're desperate for someone to acknowledge them."

"Are they in purgatory or limbo or something? Is that why they're trapped?"

"I've been around this stuff my whole life. I've read all the books in my mother's store. What I've learned is that some people, who experience a sudden or tragic death, don't know they're dead. They're confused. They don't understand why they can't interact with our physical world in the same way that they used to. It makes them frustrated and angry. It causes their energy to mutate over time, and become dangerous to us, or cause us to feel sick when we're around them. Those of us who understand the spirit world, know that when we feel this way in certain places, that it's because a spirit is nearby. Most people call it a haunting."

"That makes a lot of sense, because I kept feeling sick when I was connected to Joseph and then again in the house. It turns out he was poisoned! I felt like I was going to die, so I must have experienced what he felt. It was just *awful*!"

"That *is* awful! It must have been traumatizing to experience," he offered. It felt wonderful to be heard in this

191

way, and to be receiving answers and validation in return. "Getting rid of spirits, or setting them free, isn't easy, though," he continued. "The more mutated or evil they have become over time, the harder it is. For others, it's just a simple matter of helping them find closure, acknowledging their existence and what happened to them, then helping them face the truth. Some, on the other hand, might just choose to stay."

They choose to stay? Why? I wondered to myself.

"I don't know if they go to heaven or go to hell, in the theological sense, but what I do know is that if they can come to terms with their death, find justice, feel validated or what have you, they 'move on'. Does that mean that they've let go of the energy they were holding onto by sheer force of will, and allow themselves to become part of the universe like molecules of water or the scent of spring blossoms in the air? I don't know. But I do believe that we're part of the energy all around us."

"You just kind of blew my mind!" I responded in amazement. "I had *no* idea you were into all that stuff. Where were you this summer when I needed you?"

"I'm here now," he responded. "They say 'in life, there are no coincidences'."

"Who says that?" I asked laughing.

"Don't tease me," he laughed, realizing that he had been rambling on and on, "I don't know… *someone* said it."

"Hmmm… okay then let me ask you this, Mr. Smarty Pants, how do we help those people who died on that property, the ones in the mass grave? How do we give them closure?"

"There's a ritual. My mom has a list of things we'll need, and she'll instruct us on how to perform it," he answered. "Oh, remember that flyer you got from Judith, and how it mentioned the next full moon for the gathering of the Circle?"

"Yes, was that this weekend?"

"It was this morning. Well, they actually started at midnight and went on through the early morning hours. That's why I had to work."

"Uh, okay," I replied, unsure to how that had anything to do with what we were talking about.

"You'd asked, before, what it meant by 'Drawing Down the Moon'. It's a ritual my mother performs to bring the goddess down from the moon to inhabit her body, to offer guidance. She would compare it to the same thing as a person at church asking the Holy Spirit to enter their body, working through them and guiding them. There's really no difference, depending on what you believe. Apparently last night, the Circle sought guidance and protection for you."

"They were seeking guidance for me? So it *is* some sort of witch thing..."

"Yes something like that," he answered vaguely.

"And protection... why?"

"My mother must have seen what you experienced this summer, and knew that you're only just coming into your abilities," he informed me, "So she knew you needed

193

something more, if you were going to go back to that house."

I sat there in silence, surprised that I wasn't feeling skeptical or afraid from everything he'd just told me. I was just trying to absorb the information, as my heart danced a quick-step in my chest from the adrenaline rush.

"Does hearing all this freak you out?" he asked.

"No," I answered without hesitation. In my gut, it all felt true. "Is that why I feel such a strong connection with you, because you and I share the same abilities?" I asked, piecing it all together, my mind expanding beyond anything I thought possible.

"I'd like to think it's more than that," he interjected.

"I still remember that first time we made eye contact when you passed by in the hall," I reflected.

"Me too. It was the first time you actually noticed me, but not just that, you really *saw* me and felt something between us."

"I did, it was so weird, like I knew you somehow. When I finally let my guard down as we were dancing, the feelings were a lot to deal with. I didn't know if it was you, or if it was me, but it just felt so… right."

"It is," he answered. "And yes," he started again after a slight pause, "I *am* in love with you."

My heart sped up even faster, and heat ignited in my chest that warmed up my entire being, vanquishing that lump of sadness in my throat. I felt like a giant ball of fire just waiting to explode.

"I do. I *love* you," he said again, in a sweet whisper that came through the phone like a gentle kiss.

Hearing the words escape his lips, and really truly feeling the intensity behind what they meant, I began to understand. I understood how the word *love*, meant so much more than the intense infatuation or lust I had with Ryan, or the affectionate friendship I felt with Chris. I understood that this was entirely new, and something larger than anything and everything that had ever come before.

"I love *you* too," I whispered into the phone, feeling that ball of fire force itself up and tear open my heart to lie exposed and vulnerable to the world.

Chapter Twenty-Five
A Lightness of Being

The following Saturday, officially finished with the first week of October, Cat and I took the bus downtown again. We got off in front of the library and made our way through the busy intersection to the Kilncroft Terrace Shopping Center. It was coming up on 11:00 a.m. and Russell would be opening up the shop soon.

I was nervous as we walked across the parking lot, knowing now that Brighid was not only Russell's mother, but a High Priestess of a Witch Coven. The mere fact she'd loaned me a book, specifically to spur visions of that woman and her séances, completely astounded me.

"Gwen, you look terrible! Are you going to puke?" Cat asked, as we made it onto the sidewalk beneath the overhang.

"No," I laughed, although I did feel a bit nauseous. "Just nervous."

"Why? You've already met Brighid, and now you're meeting up with your boyfriend. So what's the big deal?"

"But in context, Brighid is now my boyfriend's mom, not just the shopkeeper," I responded. *And a witch*, I thought to myself. "I know! It shouldn't be a big deal, but everything feels different. I feel different."

"Sometimes I don't understand you," she sighed, but then laughed lightly to let me know she was just giving me a hard time. She elbowed me in the ribs, and said, "Lighten up."

We saw the door to Shanachie open up, and heard the bell jangle, as Russell stepped out onto the sidewalk. "Guid mornin', bonnie lasses," he greeted us.

He stepped back and with a swing of his arm gestured Cat into the store in front of me. As I passed by, grinning at how cute he sounded putting on the accent, he put his arm out in front of me and stopped my forward momentum.

"Not you. You can't pass through unless you give me the secret password."

"If it's some sort of a Scottish gibberish then I'm stuck outside," I responded, laughing at his playfulness.

"Aye, it is," he winked.

"*Pawkie?*"

"No, although it is a *dreich* day."

"*Numptie?*

"Who are you calling silly?" he asked, laughing. "No."

"*Auld lang syne?*" I blurted out, feeling silly.

"Is that all you got? We're definitely gonna have to expand that vocabulary!"

"We will, will we?"

"Okay, fine, I'll tell you the secret password, but only because I'm feeling charitable."

"Aw jeez thanks," I replied sarcastically.

"*Smourich.*"

"What does that mean?"

He leaned over and gave me a long firm kiss on the lips, and then smiled, "Kiss. I would have accepted the word, *winch*, as well."

"Clearly you're confused, the word is **smooch**!" I replied, overenunciating the word. Then I giggled and returned his kiss, as he ushered me through the front door. As it shut behind me the Tibetan bell rang out again, and, as on cue, his mother came around from behind the counter to greet us.

"Wylcome, hou's aw wi ye?" she asked as she walked towards me with her arms out and brought me into her embrace. This time, with my heart and mind more open than before, I hugged her back, feeling even closer to her.

"Good morning, Brighid," I replied, as she was the first to pull away from the hug.

She glanced down at my hand, nodding approval, and said, "Guid, guid, ye are still wearin the ring. Tis a braw start. A'll be right back!" Then she quickly walked to the back of the store. I heard the sound of drawers being opened and closed.

"Brighid, we brought the book back," I called out pulling it out of the large purse I had hanging from my shoulder.

"Guid, guid... just leave it on the' counter. Russell, come wig's. Wan tae write it down?"

As Russell went back to help his mother, I joined Cat at the book table. She was chuckling over a book of Scottish slang and dirty word translations.

That day the front table also had hand-carved wooden figurines placed throughout the stacks of books. There was a place-card that read, Local Artist: Fergus Carmichael.

"Look, Cat. He has the same name as our high school," I mentioned, as I picked up the nearest piece. It was a figurine about 9 inches tall of a horse rearing up on its hind legs - legs that had morphed out of an ocean wave. I turned it over to see if it had a description on the underside. The name of the piece read: *Kelpie*.

I moved around the table and picked up a second piece. A seal crawling up a rock, but in front of it was a naked woman crawling up the same rock in the same way, as if one had become the other. The surface was sanded down so fine, it felt as smooth as glass, and the details of the beautiful woman were amazing. I turned this over to read: *Selkie*.

Cat had taken notice of the art as well, and was holding one depicting that of a partially clothed man with the head of a howling wolf. The features were so well detailed, so delicate and fine, the fur looked like it was moving.

What's that one called?" I asked her.

She turned it over and replied, "*Wulver*... I guess this must be a Scottish version of a werewolf? It's really cool, huh?"

"Yeah," I said, already distracted by a shelf of other figurines. I hadn't noticed them on our first visit. These were smaller carvings: faeries, goblins, gnomes, toadstools and frogs. They were whimsical yet menacing, like they were meant to entice children, but not for good reasons.

"Gwen, can you come back here?" Russell asked as he came up to the front of the store. "My mom wants you for a few minutes. Nothing personal, Cat."

"Oh, I'm fine," she responded. "This is keeping me very entertained." Her attention had diverted to the watercolor paintings.

Russell brought me to the very back of the store, behind the curtain of cobalt blue beads, where Brighid was pulling some of the twine wrapped bundles of dried vegetation down from the ceiling.

She turned to me, smelling the loosely-bound bundle in her hand. "This is white sage. The Latin word fur sage is *salvia*, it means 'tae heal'. This haes bin uised fur centuries in mony cultures."

"Used for cooking?" I asked innocently, taken aback by the strong scent. Then I remembered some of the herbs I found crushed up in the little drawers of the apothecary in the steamer trunk. "Medicine?"

"This is uised in a ritual called smudging. It kin be performed tae clear yer emotional, spiritual an physical body as well as the energy in yer field. It kin also be performed tae clear awa' negative energy or spirits from a place. We are gang tae uise it tae dae both things."

Russell went to a large hanging tapestry, and pulled it aside to reveal the exit door to the back of the building. He opened it up, and shoved a wedge underneath to keep it ajar.

Brighid lit an incense stick. "This is made from the *Palo Santo* tree in Peru. It means 'holy wood'."

She then lit several white votive candles around the room. Another wave of déjà vu crashed over me. It was so familiar, the dim light of the candles chasing away the shadows from every corner of the room. *Could I have foreseen this very moment?* I asked myself. *Would I ever get used to this?*

In a small copper bowl were a collection of herbs that she also lit on fire, explaining, "And this is copal, myrrh an frankincense resin. This wull promote spiritual cleansing an purification, an bring us tae a heightened awareness."

As the smoke rose from the bowl, a delicious aroma filled the small room.

She moved to a second larger copper bowl filled with wood chips, and set them ablaze as she explained, "This is cedar wood, which wull offer us protection."

Russell held up the bundle of sage at an angle, lit it and let it burn for a few seconds. Then he blew out the flame leaving glowing orange embers at the very ends. He then hit that end against the edge of the table, which loosened the bundle, causing the embers to brighten as smoke filled the room.

Brighid stood in front of him as he leaned down and picked up an abalone shell, holding it in the same hand, under the bundle of sage, to collect the ashes as they fell.

He picked up a large brown hawk feather with his other hand, and she bowed to him and closed her eyes.

He started at the top of her head, bringing the smoke from the sage around her crown, clockwise, like a halo. She began reciting, "Onie energy that isnae o' mah greatest guid, yer wanted 'ere na mair…"

He continued down to her shoulders, down her arms across her palms, down her torso, ending at her feet. She continued her mantra, "Please lea me noo, it's time tae go , exit thro' the open door."

He then repeated the ritual, except that this time, from behind. Since she had no shoes on, at the very end she lifted each foot so that he, using the feather, could fan smoke on the soles of her feet.

I felt so humbled to have witnessed such an intimate moment between them, and felt almost guilty for having been in the room at all.

Brighid then took a deep breath, held it for a few seconds. When she exhaled, Russell waved the sage at her breath as he used the feather to push the smoke towards the open door.

When she turned to me she looked like she had just returned from the spa, in a completely serene state. She extended her arms out to invite me closer. Russell handed the burning sage, shell, and feather to her, as he came up alongside me and took my hand. I was surprised, yet thankful for the comfort it brought me. I had no idea what was going on. He squeezed my hand twice, which made me smile. *We got this.*

"Ah wull noo perform the identical ritual wi ye both. Mind tae recite the words tae hulp in the cleanin'. Ye want onie negative energy that might be attached tae ye tae lea, and ye want tae allow yer negative memories and feelings towards ithers tae lea ye as weel."

She then went on to perform the smudging on the two of us. We recited the words as she had, "Any energy that is not of my greatest good, you're wanted here no more. Please leave me now, it's time to go, exit through the open door."

I felt renewed somehow when she was done. I also felt in some weird way like she had performed some sort of bonding ceremony between Russell and I, and by doing so giving her full blessing of us.

I was overflowing in a joy, a lightness of being, that I had never known. So many dark things I had been carrying were gone, and literally it was a weight off my shoulders.

I looked over at Russell, who was positively beaming. I knew he felt that same sense of intimacy that I was - a bonding and a blessing from his mother, as well as an empowering for what was to come.

Chapter Twenty-Six
Preparing for Battle

Cat walked through the bead curtain to find us all standing around, with the burning sage still in Brighid's hand.

"Juist the lassie ah wanted tae see," she said warmly.

"It's okay, Cat. It's to help us be rid of the negative energy and spirits that might be hanging around," I stated, trying to make light of it so as to not scare her off.

"Oh, a smudging… excellent," she responded walking over to where we stood. She then laughed at the expression on my face. "I know a lot more about this stuff than you know."

"Apparently!" I responded. "You are always full of surprises."

Russell and I backed away, still holding hands. I honestly never wanted to let go. He started rubbing his thumb up and down along my skin. *Oh no don't start that again,* I thought to myself. I heard him snicker.

When I looked up at him he gave me a face, like, *what did I do*? Then he bent over to whisper in my ear, purposely letting his breath linger against the sensitive skin of my earlobe, "Would you like to join me around the corner for a second?"

"Russell! Haud yer wheesht!" Brighid scolded. He straightened up, and stood quietly.

Brighid then performed the entire ritual on Cat, who recited the words perfectly, as if rehearsed. Once she was done, she put the embers out in the Abalone shell, and exited out the back door, where I saw her dump the ashes in a bin.

Cat turned to me, and had that same glow about her that Brighid did. "Wow, I feel so…. so tingly," she stuttered, clearly delirious.

"Pretty cool, huh?" I responded. The words were lacking, but I just had no other way to articulate what we had experienced. *I wonder if I glow like that too.*

"Okay, now we need to collect the items we used today, as well as a few more. We are going to perform this same ceremony on the house," Russell stated.

"The whole house?" I asked, not sure I understood him correctly. "Like, as in, the entire house?"

"Aye!" Brighid responded. "Thare are a few suggested incantations as well, tae address directly tae the spirits that linger. Ah think ye wull lairn mure just throu' yer ability tae communicate wi thaim, as tae whit they may need. Remember tae come frae a place o' louv, dinnae dae oniething tae offend thaim. Ah wull send ye wi a special amulet the goddess blessed at the doo."

I looked over again to Russell, for a translation, and whispered, "A doo?"

"The ceremony they held under the full moon," he answered, placing the black stone and silver pendant necklace over my head, pulling my long hair up through the chain. "The stone is black Tourmaline which will provide a grounding energy, for when we're in the house. It'll help turn negative energy into positive. The silver Shield Knot is an ancient Celtic symbol that was placed on, well... shields, when going into battle to ward off evil spirits and danger."

"Wow, it's beautiful. Thank you," I responded.

Russell then went over and placed one over Cat's neck as well. "Yes, thank you Brighid, I feel so wonderful right now... like I could fly. I feel so light," she replied.

I heard the bell ring out from the front of the store. Brighid said, "Russell!"

"Okay, mom," he replied, stole a quick kiss, and disappeared through the curtain of beads.

Brighid then handed me a sack filled with everything we would need, as well as a sheet of paper, and said, "This is whit's wantit fer ea' mixture fur the burnin' bowls, an this is the hoo tae perform smudging o' the room. In ea' room, remember tae open up the windaes or doors, tae clear a path fur the spirits tae exit through."

Then she handed me a bell and said, "Ere is a Tibetan bell, lik' ah hae oan the front door. It wull scatter the negative energy an encourage the positive energy, sae ring it in ea' corner o' the hoose."

"Okay," I answered, taking the bell, and putting it in the sack.

"Och, yin lest thing, pay claise attention tae the doorways… energy tends tae get stuck thaur."

"We will," Cat answered this time.

"Russell will be thaur, sae ye wull be fine. Keep the ring an amulet on ye at all times."

"I will. Thank you again." I said, reaching out to hug her. Then Cat did the same, which surprised me, knowing she was not a very touchy feely person with strangers. Brighid held her in a long embrace. I was proud to see that Cat did not pull away first.

She walked with us through the store, as Russell was explaining merchandise to a customer.

"Russell, tis nae problem," she said, referring to the customer. "Ye kin tak thaim hame. Ah dinnae want thaim oan a public bus right noo."

"You're right," he replied. "Okay, hold on guys, let me get my keys."

"Dinnae dawdle, an ye better hurry back."

"I will," he replied as he met up with us at the front door. He twirled the keys around his finger by the ring. "Let's get you home!"

We walked across the drive to Russell's silver Volvo. He unlocked and opened the passenger side door, and pulled the front seat forward, so Cat could climb in the back. Once I was safely seated in the front, he shut the door and came around to the driver's side.

Only after he had the engine going, and was putting the car in reverse, did I dare finally ask, "Will you please explain to us everything she said back there?"

He laughed as he placed his arm around the back of my head rest to be able to see better in reverse. Then he came to a stop, and shifted into drive. "I was wondering when you were going to admit that you didn't understand anything she was telling you."

"Guilty!" Cat called out from the back seat, laughing also. "It was so hard to understand her that all I could do was nod and smile."

"At least she wrote everything down," I offered.

Driving through the parking lot heading towards the exit onto Ash, Russell asked, "What did you not understand? Where do you want me to start?"

"At the beginning," I responded, and Cat nodded in agreement.

We made our way through the intersection, turning left on Alder in front of the library, when he explained, "Well, in a nut shell, we're going to perform that same smudging ritual on the house. We're going to open up every door and window we can, light white candles, light up the same ingredients in the burning bowls, and ask the spirits to leave. There's more to it, of course, but we'll go through it once we're there."

"When is the big day?" I asked.

"This coming Saturday night is the new moon, which is a powerful phase for banishing and clearing out of negative energy. It's the moon of new beginnings, and the last of the waning moon. House cleansings are best under a waning moon."

"At night?" Cat asked.

"It has to be at night. The new moon will be at its most powerful at 12:04 a.m.," he answered, as we continued up Briarwood Avenue from Alder.

"I guess I'll be spending the night at your house, Cat," I stated, realizing I would be out way past curfew, and could never tell my parents where we were going.

"It's bad enough thinking about having to return there at all, but at night. Are you crazy?" Cat exclaimed, sitting back with her arms folded, shaking her head.

"You're not having second thoughts are you?" Russell asked, looking at her through the rear view mirror. "It'll be fine! Just think of the good that we will be doing, helping free those confused spirits trapped there," he offered.

"*You've* never met Jane Elizabeth," I responded, shivering at the memories I had shared with her.

Chapter Twenty-Seven
Return to the Scene of the Crimes

That whole week at school, I couldn't concentrate. As each day passed, my anxiety increased. Although I had some idea of what I was walking into, I did not feel mentally prepared in any way.

The fear of being joined with Jane Elizabeth again was ever present. I did not want to relive those memories, or actually encounter Tabitha, like I had in my dreams.

I didn't know why Tabitha was still lingering there. She had used the Ouija board to open a doorway to the spirit world in that house, so perhaps she accidentally trapped herself. Or, maybe she chose to stay behind to keep intruders from the house that she adored? Maybe it was to hide the ugly truth about the horrors that her daughter committed, and the poor treatment of the people at the farm? There were so many secrets to protect.

Russell had to remind me each morning, when we met by the lockers, to release the negative thoughts. To trust in the good we were going to do. His confidence helped a little, but the thing that helped the most was in knowing he'd be there for support.

I asked Andrea to join us, a means of closure. She wanted nothing to do with the house ever again. Before, when I had asked her if she was having bad dreams, she'd denied it. She acted, just like Cat said, as though what happened over the summer was not a big deal - it was just an exciting day in a scary house, almost as if she'd been to Disneyland. She accused us of being nuts though, for even considering going back there at night. This suggested to me that she had a stronger opinion about the house than she cared to admit.

I had to accept that everyone experienced things differently, and processed their reactions in a way unique unto themselves. Andrea's coping mechanism was denial, Erin's, anger.

~~

When Saturday rolled around, we all had our stories straight with our parents, much like we'd done the summer before. The difference this time was that Russell had found a service road straight up to the park, bypassing the gate entrance.

The park closed at 6:00 p.m., right before sunset. The expected low temperature that night was 53 degrees, with no rain. We agreed to head out around 8:00 p.m.

Kevin had made his way over to Cat's to join us for the evening, as did Russell. As luck would have it, we had Cat's house to ourselves that night. Her mother was on night shift, and Mike stuck until closing at Straw Hat. The four of us made the most of it.

We had pizza delivered, watched TV, and enjoyed the freedom of being together away from school. It was an evening of conversation about what was to come, as well as each couple cuddling on the couch and sneaking kisses. Despite the enjoyable moments, there was an unspoken tension in the air, as we unconsciously watched the clock, counting down the minutes until we needed to leave.

"I guess we should double check our supplies before we head out," Kevin suggested when it was 7:50 p.m. He lifted Cat up off his lap, dropping her playfully on the couch cushions.

"Hey, meanie!" she complained. She then tried to push me off the couch cushion that I was on.

As I rolled off dramatically, I grabbed her leg and dragged her down with me. We then began to grapple with each other to see who could untangle first to stand. Each time I thought I was winning, Russell pushed me back over gently, until Cat stood up victoriously.

"No fair! I call foul!" I complained, staring at Russell, playing at being an innocent bystander.

"Seriously, guys! Enough playing around, it's time to get serious," Kevin chided. He was going through his pack, double checking some mental list in his head.

"Cat, you have extra batteries for your flashlight, right?" he asked ticking off his "list" using his fingers to count. "Hat and gloves in case it gets colder tonight than the weather man said?"

"Yes, and yes," she replied, flipping open, in turn, her thumb and forefinger, playfully mocking him. "I also have matches, just in case, and water to drink."

"Me, too," I answered sarcastically, "just in case you were worried about me."

"Well, *I am*, so that's good to know," Russell responded. "Did you remember a bunnet n' pawkie?"

"*Bunnet*?" I asked, giggling at his Scottish slang.

"That's what my mom calls a hat, like a bonnet."

"Oh, okay, yes, hat and gloves. Check," I responded. Turning to Cat, I asked, "Box of keys?"

"Yep, in the pack," she answered. Then she turned to Russell. "What about the… supplies?" she asked.

"Everything's accounted for," Russell answered. "This is it, guys," he said as he reached out for my hand, and squeezed it twice.

Cat left a note for Mike in his room, so he wouldn't worry when he got home, and we headed out.

~

Twenty silent minutes later, Russell slowed, squinting into the darkness along the rural highway. The service road was hard to find at night, even with me, in the front seat, trying to read the map by the dim interior light. Kevin tried to help, from the backseat, by turning on his flashlight to shine it over one shoulder, while Cat peered over the other.

"I think this should be the area, right here on the left. Up there looks like it could be the summit," she pointed to the dark wall of forest. Russell had circled where the service road would be, because it was not printed on the official map.

"It's a lot darker out here than I was expecting," I observed, looking out the front windshield into the night.

"That's because there's no moonlight," Cat answered.

Russell slowed down, even more, and we all peered out the windows looking for a visible break in the trees that might suggest a turnoff.

"There," Kevin called out, pointing to a small opening. Russell turned into it, and followed the twisting dirt track. The crunching sound of loose rocks beneath the tires reverberated throughout our confined interior, and the unexpected holes and bumps in the road caused us to bounce around. Russell slowed way down, his knuckles clenched tightly to the steering wheel. As we crept along, the Volvo's weak headlights were barely able to penetrate the unrelenting darkness before us.

"How are we supposed to know if we're on the right road?" I asked, turning off the overhead light.

Russell, who had been quiet and concentrating on each winding turn, answered, "I guess when we get to the top, and we see the house."

"Sounds reasonable," Kevin responded.

Despite the warmth from the heater, my face started to feel cold and clammy as something began to twist its way through me.

Russell sensed the shift within me, and without taking his eyes off the road, asked, "You okay, Gwen?"

"Are you getting car sick?" Cat asked, concerned.

214

"No, I'm okay. We're definitely on the right road. The house should be coming up now just around this corner," I replied quietly, trying to quell the incessant waves of nausea.

"How would..." Kevin started to ask, but then he stopped as the top of the house came into view, its witch-hat tower silhouetted against the starlit sky above the tree line.

Russell pulled the car to a stop. The headlamps illuminated a metal "No Trespassing" sign hanging from a metal chain. It hung about waist high, strung between two trees where the service road ended. A foot path continued on from there, opening up to the grassy plateau that became Douglas Park.

We took out the flashlights we each brought, checked that they worked, and then zipped our bags up tight. Russell and I held the car seats forward for Cat and Kevin to climb out of the back.

"So everything we need is in there?" Cat asked, pointing to Russell's pack.

"Yep. We've gone over this a dozen times tonight," he replied, squinting as Kevin flashed his beam around. "We'll start the smudging downstairs and make our way through every room, clearing the door ways, the nooks and crannies. We'll ring the bell in each corner." He started around towards the trunk of his car, unlocked it, and lifted the lid.

"And what exactly is the bell for? I hadn't heard about that yet," Kevin asked.

"The bell's vibrations can banish stagnant and negative energy of unwanted spirits, in any space throughout the house. Sound affects energy on a physical level, because sound *is* energy," he responded, as he lifted from inside the trunk a broom with a dark wood handle and long thin twigs at the end.

"What is that for?" Cat asked.

"This is a *Besom.* The handle is made from an Ash tree, and the Birch twigs are tied with Willow. It's going to be part of the house cleansing ritual," he replied. "It's called a 'Broom Out'."

"So it's a broom?" Kevin asked, laughing in surprise. "I hope we aren't going to have to scrub the floors as well," he joked. I think we all appreciated his attempt at a bit of levity.

"You will if you want your supper, young man!" Cat scolded him in an elderly voice, smiling as she wagged her finger at him.

Russell closed the trunk, slung his pack over his shoulders and tightened the straps. "We ready?" he asked, shining his flashlight beam at each of us.

"Yep," I lied.

"Like, totally!" Kevin responded with his best *Valley Girl* imitation.

"Fer sure, fer sure!" Cat answered back giggling.

Kevin aimed his flashlight beam at the reflective metal "No Trespassing" sign. It was practically yelling at us, *Turn back now, you stupid idiots!*

We didn't though.

We followed Kevin as he led us along the footpath through the last line of trees out onto the open lawn.

Before us loomed the shadowy silhouette of the old Victorian house, ominously awaiting our arrival.

GINGER G HOWARD

Chapter Twenty-Eight
Gaining Entry

With Kevin in the lead, we cautiously made our way across the open area. The nausea continued to build, the same feeling I'd experienced last summer, but stronger. Each step closer also brought waves of foreign emotions, as if the very ground I was walking on was alive with the people who had been there before. It was confusing... dizzying. It took all my focus to continue moving forward.

Suddenly, I heard a single voice break its way through the psychic onslaught, reminding me of the amulet. With my free hand I instinctively reached for the stone around my neck, and everything began to subside.

"*Blessed by the Goddess,*" Brighid had said. I focused on its power of protection, and gradually felt myself strengthen. I then thought of the lightness I felt after the cleansing Brighid had performed.

My hand found its way to the Celtic shield knot pendant hanging with the stone, and as I traced along the unending loops with my finger, I remembered I had been given these tools to keep these energies from attaching to me.

218

Again, the voice broke through, "You have the power to help them. You have the strength to shut the gate... to close the door."

I don't know whose voice it was, but I held onto it, like it was the only light in that dark night.

"Gwen," Russell said quietly to me as we walked along, "If you feel under attack at any point, you need to let me know. I came prepared. I've helped my mother with this sort of thing many times before. But I can only help if you tell me."

"Attacked, like a spirit trying to physically hurt me, or are you referring to my visions?"

"Anything. Tonight's not the night to mess around with this stuff, okay? I know you aren't completely sure of your abilities yet, but I believe in them. The power will come when you believe it too. But just in case, I'm here for you."

"Okay," I answered quietly. I wished I had his confidence!

As we approached the house, Kevin said, "Let's walk around the back first, where we got in last time. We can see if that window is still open."

We followed him as he disappeared into the black blanket of shadow behind the house. All I could see was his flashlight bobbing up and down. Then Cat disappeared, swallowed up in the abyss. I felt an un-reasonable fear walking into it, even knowing that it was nothing but the area beneath the canopy of trees.

"It's okay," Russell said, noticing my pace falter, and holding out his hand. "I'm right here with you. Nothing bad will happen, I promise."

I dropped my hand down from the amulet and once he had hold of it, he boldly walked through the dark barrier, dragging me in behind him.

I heard Kevin talking to Cat from ahead of us, "They sure have cleared a lot away from the base of the house. Remember all that ivy that was choking everything?"

By the time Russell and I made it around beneath the kitchen window, their beams of light disappeared around the other corner.

"I guess we won't be getting in that way," I pointed my flashlight up. The window we'd entered before wasn't just shut, it was boarded over. "That's where we got in last time. The kitchen," I explained to Russell.

"Guys, over here!" Kevin whispered loudly, peeking his head around the corner.

"Seriously, Gwen. Come look," Cat said.

As Russell and I rounded the corner, we saw what had once been a mound of ivy and shrub. It had been cleared away to reveal a wooden hatch with two doors that opened out.

"Does that go down to the cellar?" I asked in amazement.

"I think so," Kevin responded. He then tugged at one door of the hatch, but it didn't give. "The hinges are rusted shut," he said.

"Here, let me help," Russell offered, and walked to the other side, put down the broom, and pulled at that door. It didn't budge. "Let's try together at the same time, maybe it'll jostle something loose."

They stood opposite each other, placed their flashlights on the ground, and using both hands pulled at the doors with all their strength. There was a loud *snap,* followed by a *thud* and an exclamation of "Shit!" as Kevin went flying back and landed on his butt.

Cat swung her flashlight beam towards where she thought Kevin would be until she finally found him standing up dusting the dirt from his pants, metal handle still in one hand.

"Are you okay?" she asked, trying to stifle a giggle.

"Yes, and it isn't funny. That actually hurt," he groaned, rubbing his back end.

Russell had better luck, as his hatch did twist under the stress of their combined effort. He continued to jiggle the one hatch door back and forth until some of the rust started to break free from the hinges, loosening them up. Kevin came back over, and the two of them worked on the door until, with a reluctant *creak,* it finally started to give.

Down inside the opening was a thick darkness, worse than the shadowed area behind the house. "Oh my god, please tell me we aren't going down there?" I asked. All pretense of bravery had been tossed aside.

"I'm with her," Cat said. "There has got to be another way!" She aimed her flashlight beam down, illuminating a set of dirt-covered steps descending into what might as well have been the pit of hell.

"I'll take a quick walk around the perimeter. You stay here," Kevin offered, back in full Boy Scout mode, and then headed up towards the front of the house. We could hear his footsteps climbing the front porch.

Russell, meanwhile, had been working on the other hatch door, jiggling it back and forth on its hinges until the rust loosened up enough to force it to open.

"Not very inviting is it?" he asked, trying to penetrate the depths with his flash light. "Well, no time like the present, is how I've heard it said." He proceeded to step down into the mouth of the stairwell, as if he were offering himself up as a meal.

"Please don't," I begged. "Wait for Kevin to get back. There might be another way."

"Yeah, you're nuts. Don't go down there," Cat concurred.

"We're wasting time. We can just start the rituals down here, and then make our way up, floor by floor."

"I don't even remember there being a doorway to the outside when we were down there, do you Cat?" I asked.

"No, but then again I was pretty distracted by all the spiders."

"Russell! Oh my god, watch out for spiders," I called out.

"Ladies! Ladies! I'll be fine," he chuckled. "There *is* a door down here," he called out when he made it to the final step. He then walked forward into the shadows.

I heard the sound of him pushing against something, and the sound of his feet slipping in the dirt. In my flashlight beam I could make out dirt clods being flung back towards the steps.

"What's going on?" I asked. Just then I heard a **WHOOSH** as the interior door flung open, followed by the *clank* of what must have been his flashlight hitting the floor, and then I heard, immediately, "Oof! Damnit!"

"Well, I guess he got the door open," Cat mused, craning her head to see down the narrow stairwell.

His face popped back into view of my flashlight beam, covered in dirt, smiling. "See, no problem."

"Guys, this is the only way. The windows are all boarded up on the outside," Kevin mentioned, coming back up alongside Cat.

"Damn, I was afraid you were going to say that," she grumbled, picking up the broom Russell had left behind.

"Come on Gwen, it's just a cellar," Russell coaxed, holding up his hand for me to join him at the bottom.

I took a deep breath, and descended down the foul mouth to the belly of the beast. With each step I told myself over and over again, *I am protected. Nothing can harm me.*

Russell grabbed my hand when I reached the landing, and walked with me through an old wood door into the cellar.

I swung my beam around the room, recognizing the space just as we had left it. I finally stopped when the light landed on the leather case cut open by Kevin's Swiss Army knife.

"I am surprised it's still here," I remarked.

"See how calm you are now? It's just a room. I believe the fear of the unknown is always the worst part. You can't let that stop you from getting to the other side, right?"

Chapter Twenty-Nine
The Cellar

Russell set about unpacking the ritual supplies. First, he handed me four white votive candles, and explained, "White candles are for protection and purification against negative energies. They also represent one of the four elements, fire. Place them in four corners of the room: north, south, east and west."

"Okay," I responded. I placed them around the cellar and lighting them along the way. One on the shelf next to the broken jars, one on the pile of firewood where the spiders lived, one on the bottom wood step leading to the first floor, and the last one on the suitcase I placed by the open exterior cellar door.

"It's a lot colder down here than outside. Dang," Cat complained holding her arms closer to herself despite her turtleneck, thick sweater and scarf.

Next, Russell produced two paper bags, and two copper burning bowls. "Cat, here are the instructions for what to do with these. Only put in a little. We have to have enough to get us through the whole house."

From the first bag she took a couple pinches of copal, myrrh, and frankincense resin, placed them in one bowl, and set it aside. From the next bag she grabbed a few cedar chips, and put them in the second bowl. "Do I go ahead and light these?"

"Yes," Russell answered as he lit a *Palo Santo* incense stick.

Russell took the bell from the bottom of the sack and handed it to me. "You will ring this in each corner of the room after I have cleared that area, okay?"

"Got it," I replied.

He grabbed the broom, which Cat had rested against the wall, and handed it to Kevin. "You're going to symbolically sweep the energies out the door when we're done with the smudging okay?"

"That's when you wave the smoky thing around the room, right?" Kevin asked.

"Yes, the smoky thing," Russell replied patiently, "but first you'll need to be cleansed as well."

"Me?" Kevin asked.

"Yes, we need to clear any negative energy in your field, heighten your spiritual awareness, and empower you for what's to come," Russell stated.

Kevin was taken aback by the seriousness in his tone. It occurred to me that moment might have been the first time Kevin truly grasped the gravity of what we'd come to do.

He then pulled out the sage bundle, the Abalone shell and the large hawk feather. He held the sage at an angle with one hand, while he struck the wheel of his Bic lighter with the thumb of his other hand, and lit the end of the sage. He let it burn for about 10 seconds and then gently blew it out. I could see the orange embers still glowing at the ends.

Russell put the lighter back in his pocket, and then grabbed the abalone shell with the same hand that he held the sage, so as to catch the ashes as they fell. With his free hand he held up the hawk feather and gently waved it back and forth in front of the embers making it smoke a little more.

"Kevin, stand here for a second and close your eyes. Then I want you to repeat after me, okay?"

"Um, okay," Kevin responded hesitantly. "That's all I need to do? Just repeat what you say?"

"Yes, but it would be helpful, for the cleansing to work well, for you to imagine whatever's holding you back from being at your strongest of mind, heart and body, and then let it go as you recite the words. We're trying to rid you of bad energy, and only allow in the good as we go through this house. Do you understand?"

"Hmmm, understand, I do!" Kevin replied, doing a poor impersonation of his favorite Muppet.

"Kevin, be serious," Cat scolded.

"Okay, okay. Yeah, I get it."

Russell began at the top of Kevin's head, circling his crown clockwise with the sage, and fanning the smoke with the hawk feather. He then went slowly down each section of Kevin's body, just like Brighid had done with us. "Any energy that is not of my greatest good," he began.

Kevin repeated the phrase.

"You're wanted here no more," Russell continued, now making his way to Kevin's back side.

Kevin repeated the phrase.

"Please leave me now, it's time to go, exit through the open door," Russell concluded, waving the smoke towards the exterior cellar door.

After Kevin had repeated the last part of the incantation, he asked, "Can I open my eyes now?"

"Yeah," Russell answered, "And you'll want to wear this." He put the same amulet that Cat and I wore around Kevin's neck. "Think of this as armor."

"You expect a battle?" Kevin asked a little taken back.

"I thought you were a Boy Scout once?" Russell teased, "Always be prepared."

Russell then leaned back into his pack and pulled out a glass container of a white substance, and a silver flask.

"What are those?" I asked.

"This is salt that has been blessed. It represents earth, and it will absorb the negative energy." He poured some into his hand and sprinkled it lightly around the room.

"This is Moon Water that has also been blessed. It will dispel any bad energy and invite in harmonious ones." He poured a little into his hand and flicked it lightly around the room.

Then he turned to Cat and I. "Now we will go around the room in a clockwise direction, starting and ending at the door. Cat, do you want to be in charge of fanning out the smoke?"

"Sure," Cat responded.

"Kevin, follow behind Cat as you sweep up the negative energies, and when we're done, sweep it out the door."

"Wait," Kevin responded. "Really sweep up the dirt? Do I push it behind you, or do I sweep side to side?"

"You are *figuratively* sweeping away the negative energies out of the room. So... no you don't have to literally try to sweep up the dirt. It's in the intention of the motion." Russell answered.

"Okay, got it," Kevin replied, then repeated, "Intention in the motion."

"Okay, and Kevin, one more thing," Russell continued, "Repeat this chant as you go: Sweep, sweep, sweep the ground. All that's negative shall be bound."

Kevin repeated the lines.

"I banish from here all that's profane. Only what's positive shall remain," he concluded.

Kevin repeated the lines.

"All right, here we go," Russell stated as he started walking forward, fanning the sage from floor to ceiling as he chanted, "I am cleansing this house! Any unwanted spirits or entities in this place, please leave now."

As they rounded one corner of the room and turned, I felt compelled to speak out as well, "You don't belong here. I'm sending you home." Then I rang the bell.

Once Russell had completed his circle of the room, he said, "Okay, now let's hurry and gather up everything. We have a lot of space to cover before midnight."

Thump! Thump!

"Oh crap!" Cat exclaimed, as we all jumped at the sound. "That's exactly what I didn't ever want to hear again!"

Kevin put his arms around her, as she covered her ears. "Me neither."

"Gwen, you're going to have to speak with these ghosts. Remember, you're a natural medium. They'll come to you like moths to a flame," Russell explained.

"I don't know who I'm talking to you," I responded, feeling both overwhelmed and overstimulated. "I don't know what to say."

Scraaaaatch! Scraaaaatch!

I suddenly had a flashback to the sounds from my reoccurring dream. This wasn't quite the same though. It wasn't the sound of bricks being laid, and the mortar being scraped across.

Holding my amulet with one hand, and rubbing the stone of my ring with the other, I reminded myself, *I am protected!*

Once Russell realized I wasn't going to say anything, he called out into the darkness, "All unwanted spirits and entities we ask you to leave *now!*"

Thump! Thump!

"You are *not* welcome here! Go back to wherever you came from," Cat screamed up at the sounds coming from the room above.

Scraaaaatch! Scraaaaatch!

I suddenly knew the origin of the sound - the library, in the space beneath the stairs. We were exactly beneath that spot.

Chapter Thirty
Uniting as One

When we made our way up the cellar steps into the back hallway of the house, Kevin reminded us of the floorboards that had broken away last time we were there. But when he shined his flashlight beam down the hall, we were surprised to see new planks of wood had been laid down as part of the renovations.

He shone his light upwards at the ceiling, and sure enough, those boards had been replaced as well.

"That's one less thing to worry about," he sighed in relief.

As we walked along the sturdy new flooring we came up to the entryway of the kitchen, and Russell immediately went into the room. The new flooring extended throughout, and the overwhelming stench of mildew and rotten wood was gone.

"Alright, so we'll repeat the same steps in here, as we did before, but we need to open a window first. The smoke has to be able to escape and lead the spirits outside." Russell looked at the nearest one, boarded up from the outside, and went over to see if he could get it to open. It was the same window that had spilled bugs on us before.

This time it slid up easier, and he lifted it mid-way up without too much effort. There were long gaps between the exterior wood planks that allowed the air to flow freely. The cross breeze, created from the open cellar door and the window, felt like the house had taken a huge breath.

"I really think we need to be in the library," I commented, feeling a pull I struggled to ignore.

Russell came over to me then, and placed his hands on my face. I could see no details, just his silhouette. He whispered gently, "I feel it too. Just let me know if it becomes too much to fight off, okay."

He then turned to Kevin and Cat, "We have to focus our attention on each room, one at a time, to release as many spirits from this place as we can." Turning back to me he added, "Don't be afraid of talking to them. It won't be like last time, I promise. Just talk to them."

"Out loud?" I asked, feeling self-conscious.

"Any way that works," he said. He then leaned in and kissed me chastely, which surprised me. I was used to feeling the fire from his intentions when we kissed, but this time it felt... familial. I thought about it for a second or two, and then realized there was a time and place for such things, and this was clearly neither.

I picked up the four votive candles and took one to a closed window and placed it on the sill. I whispered quietly as I lit the flame, "All of you who lived and worked here once, in this house, or on this land, you need to realize that you are no longer alive. Your duties are finished, and you can now rest. Go be with your loved ones. It's okay to move on. To leave this place... I release you."

I repeated the phrase with each candle I lit, remembering what I had learned about the people who had worked the farm, and remembering the abandoned children who had made their way there by train.

"Children, if you still linger, please know that your grave has been found. You are no longer forgotten, we know of your struggles, we know of your pain, and you are no longer bound to this place. Go be with your loved ones. I release you!" I called out loudly into the air, feeling a tear streak down my cheek.

I heard Russell then begin his cleansing incantation. "I am cleansing this house! All unwanted negative spirits and entities please leave now! All of you who worked this farm, who lived on this land, who toiled and suffered, we acknowledge you. It is okay to move on now."

Cat then picked up the hawk feather, Kevin picked up the wood broom, and I picked up the Tibetan bell, and clockwise we walked the room behind Russell.

When I rang the bell, unexpectedly, the four of us said in unison, *"We release you!"* It was powerful. I felt goosebumps all over my skin.

In the candlelight we looked at each other with a new sense of wonder. The power in our coming together as one voice, with one purpose, had just amplified the energy in the room. Even the candle flames flickered in response.

After that, with each ring of the bell we called out together, *"We release you!"*

～

We cleansed the hallway after we finished the kitchen, and then moved everything into the dining room.

The window in there put up more of a fight, even with Kevin and Russell lifting it together. Once lifted halfway, I could feel the fresh air coming in through the gaps in the haphazard placement of the boards on the outside. The house seemed to inhale again.

As I lit each of the four candles in the dining room I said, "If you still linger in this place, please understand that you are no longer among the living. Your hard days of work are over. You can rest now! Please know that your graves have been found. You are no longer forgotten. We know of your struggles. We know of your pain. You are no longer bound to this place. We release you!"

Thump! Thump!

"I guess we better keep working fast," Russell reminded everyone, waving the sage in the doorway between the hall and dining room. Then he started from the floor board and made his way up each wall to the ceiling, taking extra time in the corners to remove any stagnant energy.

Kevin continued sweeping, and chanting, "I banish from here all that's profane. Only what's positive shall remain."

I went to the corner behind them, and rang the bell.

TING! *"We release you!"* We called out.

Scraaaaatch! Scraaaaatch!

"I really don't want to know what's making that sound," Cat whispered, fanning the smoke towards the open window.

"Don't worry about that spirit. We'll deal with her soon enough," Russell responded. "Focus on our intent in this room."

I continued to follow behind then, and at the next corner, rang the bell.

TING! "*We release you!*" We called out in unison.

As Cat finished fanning the last of the smoke out the window, it appeared to be moving unnaturally against the flow of air coming in from outside. "Haunt this place no more! Leave now through this open... window."

I saw Russell smiling from the faint light of our collective flashlights as he said to her, "See, I knew you'd find that power within you. You're a natural." This made Cat grin from ear to ear.

Kevin finished his sweep of the room behind her, and made his way out to the foyer, between the front door and the main stairwell.

Without warning, Cat's whole body went rigid. "Oh, damnit," she groaned, a strange expression fixed on her face. She looked as though straining to hear something.

"What is it?" I asked in concern, coming over to her side.

"My dad," she fretted. "He's trying to talk to me, but something is wrong." She staggered out of the room into the foyer, as Russell and I gathered up the supplies and followed.

"We won't banish his spirit will we?" I asked Russell. "She doesn't want him to leave."

"He's attached to Cat because of their love for each other. He wouldn't be affected by the cleansings, because he isn't attached to the house," he reasoned.

"Oh, good," I sighed in relief. After a brief pause, I mentioned reluctantly, "We need to take care of this entity soon, I can feel her getting more and more worked up the closer we get to her space."

"I feel that too. Just one room at a time, though. We need to focus our energy on our intent within each space," he replied. "Can you do that?"

"Yes, but I am getting really tired. Is that normal?"

"You're using up a lot of psychic energy, so yes, you're going to start feeling drained," he answered. "But you've got to dig deep, okay?"

"Okay," I replied, gathering up the last candle.

In the foyer, we walked up on Kevin holding Cat in his arms, and Cat was crying, "I can't reach him, Gwen. Did we drive him away?"

"No, Cat," I responded, wrapping my arms around her. "I think we're in the middle of a tornado of spirits - all competing to come through. It makes sense that you wouldn't be able to hear him over all the noise, ya know?"

She sniffled then sagged against Kevin's chest, her energy waning as well. "I guess that makes sense," she sighed. "I just want to get out of here!"

Russell laid out the copper bowls, and lit the incense, right there in the foyer. He poured out a pinch of salt and flicked it about, and followed by a sprinkling of the Moon Water.

Thump! Thump!

"God, make it stop," Cat cried out putting her hands over her ears.

Russell divided up and set fire to the ingredients in each bowl, lit the sage, and carried the feather over to Cat. "Let's keep our minds focused on clearing this room."

"Okay," she sighed in resignation, taking the feather.

Scraaaaatch! Scraaaaatch!

The spirit knew we were closing in, clearing the space around it. I proceeded to declare my intent as I lit each of the four candles.

Cat then fanned the feather behind Russell as he recited his incantations and cleansed the room. Kevin followed behind Cat, continuing to sweep and chant, while I rang the bell in each corner.

We then moved to the parlor and opened the window between the fireplace and the door to the library. We went through the same smudging routine as before. When we were done, Kevin, who had managed to crack the front door open, was sweeping out the collection of negative energy from the house, out on to the porch.

A burst of air came through and a cold vortex sprang to life. The smoke from the sage twisted in the air, and the candle flames bowed and bent.

We took it as a sign, joined hands and began to chant, *"We release you. We release you!"*

The wind swirled in circles around us, like a cyclone. It was as if the house was trying to help us by sucking in the pure night air and expelling out the toxic spiritual residue.

As quickly as the chaotic storm arose, it dissipated, leaving us peering around the room, to ensure we were alone. Once we were sure we let go of each other's hands.

"Should I just leave the door open?" Kevin asked.

"Yes," Russell responded. "The more exits we can create, the easier this will be."

"Cat, are you okay?" Kevin asked in a concerned tone. I turned my flashlight to where he was looking, and saw Cat staring up at the mirror above the fireplace. I passed the beam over the mirror... nothing.

"Turn those off for a second," Russell whispered. Astonishingly the four candles continued to flicker, having survived the maelstrom. Their light made it look as though there were shadow people walking around in the dark corners.

I approached Cat, and stood next to her looking up into the mirror. "I had hoped to see him again in the mirror," Cat said sadly, "but can't."

An idea hit me, so I reached out to take her hand, and gasped!

In an instant I saw the image of her father, just like he had looked this past summer. "Cat," I whispered, "I can see your dad!"

He stood in the center of, what appeared to be, a whirlpool of oil paints - a whole palette of swirling colors. I was transfixed. The longer I focused on the space around

239

him, the more I noticed that the colors weren't meaningless.

It was hypnotic, the various colors moving and pulsing through the mishmash of vague shapes. Shapes were attempting to form as they pushed their way up through the oily whirlpool. They would morph and then collapse, then try to form again, trying to become something of substance.

Here and there a face would materialize. It was as if people were trying to break free of the current, reaching up to grab hold of something... anything.

"I will try to keep this connection open so that you can talk to him, okay?" I told her.

She didn't reply, but she squeezed my hand in gratitude. Then I heard Kevin come up beside her, and say, "I'm here for you, babe."

Russell came up to my side, and grabbed my hand. I closed my eyes then, focusing all our shared energy on pushing aside the oily blur around him. I stood there, between the two worlds, holding open a door. I remembered Russell's explanation: *You can see the ordinary world and the spirit world: two sights.*

Suddenly, I heard a voice, the same voice that had spoken to me earlier, and realized... it had been Cat's father.

I had to keep my focus, and hold the door open for Cat and her father. Finally, her voice resonated into the place he was.

He turned to the sound of her voice, and a huge smile brightened his face. In my mind's eye, I saw him make his way closer until he stood in front of her.

I heard him say, *It's working! The door is opening, and they can see the way out. But you have to make Tabitha leave. You can't open it enough with Tabitha fighting to keep it shut. Until she's gone, they're all trapped.*

I heard Cat ask him, *How? How do we force her away?*

A shadow crossed the vision, and for a moment he went out of focus. When he came back into view, he responded, *Gwen will have to contact her. It is the only way. Find a way to connect with her. Make her face what she has done.*

I called out to him then, *Open it? You said I would be able to close the door, what do you mean?*

THUMP!

The sound of pounding on wood resonated louder than ever throughout the room, jolting us from our shared vision.

THUMP!

Wide eyed, the four of us spun around, gaping at the darkened doorway.

"The library," Kevin stated quietly, a slight quiver to his voice.

Chapter Thirty-One
Parting the Veil

When Russell first crept through the library threshold, I wasn't sure what to expect. I remembered a broken window, torn curtains, and swollen mildew-covered book carcasses on the floor before. When he panned his flashlight around the room, it looked cleaned up. Then he stopped, and my breath caught in my throat.

"Oh, no," I gasped.

Sitting on the other side of the room was the steamer trunk. The secret bookcase door was ajar, and the once hidden room was hidden no more.

"Shit!" Kevin exclaimed, as we all made our way into the room to stare down at the trunk. It appeared to have been unopened, though it was hard to tell in the dark. Kevin knelt down and tugged at the lid.

"It's still locked! Oh thank goodness," Cat sighed.

THUMP!

All four flashlights snapped to attention, beams converging on the bookcase.

"What was that?" Kevin asked.

Russell walked forward into the secret room to investigate. He disappeared through the opening for a second, before he stepped back out and declared, "There's nothing in there."

Cat and I exhaled simultaneously in a huge sigh of relief. "My heart is pounding so hard I think I'm going to have a heart attack," she exclaimed.

"Cat, can you get me out the key for this thing?" Kevin asked, turning his attention back to the trunk. Cat took the puzzle box out of her pack, going through the process of pushing on each panel to get it to open.

"I won't be able to remember which ones went where, Kevin, so you'll just have to try them all," Cat confessed. "Here, let me hold your light."

She held up both flashlights as Kevin grabbed the smaller keys, and one by one tried each one in the metal lock. Finally, we all heard the loud CLICK of the locking mechanism disengaging within the trunk. He put the key aside, to keep it from getting confused with the others, and lifted the lid.

I swung my light down illuminating the familiar pink satin lining. Everything was just as we had left it, even the doll, lying sideways across the top of the wood boxes.

"That thing again," Kevin complained.

I didn't want to touch it. I couldn't bear the thought of seeing Joseph and the other orphans murdered all over again.

Joseph, I thought, remembering his sweet little face beaming at the sight of his beloved marble. *I sure hope we set you free.*

"Gwen, what do you need to help you contact Tabitha? Will something in here work?" Cat asked, pulling out the hat box and the perfume bottles.

I turned to Russell for guidance, not knowing how we should proceed.

"First things first, Cat. Before she tries to communicate with anyone, we need to prepare the room," Russell reminded us, "exactly like we've been doing."

"On it," I replied. Then I set about to lighting the candles and reciting my incantation.

"I will try to get this window open," Kevin said, standing up from the trunk and making his way across the library.

"It's already so cold," Cat grumbled, as she prepared the burning bowls. "Is it just me? This room is freezing."

After Russell lit the incense he said, "We'll form a circle around Gwen as she tries to talk to Tabitha. Once we know her spirit is present we can start the smudging ritual to move her energy out."

Kevin stopped and asked, "Wait… we're not doing the smoky thingy first? I thought…"

"No, we need to be ready to… but we need her here first, "Russell clarified. "Let's circle around Gwen."

I could feel energy collecting around us, and the hairs on my arms began to rise. I caught the faint scent of that same aroma that had been in the library before. It meant Tabitha was nearby. "The perfume bottle will work, the heart-shaped one."

Cat plucked it out from the trunk and set it out. The contours of its delicate shape refracted in the gleam from our flashlights.

Russell waved the incense around the room, then crouched down, and brought out the jar of consecrated salt, and the silver flask of Moon Water.

"Gwen, go ahead and sit down next to the perfume."

I did as he instructed, making sure not to touch anything from the trunk. He started to pour the salt in a circle around us.

"Inside the circle next to Gwen," Russell motioned to them.

Cat and Kevin came in on either side of me, as Russell finished, enclosing us all in. "The salt will form a protective circle around us, as you make contact. Another shield against negative energy wanting to do us harm, or attach itself."

"Attach itself?" Kevin worried aloud.

I reached out for the perfume bottle, closed my fingers around it. The scent grew stronger as Tabitha's memories took hold, but this time I knew how to distance myself. To not get pulled completely in.

She sat at the small table in the nursery, with Jane across from her. Jane wore her favorite blue dress, and across her face, a pronounced angry bruise - punishment for the murder of the baby. However, the child seemed completely unfazed by it.

I felt Tabitha's confusion. How could Jane, this... thing, be so oblivious to the unforgiveable sins she'd committed.

245

"*Mother, I am so pleased you are having tea with me,*" *Jane announced gleefully, reaching for a piece of almond cake and putting it onto the small plate of fine china. She smiled to herself as she nibbled at the edges of the cake, closing her eyes and savoring the sweetness.*

"*Are you not going to try some, Mother? You really should, it is the best cake the kitchen has ever made.*"

*After a few moments of silence, Jane started to appear agitated. "Mother, are you not going to speak with me? After all, it **is** a special occasion.*"

"*No, it is an occasion as **far** from special as any could be!*" *I felt the cold anger course through her heart, and I heard Tabitha's voice speaking as if it were coming from my own mouth. She then looked down at her china cup, the tea untouched, growing cold.*

"*Yes, Mother, it is. That horrible crying has finally stopped, and you and I can now spend all of our time together,*" *she said, smiling in satisfaction. The child took a sip from her dainty cup, and grimaced, tasting something bitter.*

"*Do you need another lump of sugar, Jane?*" *I heard Tabitha ask, and felt her heart skip a beat. She took the small silver tong, lifted a lump of sugar from the delicate bowl, and then placed it in Jane's cup.*

For a brief moment I felt as though I were swooning, as the light from the nursery faded into the darkness of the library. Physical reality broke in, with a wave of nausea, and I heard the room around me rumbling, and glass rattling against its wooden frames.

Russell called out, "Cat, ask your father to help protect us. Help us keep negative spirits from penetrating the circle. Kevin, repeat after me, 'We are surrounded with a shield of protection. We are safe within this space'. Again... Really believe it! Mean what you say!"

The world swayed, and fell away. The nursery came back into view, and light streamed through the bright curtains once again.

"Yes, Mother, another sugar would be lovely. The last time I had a tea party was in the attic with those dirty gutter snipes," she reminisced without an ounce of regret.

"Do you understand what you have done, Jane?" Tabitha asked sternly, waiting breathlessly for the moment to come.

The child merely cocked her head to the side, feigning ignorance.

*Tabitha pressed. "**You** caused them to fall ill," Tabitha accused, the well of hatred rising higher and higher. I could feel her steely nerves pushing it back down into the bowels of her being. "You, Jane, are the reason the children have died, all of the children. My baby... YOU killed my baby. WHY?"*

Jane batted her eyes, looking around the table for another piece of almond cake, ignoring the outburst.

*"Mother, your tea is getting cold," she mentioned, raising her cup up to her lips for another sip. "Oh, that **is** much better."*

Tabitha's mind reeled in protest. Could she bear as much responsibility for these tragedies as the child? It was she who brought Jane into this home; therefore, had she not helped create the monster the child had become?

"No matter," the woman steeled herself, repressing the misplaced guilt. "It will be over soon enough," she soothed herself.

Jane took another bite of cake, followed by a large sip of tea, when a strange look came over her face - a startled wince.

"Mother, I suddenly don't feel right," she moaned, as she doubled over in pain.

Tabitha slowly stood up, calmly gathered every item from the small table, and then arranged them carefully on the silver serving tray.

"Mother," Jane cried out fearfully, "please help me! I think I am becoming sick." Her face had gone pale and damp, as she slid off her chair. She then lay on the floor in a fetal position.

Tabitha, ignoring the child's pleas, lifted up the serving tray and silently walked across the room to the door.

"Mother," Jane groaned, reaching out in vain, as the convulsions began.

A nauseating swoon took over, the image of Jane lying on the floor of the nursery faded away into the darkness and noise of reality.

The air was whipping around, rattling the glass, and banging the door back against the wall.

"We are surrounded with a shield of protection. We are safe within this space," they chanted over and over again.

Their voices fell away as I suddenly felt like I was dropped down a never-ending chasm, and I was drowning in the nausea of vertigo.

"Agnes, can you please find Edward? He should be at the barn loading produce onto the wagons to take into town." Tabitha asked the maid, later that day. "Tell him to bring bricks and mortar up to repair the fireplace in the nursery. Some have come loose and broken. There is a terrible draft."

"Right away, Mrs. Briggs," Agnes responded and hurried away.

She then turned towards the stairs and made her way back up to the nursery. When she entered the room she glanced numbly at the rolled up rug that used to lie beneath the bassinette.

She felt no emotion at the death of the little girl. Only relief she was finally rid of her. That child had everyone fooled.... everyone but Tabitha. She alone knew the horrible acts the girl had committed. She had to put an end to it. Tabitha knew this in her soul. She only hoped Samuel could forgive her. He had only seen the darling girl he wished to her to be, not the monster she truly was.

Tabitha struggled to lift one end of the rolled up rug. It weighed a good deal more today, than it had previously. She leaned back and dragged the bundle to the open fireplace and dropped its dead weight to the floor. She carefully lowered onto her knees and, with both hands, shoved the rug and its contents all the way to the back of the open cavity. She stood up, surveyed her handiwork, and realized how easily the rug could be seen.

She then took some of the cut firewood that had been stacked in the corner and placed one on top of the other to completely cover the roll.

249

She heard the heavy footsteps of Edward coming up the stairs, so she dusted off her hands, straightened her dress skirts, and made herself as presentable as possible.

Edward, with his long white beard, wide straw hat, and work overalls made his way up to the first floor landing, where Tabitha greeted him outside the nursery door.

"I have decided to close off the fireplace entirely. I just can't bear that draft. Could you please fetch enough brick to accomplish this?"

"Yes, ma'am," he replied.

Tabitha reached out for the trowel and bucket filled with mixed mortar.

"Oh, ma'am!" he said, resisting letting the woman carry the supplies. "I can set these inside, then fetch the rest."

"Nonsense, Edward! I will take these. Now please hurry along and fetch those bricks," she insisted.

He leaned around her, to view the fireplace opening, gauging the number of bricks he'd need to gather, but she leaned with him, gently scooting him along.

"Hurry now, before the mortar dries up!"

"Yes, ma'am," he answered, and lumbered back down the stairs.

I swooned into reality, with the nauseating vertigo, as I felt Russell pulling me to him. Then I heard his voice calling out, "Gwen, hurry up. We are running out of time."

I heard Cat and Kevin continue to chant, "We are surrounded with a shield of protection. We are safe within this space."

Then I dropped away again...

I heard Edward's heavy footsteps climbing up the steps and crossing the hall to the nursery. This time she knew she had no choice but to let him in to drop the bricks.

"Over here, Edward," she told him as he toiled with a sling full of bricks. "Just place them there."

Once he slowly eased them to floor level and got his hands free before letting the stack fall, Tabitha instructed him, "I do fear that this might not be enough. You will need to gather more, just in case. But, there is no hurry. You can come back with them after you've finished with your other duties."

"Are you sure, Mrs. Briggs? This looks like it could do the job, and I am right here. I can get this walled up in no time."

"No, tend to the workers and filling the wagon, and then you can come back."

Once he'd left the room, she shut the door behind him. Lifting her skirts so as to not soil them, and pulling up her sleeves, she knelt down in front of the fireplace and set to work.

She took the hand trowel and scooped up some mortar. She slopped the mud down across the opening, which made a sickening sound, and then spread it across. SCRAAAAAPE!

She dropped the first brick into place. THUD!

Followed by the next. THUD! And another THUD!

Once she had a complete row, she scooped up some more mortar and slopped it down on the top of the layer of bricks. She took the trowel and then spread it across. SCRAAAAAPE!

Over and over again, she repeated the motions, slowly closing Jane Elizabeth behind a wall of brick.

When finished, she tidied the nursery, and readied it as if children would be there again one day. She locked the door behind her and crossed the hall to her room to clean up.

In anticipation of this moment, she had begun collecting items she wished to keep safe. She had been placing them in the library, hidden away in the secret room behind the bookcase. She imagined, upon finding her body draped across her husband's grave, nothing would be found to point to the deaths of the children, and it would bring no attention to how or why Jane disappeared.

After locking each room, she descended the hidden staircase to the library, the Chinese puzzle box in her arms. With all the keys collected, and everything in its place, she could go to Samuel in peace. She felt certain that her acts were just, and that she could be released from her responsibilities in this world.

In the small darkened chamber, fashioned from the space beneath the stairs, hidden by the trick bookcase in the library, Tabitha bent over to lock the steamer trunk. She stood up straight when she heard footsteps in the library, quickly placing the last key in the box, before placing it atop the trunk.

Edward stepped into the frame of the false door, "Mrs. Briggs, I am afraid we have a problem."

"Oh, Edward, you startled me. You know I don't allow anyone into the library. Let's take this out into the parlor," she stepped forward expecting him to back away and obey her.

"Agnes has informed me that the cook is dead. Apparently she finished the tea you brought back down," he replied in a flat tone. A look of anger flashed across his sun-weathered skin, a glint of dawning awareness in his eye.

"Oh dear, that is dreadful news! Here, let us go see to this right away," she insisted, but he would not back away. "Edward! Kindly, step aside so that I might make my way into the main library!"

"No, ma'am, I can't let you do that just yet. Where is Miss Jane, might I ask?" he inquired, accusation in his voice. "And why is the nursery door locked?" He moved forward, blocking her way out from the secret room. "What did you need those bricks for, Mrs. Briggs?" He took another step forward.

"Edward! Step away this instant!" she demanded.

"No, ma'am, I can't do that. You see, I believe that you put something in that tea. The cook is dead now," he stated. "I will ask you again, where is Miss Jane?"

"AGNES! AGNES!" Tabitha called out, suddenly realizing she was trapped.

"I am afraid Agnes won't be helping you. No one will," Edward said, with a sneer. "I saw that bruise on lovely sweet Miss Jane! How could you hurt her? Where is she now?"

"Jane... she did horrible things," Tabitha fumbled as she backed up against the trunk. "My baby... it was Jane."

"How could you even suggest such a thing? I am afraid I cannot let this stand." He reached behind him and brought out a china tea cup filled with cold tea. "Drink this now. All of it!"

"No, thank you. I don't want any! Now please, step aside and let me out of here!"

"If there is nothing wrong with this, then drink it. There isn't a problem, is there?"

"Drink the tea, Mrs. Briggs!" Agnes demanded, as she came through the library, and stood behind Edward outside the bookcase door.

253

"What? No, Agnes!" Tabitha gasped. "Both of you step aside!"

Edward then came at her and grabbed her hair in a violent twist. "Your days of terrorizing us are over. We are starved, and dirty, and haven't a penny to our names! Not even the things we came here with. You have taken it all. Drink the tea, Mrs. Briggs!"

"Drink your tea, Mrs. Briggs!" Agnes repeated angrily. Stepping into the space, she gripped Tabitha's face, took the cup and forced the liquid down her throat. "Nothing to worry about, right? It's only tea." Pinching Tabitha's nose and holding her hand over the woman's mouth, Agnes made sure she swallowed.

Choking, Tabitha tried desperately to inhale air, but Agnes kept her hand over her nose and mouth, while Edward held her head back.

"Would you like to stay in here with all your fancy things? We can manage that!" Agnes exclaimed. She got down on all fours and pulled at one of the boards covering the narrowest part under the staircase. "You didn't think we knew about your secret hiding spot?" Agnes proceeded to pull out a large carpet bag, and opened it up to show Edward.

Inside were watches, jewelry, leather wallets, glasses, dozens and dozens of things belonging to the paupers who had passed through the Briggs' Farm. They were forced to leave their most prized possessions as payment towards their room and board, then expected to stay on as they worked, and worked, and worked.

"We'll be taking these," Agnes smiled.

"A fitting place for you ma'am," Edward sneered. "Nice and cozy!"

He then kicked Tabitha in the stomach, and, as she cried out and doubled over in pain, the two servants shoved her back into the tight space.

Tabitha began to wince as the poison coursed through her body. She felt nauseous and dizzy. She knew that it was only moments before the convulsions started.

She tried to fight as they forced her further into the space, but it did no good. Edward took the loose board and pressed it against Tabitha's weakening efforts, holding it firmly in place. She pounded on it, and scratched at the edges trying to get her fingers around it somehow to get free.

"Agnes, be a dear, and bring me my hammer and nails from out on the porch."

Thump! Thump! The sound rang out as her fists banged against the wood board. "Let me out!"

Scraaaaatch! Scraaaaatch! The sound echoed as her fingernails clawed the wood grasping the edges of the boards, only succeeding at creating slivers and causing her fingers to bleed.

Thump! She was about to pass out, her energy waning, but she kept holding out on hope they would come to their senses and free her.

She pounded again. **Thump!** "Let me out!"

A violent tremble took over her muscles, and she began to seize.

Bang! Bang! Bang! The nails went in on the outside of the panel.

The final sounds she heard before Agnes said, "May you never rest in peace."

Chapter Thirty-Two
Confrontation

When I opened my eyes I saw my friends holding hands in a circle around me. Their shadows danced above them on the ceiling. It took a second to register that I was lying on the floor in the library. The perfume bottle had rolled free of my hand a few inches away from my outstretched finger tips.

Slowly I sat up. Russell's voice made it through my foggy brain, and I heard him say, "She's coming out of it. Keep the circle strong. Keep giving her your energy. Gwen, are you with us now?"

"Yeah..." I answered groggily. I felt as though I'd been run over by a bus... after having not slept for a week.

"Did you connect with the spirit?" Russell asked.

"Yes," I replied.

"Did you talk to her? Did you get her to leave?" he asked with a strain in his voice I hadn't heard before.

"No, not yet," I answered, trying to get my bearings.

"Hurry, Gwen. Hurry," Cat pleaded. I had no idea what had been going on.

I wearily rose to my feet and pointed. The three of them turned, following my gaze. "I have to go in that room," I said. "I'll need your help though."

"Gwen we can't break the circle. There's a lot of violent energy in this room. We need to finish the cleansing. Get whoever is here to leave."

"We will, but we have to set her free first," I answered. I bent down underneath Cat and Kevin's clasped hands, and left the protective circle of salt. I felt the psychic hit in my temple first, then a wave of nausea, then a flow of anger, then a well of sorrow, all in the seconds it took to close the distance to the secret room.

"I am protected. I will not allow you to do me any harm," I called out. I could feel the tentacles of insanity trying to wriggle their way into my psyche, as well as heavy blankets of despair trying to suffocate me.

"I am protected. I will not be harmed. You are not welcome. Leave here now!" I cried out as I toiled to find my way to that board at the back of the closet.

"What do you need, Gwen?" Russell asked coming up behind me.

"Help me pry this loose," I answered. We groped around, searching blindly for some edge we could grab, but found none.

Kevin flicked open his Swiss Army knife, and handed his flashlight to Cat. "Aim at that corner," he instructed.

He went to work jimmying the knife between the boards, working back and forth until the blade slipped between. With a bit more pressure, using the knife as a lever, Kevin managed to wedge the two boards apart. Once the gap opened, Russell wriggled his fingers in a little, and pulled. With a loud creak, followed by the scratch of the nail from the wood, the panel came loose.

I spun around, away from the cavity, and faced my friends. "This might not be easy for you…"

Cat shined her light around me, illuminating the cramped cavity. "Are those buttons?" she asked in dismay. "Oh my god, those are buttons on the back of a dress!"

"Meet Tabitha. The mom," I responded, completely exhausted. I sagged against Russell. He wrapped his arm around me and gently kissed my forehead.

With a start, he let me go, and scuttled out into the library. I heard the flick of his lighter, and, a few moments later, the familiar scent of sage filled the room. "Come on guys, it is time to take care of this whole area."

We all emerged from the enclosed space and joined Russell. Cat picked up the feather, Kevin the broom, and I grabbed the Tibetan bell.

Russell chanted, as he waved the sage throughout each corner, "I am cleansing this room of any unwanted negative spirits or entities. You are no longer welcome here, please leave!"

I knew I had to speak directly to one spirit and one spirit only. "Tabitha Briggs, you are free to leave this place." I rang the bell.

TING! *"We release you!"* We chanted in unison.

At the next corner I called out, "We will make sure your daughter does not harm another soul. You no longer have to guard this place, or keep your secrets. We know what happened here, we understand and acknowledge your grief and your anger, but you can go now."

TING! *"We release you!"*

Kevin continued to sweep behind Russell and Cat, chanting out his incantation. When we rounded the third corner I called out, "Tabitha, dwell here no more! You are no longer among the living, and this is no longer your home. You are free to go be with your beloved Samuel."

TING! *"We release you!"*

At the last corner I addressed the others, "Any spirit that may still linger, please hear my voice. Know that your graves have been found. You are no longer forgotten, we know of your struggles, we know of your pain, and you are no longer bound to this place. Go be with your loved ones.

TING! *"We release you!"*

We stopped, and looked at each other, taking a moment to get a feel for the energy left in the room. "Did it work?" Cat asked tentatively.

"It feels better in here to me," Kevin responded, "And I don't even know what it was I was feeling before, but it wasn't good."

"We need to get up to the séance room and the nursery," I said.

"Guys, we are at 11:30 p.m. now. The height of the New Moon is at 12:04 a.m." Russell replied with a renewed sense of urgency. He gestured for all of us to start gathering up the supplies.

"Cat, we'll need the large keys. One of them *has* to work for the séance room," I said.

"Is that the room we didn't explore last time? It was used for the séances?" she asked. "Okay, great. The worst room, probably."

"Kevin," I pleaded, "I hate to ask this, but I need you to bring the doll. We'll need it in the nursery." His face pulled back in disgust.

"No way!" he protested.

"I'll do it," Russell offered. He went to the trunk, grabbed the doll and placed it in his pack.

"Okay... short cut?" Kevin offered, shining his light at the case covering the hidden stairwell.

"Only if we have to," Cat grumbled. Kevin pulled away the panel, revealing a recess in the wall, only the bottom step in view. Cat brought her beam of light to the recess and illuminated several more steps spiraling away into the darkness.

"Cool," Russell stated coming up behind me, ready to go.

"It's really not," I responded, remembering how dizzy it made me feel last time.

"I got you," he said.

Kevin and Cat were already slowly ascending, when I finally took my first step. I closed my eyes and let my left hand guide me up the wall, not thinking about how tight the space was, not thinking about going around in circles. *Just keep focusing on each step*, I told myself. The next thing I knew, my hand was reaching out into the open space of the upper hallway.

"You can open up your eyes," Kevin said.

"Thanks," I answered, squinting against the glare of his flashlight beam aimed at my face. "Hey, are you trying to blind me?"

"Sorry." He swung it away. "Okay, then. Which room?"

"That's the one we didn't try," Cat responded, pointing to the right. She walked over, knelt and brought out the keys. She proceeded to try each one until, CLICK. "Yay! It worked."

Kevin pushed the door inward while Cat gathered the keys back in the box, then followed in behind. The room contained only a single table and four chairs. Empty shelves lined the walls. I remembered, from my vision, that those were where candles had been placed. I could still see Tabitha and the clairvoyant sitting, holding hands with two other townspeople. They were inviting any spirit nearby to join them, welcoming them, opening the door to the spirit world.

"This is the gateway," I said aloud. "This is where the medium invited all the wandering spirits to come in."

"All right then, you know what to do. Hurry," Russell said. We then took to our designated tasks.

I went around and lit each candle, as I had done before, saying, "Spirits, if you still linger in this place, please hear my voice. Know that you are no longer among the living. Your hard days of work are over, and you can now rest.

262

Please know that your graves have been found, and that you are not forgotten. You are no longer bound to this place, I release you."

We followed behind Russell in a clockwise direction, starting at the door, and finishing at the door, where Kevin swept the negative energy out.

As I rounded the last corner I rang the bell. **TING!**

"We release you!" We chanted together.

When we finished, Russell exclaimed. "It's almost time. Next room!" We hurriedly went about gathering up all the supplies… feeling the urgency of diminishing time.

Surprisingly, we found the nursery door ajar when we arrived. I pushed at it timidly, not sure what I would find on the other side.

The flashback from my dream hit me full force. I watched my hand push the door all the way open taking in the full view of the room. Unlike that dreamscape though, it still had the nursery wallpaper, and in the far corner, nearest the window, all the furniture was stacked up neatly. I swung my flashlight beam around making sure there wasn't a person hiding in the corner.

"Are you going in?" Cat asked me. I startled at the sound of her voice breaking through my memory of the dark veiled figure, hiding in the shadows.

"Come in with me, at the same time," I pleaded, grabbing her hand for support. "This is like the scene from my damn nightmare!"

"Oh! Okay, we'll go in together."

263

"Gwen, you're going to have to be really strong. Can you dig deep?" Russell asked, as he walked in behind us, placing his pack on the ground. He got out the silver flask, as well as a cross, and a black chord, then laid them out next to the bowls.

"What's that for?" I asked, pointing at the black chord.

"If we need to, we're going to do a binding ritual between Jane Elizabeth and the doll, in case she refuses to leave. But for the ritual to work we need to use the power of the new moon." He checked his watch. "We're closing in on midnight."

"Jane Elizabeth is in here?" Kevin asked, looking around.

"Yes. Her mother buried her behind those bricks." I pointed, and they followed my gaze. "In what used to be the fireplace," I answered. I heard them gasp in surprise.

I looked at Kevin, and asked, "Can you work your knife between any of those bricks and see if we can't loosen a couple, give her a way to leave?"

"Oh damn," Cat recoiled, shaking her head in disgust. "Her mother walled her up in there? When did you find this out?"

"It's what my dream tried to show me, but I wasn't sure, until I saw the whole thing happen through Tabitha's memories downstairs."

"What exactly happened?" Kevin asked.

"Guys," Russell urged, "There's literally no time for this. Let's move!"

"I'll tell you the whole story once we get the hell out of here," I replied, trying to rally every ounce of energy I had left.

I went over to the covered fireplace and touched the bricks. I didn't experience any visions, or feel any emotional energy. Meanwhile, Russell was lighting the bowls and the incense, Cat was lighting the candles and reciting an incantation of her own, and Kevin was trying to get a window to open.

"Russell, I guess I am going to need that doll for this to work," I said. The thought of even touching it made me recoil.

He pulled it out of the pack and brought it over, unceremoniously holding it by one of its long blonde curls, and flung it to the floor at the base of the fireplace. He quickly grabbed the black chord and came back over.

"Okay, we need to do this *now*," he insisted.

Chapter Thirty-Three
New Moon

K evin began to work at the crumbling powdered mortar between the bricks, wedging the blade in and applying pressure, just like he had with the board. I could see he was going to get at least one brick loose, which might be all we needed.

Before I grabbed hold of the doll, I held the amulet, and took several deep breaths, reminding myself, *I am protected, I am surrounded by a shield of positive energy, and nothing can harm me.*

Then I reached out and grabbed the doll's hair, the real hair that once was part of Jane Elizabeth...

I saw the nursery from her perspective as she sat across from Tabitha in those last moments before her death. The taste of the almond bread was sweet on her tongue, and she was happy. I had not felt this emotion come from her before. She was so happy to have Mother all to herself, giving her so much attention, and agreeing to finally have a tea party. It was the best day she could remember having in such a long time.

When Father had been alive, before the baby arrived, she had him all to herself. She was his special little girl, and he always told her how pretty she was, and what a wonderful dancer she was. He loved for her to sing in front of the fire at night, or recite poems. It had been such a happy time.

But the farm and all the workers took his attention from her during the day. When the orphans from the trains started showing up, she also lost Mother's attention. She was alone. She was told to stay in the nursery, to not be underfoot, and to stop being a nuisance. Then Mother and Father had their own baby that cried all the time, and then Father died.

She found herself very alone in a big lonely house with no one to tell her how pretty she was, or to watch her dance, or listen to her recite poems by the fireside.

The tea party, though, meant that she had Mother all to herself. Mother could love her now, and would ask her to sing, and they would have so much fun spending time together.

But suddenly, she felt sick. So very sick. She couldn't understand. She wanted to vomit, and she felt dizzy. Something was horribly wrong. Why wouldn't Mother help her? She kept calling out to her, but she was being ignored.

You can't ignore me anymore, Mother! It is just you and me now. You can't ignore me now. You will not ignore me now.

I could feel her confusion and hostility right before she began to convulse. I felt the same tremors run through her body as I experienced with Joseph and Tabitha.

I let go of the memory before it could pull me down with it into the darkness of death…

Coming out my vision I spoke out loud to her. "Jane Elizabeth, if you can hear me, I know what your mother did to you. I know you feel hurt and confused. I know you feel sad you lost your father. You loved him so much. I'm here now to tell you, you can be free of this room. You no longer have to be alone. You can be with him. Join your father, be free of this prison."

Suddenly, I felt hatred wash over me. So overpowering, rich and sour and seething. I collapsed to the floor. The menacing glare on her face from the mirror in the attic flew towards me in my minds' eye, filled with rage. It beat itself against me over and over, threatening to fill every cell in my being, to take over every part of me.

"Cat, hand me that flask, quick!" Russell called out.

I felt sprinkles of the Moon Water splash around me, and heard him yell, "I remove your power until there is not a trace. Flee evil being, through time and space."

TING! "Leave here! You are not welcome!" Cat yelled out.

I heard the sound of Kevin pulling a brick away and letting it fall to the floor, as Russell called out, "Fight, Gwen. Tell her to leave!"

"Jane Elizabeth! You are no longer alive! Your father is dead. Your mother is dead. There is nothing to keep you tied here to this world. We've made a path for you to follow! Leave your prison. Fly out the window. You are free to go wherever you want. Be with your loved ones. *We release you*!" I yelled out.

A wind suddenly swept through the room, rattling the window against its frame, causing the smoke from the incense to whirl like a dust devil.

Again, I was hit with rage, like a punch to the gut, and I doubled over, moaning. *How could be she dead? She didn't want to be alone anymore. She felt lost.*

"Jane, we mean you no harm, but you are no longer welcome in this home. You need to *leave* NOW!" I tried again.

"Gwen," Russell cried out, "this isn't working! Take this cord and wrap it around the doll as you say these words, 'I bind thee Jane Elizabeth Briggs from ever doing harm to others', and then tie a knot. Do this three times."

Russell jumped up, grabbed the bundle of sage, lit it for 10 seconds, blew it out, and picked up the Abalone shell. "Cat, are you ready?" he asked.

She picked up the feather, and the bell, and replied, "Yeah, let's do this."

Once Kevin loosened and removed a few bricks, the rest tumbled from the hole and scattered on the floor around him. As the dust settled, the contents of the fireplace came into view... a disintigrating rug around a pile of bones and scraps of clothing. "Oh my god!" he exclaimed.

"I know, Kevin! We need you here with us. Focus. Pick up the broom and help us clear her negative energy from the room," Russell directed.

"I bind thee, Jane Elizabeth Briggs, to this doll. I bind thee from ever doing harm to others," I said as I tied the black cord into one knot.

The candles flickered violently in protest, as the wind continued to swirl around us, and the house creaked and moaned.

"Again, Gwen," Russell instructed.

"I bind thee, Jane Elizabeth Briggs, from ever doing harm to others!" I yelled louder, and tied another knot.

The bile of rage began to ebb... the energy waning.

"Say it one last time, and then say, 'Three by three, I bind thee, from ever doing harm to others'."

I did as he instructed and then sat there with the doll in my lap, as Russell continued to sage every crevice of the room. He then went to the fireplace and waved the smoke around the opening.

TING! Cat rang the bell. "*We release you!*" We cried out in unison.

"Again!" Russell declared.

TING! "*We release you!*" We yelled again.

They each collapsed to the floor next to me, and the house fell silent. The creaking and whining... everything ceased. I could literally hear my heart slowing down, resuming its normal rhythm in my chest. Moments passed as we simply sat and caught our breath, the relief palpable.

I saw Russell glance at his watch, "It's 12:06 a.m.! Just. In. Time," he sighed.

Everyone looked as exhausted as I felt.

"Can we be done now?" Cat asked.

"We've still got many more rooms to go, as well as the attic."

"What?" Kevin exclaimed. "Anywhere, but the attic! I hate that place!"

"We still need to finish releasing the trapped innocents," Russell responded. "But the hardest part's over!"

"I think if all that stuff is still up there we should just burn it!" Cat announced. "Except the jewelry box. We should give it to the reporter. Maybe she can see that it gets laid to rest with the children's bones."

"That's a *great* idea!" I responded. *Joseph*, I suddenly thought. *What about the marble?*

"Kevin, would you be able to find your way back to where the marble is buried?"

"You have got to be kidding me! I'm not going to go looking for that in the middle of the night. No way!"

"Gwen, we always have tomorrow," Russell said as he held out his hand. "It isn't going anywhere. But tonight, we need to finish what we started." As he held out his hand, I thought he wanted to hold mine, but instead he gestured towards the doll. I gladly handed it over to him, and he placed it in his pack.

"You're going to keep that?" I asked, completely in shock.

"There is one more thing we'll need to do, but not tonight," he responded. "Let's finish with this floor then head up to the attic. We don't want to be here all night."

"Please god, no," Cat grumbled again. "My body feels like it weighs 2 million pounds. Is that even possible? To feel heavier than the whole universe?"

"I know what you mean," I responded, grabbing her hand and helping her stand up.

"One more floor. We can do this!" I said, trying to rally her, but also to rally myself.

Chapter Thirty-Four
Coming to a Close

To make our way out through the front door, and sweep out the last of the negative energy, it had taken everything we had. We left everything we could open, to allow the spirits a chance to leave. We'd taken down the boards off the front door, and wedged it open with a toolbox from the renovation crew, to bring attention to our visit. We wanted the bodies, buried within the walls, to be found.

Cat left all the keys behind except for the one to the jewelry box. That she had safely tucked away in her pack. Russell and Kevin also had items taken from the attic tucked away in theirs.

Once we had made it to the car, Cat immediately fell asleep against Kevin's shoulder, and he passed out with his head against the glass of the backseat window, bouncing off it with every bump in the road. He didn't even stir.

I felt tired enough to sleep for a week, but my head was swimming with everything I'd seen. I was still trying to process it all, acknowledging each aspect of the encounters

273

with the spirits, what it felt like to be attacked, nearly invaded by an angry and confused child spirit.

"Do you think we closed *the* door? You know, so nothing can come back? Did we do enough?" I asked, my head resting against Russell's shoulder. "I mean, we dispersed the energy, we cleansed the house, we acknowledged the spirits, we gave them permission to leave, and we even showed them the way out."

"We'll have to wait and see," he responded. He sounded tired, and was struggling to keep his eyes open as he drove.

We made it back to Cat's house. Luckily, her mother had not yet returned from her graveyard shift.

"Kevin, dude, I'll drop you off. You don't need to walk home from here," Russell offered. I got out and held the seat up for Cat to climb out. Russell, despite his own exhaustion, got out to help us with our stuff and see us to the door.

"I'll call you after I have a really long nap," he offered, leaning in to kiss me gently. "You were amazing tonight. You both were." He looked at us, smiling. "Sleep well."

With that he stumbled back to the car, while Kevin waved good-bye from the back seat.

∿

After sleeping in at Cat's house, I went home that Sunday afternoon. Immediately I took another nap. I barely could rouse myself for dinner, and my parents wondered if I might be getting sick. Afterwards I returned to my room and slept again until my alarm went off for school on Monday morning.

When I met Russell at the lockers, he looked renewed, back to his old self.

"You missed my call yesterday," he said.

"I did? I didn't know you called. My mom thought I was sick, because basically all I did was sleep until my alarm went off this morning. Sorry," I replied.

"Yeah, that's what she said. She didn't want to disturb you. Are you feeling better today? You look great by the way." He smiled, and that impish sparkle had come back into his eyes. He reached over and grabbed me into his arms, "Come here."

Then he kissed me like he hadn't seen me in a year, and that old familiar buckling of my knees came back. I could feel the intensity again, and I loved how intoxicated it made me feel.

"Mmmm, where was this Russell on Saturday night? I was starting to feel like your sister or something."

"What? Now, that would be really, really gross. Never," he squirmed at even the thought of it.

"I wasn't meaning literally. It's just that you were a different Russell than this one," I replied nuzzling my nose to his, as we swayed back and forth in each other's arms.

"That was business. This, my dear, is pleasure," he whispered in a sultry, come hither, tone, and kissed me again.

"Hey guys," Kevin said as he came up on us, with Cat at his side.

"Oh, hi," I answered, wiping the slobber from my lips, feeling my face turn several shades of red.

"I was just wondering what we were going to do with the stuff we brought back from the house? I don't want to keep them," Kevin admitted.

"We'll take care of it Halloween night," Russell answered.

"What're we doing?" I asked.

"I'm taking you guys to the party house out in the fields. There is going to be a full moon and there will be a bonfire. The perfect opportunity to bring all this to a close," he answered.

"Ohhh, Mike is going to hate that!" Cat grinned.

Russell addressed Kevin, "But if that's too long to hold them, I'll take them off your hands."

"Thank god, I thought you would never ask," Kevin replied, and immediately dropped his pack, unzipped the top and took out the heavy occult books and Ouija board.

"Can you at least bring them to my locker?" Russell asked, laughing at how quickly Kevin was trying to toss them onto the ground.

"Okay, where is that? First bell is going to ring soon."

"Dude, chill out! This way," he said, gesturing Kevin to follow him. "Talk to you before 4th period," Russell said to me, as he led Kevin from the quad to the next cluster of buildings.

"Okay!" I responded.

~~

The following Sunday, Russell and Kevin made a plan to drive up to Douglas Park and sneak their way across the grassy plateau and down onto the tracks in the forest.

When they reported back to us at Cat's house, they said they had no trouble finding it, and when I asked about Joseph, they said they didn't see him.

"So I can only hope that means he was freed when the bones were uncovered," I said aloud. Kevin pulled the marble out of his pocket, and tried to hand it to me.

I was afraid to touch it. I just couldn't bear finding out we'd failed. "No, could you just put it in the box where we found it?"

Cat then placed the jewelry box and key inside a plain brown box addressed to Claire Beaumont, care of the TV station. Cat and I included a note of explanation, signed "Anonymous", of course.

Russell drove the four of us to the studio, and Cat and I did the honors of handing it to the receptionist. It was not the same woman who had seen us that summer, so we got lucky. We pulled the same act as before, saying we just happened to be walking by and noticed the box sitting out front. We didn't want anything of importance to be stolen, so we thought we'd bring it inside.

This particular receptionist seemed a little more cautious, wary of accepting a package from a pair of strange girls, and called for security to handle it. I am not sure what she thought might be in the box. But we played up our ignorance.

"Hey, we just thought we were being helpful," we explained. We wished everyone a nice day and walked out.

When we got back in the car, I sat back in the seat and felt all my muscles unwind. A huge sense of relief washed over me.

"I am so glad that is over," Cat sighed.

"This isn't over until all the rest of the stuff is tossed in the garbage or destroyed. THEN it will be over." Kevin concluded.

"Let's hope so," I sighed, feeling Russell's hand come over to mine and give it a loving squeeze.

"The worst *is* over," Russell assured me, then put the car in drive.

Chapter Thirty-Five
Exclusive Report

The Friday before Halloween everyone did dress up at school. I was thrilled. Apparently it wasn't lame to want to pretend to be someone or something else for the day.

That night, after the football game, was a dance. Cat and I blew them both off to stay in and watch *An American Werewolf in London* with Kevin and Russell.

We ordered in pizza again, and just before starting the movie, we took up separate sections of her couch for blanket cocoons of cuddling.

"Wait!" Russell suddenly called out, as Kevin was just about to hit play on the VCR. "Turn it to Channel 13."

"What is it?" I asked in concern.

"Hurry, Kevin! It's started..." he trailed off.

"How would you know..."Kevin started.

"Shhh... listen!" Russell scolded.

Good Evening! I'm Claire Beaumont, and this is an exclusive report. Thanks to the hard work, and really, the dogged determination of the staff here at KTVL, we can now close the loop on a local mystery.

279

You may remember a story we ran earlier this summer, concerning the discovery of the mass grave near the Douglas Zoo...

"Hold up... their hard work?" Cat protested.

"I know, right?" I replied.

"Shhh..." Kevin scolded this time.

... in the 1800's called the Orphan Trains. Orphans from the New York area who would otherwise be placed into institutions filled with juvenile delinquents, were given the opportunity to find refuge on farms. The belief, at the time, was that fresh air, open spaces and hard work was a better environment for these unfortunate castoffs.

These children were loaded onto trains and taken to various cities across the country, where they were trotted out for potential adopters to inspect, dressed in their finest, and coached to impress. Organizers assured applicants would be screened and there would be follow-up visits to ensure the children were taken care of properly. Sadly, these rules were rarely enforced.

By the time the trains made it to the West Coast, the remaining children were treated more like cattle at an auction. People checked their teeth to see if they were healthy, checked their muscles to see if they were strong enough to work, and if they passed those tests, the 'lucky' few were selected for adoption.

Unfortunately, many of the adoptees were given new names, and subsequently, lost from the well-meaning organization.

"Or... murdered!" I yelled at the TV. "Don't forget about that, Claire!"

"Kevin, can you hand me another piece of pizza, please?" Cat asked.

"You'd think the two of you would want to hear about this?" Russell complained trying to get us to stop talking over the broadcast. He moved forward and dialed up the volume, playfully glaring back at us.

... claimed that the children on these trains were homeless or abused, but mostly they were children of new immigrants and families that were destitute. Accusations were made, that they were deliberately separating families of Catholic immigrants, placing the children into Protestant homes, an extreme form of conversion.

Older children were frequently placed with farmers who could profit from the labor. Critics pointed to this indentureship as just another form of slavery. Stories of horrendous abuse began to circulate.

Sadly this seems to be the case of the children found right here in Douglas!

"Thanks to Kevin Maxwell!" Cat blurted out.

"Yeah, we should have told her about you, Kevin. You could be famous!" I added.

"Shhh..." Russell said.

Newly discovered I.D. cards found hidden inside the old Briggs' Victorian House closely match the basic details of the remains recovered near the zoo. These children, adopted by the Briggs family, arrived by way of the New York Catholic Protectory. This institution welcomed the destitute, the neglected, the delinquent, as well as the orphaned. Using the information provided to us, our staff has uncovered a sobering and awful fact: they weren't all actually orphans...

"Joseph..." I lamented.

"I know...poor guy," Kevin sympathized.

"It just kills me to think his mother never knew what actually became of him," Cat commented sadly.

A few weeks after this tragic discovery, a secondary grave was uncovered, with dozens of adult individuals. Soon after that, a third grave, also with dozens of adult individuals.

What do these graves have in common you may be asking yourself? I asked myself the very same question.

What we learned was that the Briggs's property was used as a working farm for the poor of Douglas County. In exchange for room and board, these paupers toiled long hours tending to livestock, picking fruit and vegetables, and maintaining the property. The Briggs' also took in the ill and infirm, as well as adult individuals with mental illness. It became a sanatorium, where many patients with tuberculosis went for long-term care, and had separate housing to quarantine the contagion.

"Oh damn! I didn't know that," Kevin exclaimed. "That explains why the men I saw just seemed so… off!"

"Yeah," Cat confirmed. "Totally creepy!"

Eventually, the farm came under scrutiny, after a routine inspection by the county. It revealed residents suffering under atrocious living conditions, likely no better than the squalor from which many came, a stark contrast to the lavish Victorian house where the Briggs' family resided.

Word of the untenable situation quickly spread, and under increasing pressure, officials decided to step in. However when they finally arrived to shut the program down, they discovered the property abandoned.

These mass grave sites are believed to be the unidentified and unclaimed bodies of those people from the Briggs' farm.

After a thorough search, only Samuel Briggs, the family patriarch, and their infant son, could be accounted for, having clearly marked plots in the family cemetery.

"Because, the others were murdered and buried in the house!" I heckled.

The disappearance of Samuel's wife, Tabitha, and the couple's adopted daughter Jane Elizabeth remained a mystery.

Soon after, the county reconstituted the "poor farm" program at another property on the opposite end of town. The Briggs Farm fell to ruins, eventually swallowed up by the forest where it has sat forgotten. That is, until the events of this previous summer grabbed our collective attention.

Now, just this week, we received more information from our anonymous source, including a disturbing object...

"The jewelry box!" Cat exclaimed. "Is she going to talk about all the teeth?"

"I don't know. You have to use your ears, my dear," Kevin teased.

...two more bodies were discovered, this time within the very walls of the Briggs' house itself. Found, in a walled off fireplace, was the body of a young girl. Located in a covered crawl space, within a hidden room beneath the main staircase of the home, was the body of an adult female.

Experts speculate that these are likely the remains of Tabitha and Jane Elizabeth Briggs. And while as yet unconfirmed, this evidence suggests only one thing… murder! What on earth went on in that home? We may never know.

"You should ask your anonymous source, lady. We did all the hard work!" Cat heckled.

"But if we didn't stay anonymous, then we'd get in trouble," I reasoned.

"Okay, yeah. You got a point," she responded. "Still…"

"Girls!" Kevin shushed us again.

Without a way to truly match the names on the I.D. cards to the bones of the children, the Northwest Investigators of Archaeology have at least identified the boys from the girls and proposed approximate ages. From the names on the I.D. cards we were able to determine that several families of these children are buried in the cemetery at St. Raphael's Church in New York City. This cemetery is located adjacent to where their orphanage once stood.

The recovered remains, and the newly discovered belongings, will be transferred there for final interment…

"Okay! So they *will* bury their belongings with them! That's awesome!" Cat said.

"Yay! Joseph will finally be reunited with his family!" I exclaimed.

"Right on!" Kevin yelled. Leaning in to the middle of the couch we gave each other high fives.

Meanwhile, at the Douglas Zoo, a plaque is being erected to pay respects and give acknowledgement to the unidentified souls buried in those mass graves.

"That's awesome," Russell responded.

Finally, remodeling is set to commence on the old Victorian House to make it into a local museum, which will include this newly discovered history in a very dark chapter of the town of Douglas...

Chapter Thirty-Six
Samhain and the Bonfire

The next day, Russell came by my house first before we headed over to Cat's. Mike and Erik were there when we arrived. They weren't pleased Russell had invited us.

"Pretty bogus, Russ," Erik scolded. "Not cool."

"Well, it doesn't matter if you don't think it's *cool*," he scolded back. "It's what's happening, so... just chill!"

"Cat, just don't tell anyone that you're my sister. Pretend like you don't know me," Mike urged, as he and Erik headed out the door.

After he was out of earshot, Cat started to laugh. "He's going to shit when he finds out I invited everyone else."

"When he comes for you, and he will, you keep my name out of this," Russell laughed, shaking his head in disbelief, grabbing my hand gently. "You have everything you need?"

"Yep," I answered, smiling back. I was really excited for my first real party.

"Okay, so let's go howl under the full moon!" Kevin said, grabbing Cat's hand and following us out her front door.

We passed over the Douglas River on the road leading out to an old abandoned farmhouse. The road seemed like it went on forever. The sky was bright with moonlight, and the miles of open fields stretching out before us had an eerie glow. After what seemed like ages I finally could make out the light of a giant bonfire in the distance.

"Is that it?" I asked, leaning forward, my hands on the dashboard.

"Yeah, pretty cool, huh?" Russell responded. "That was MacLean's original homestead."

"MacLean. As in Angus MacLean, the founder?" I asked, making the connection.

"Yeah," he answered.

We pulled off the main road, across the shoulder, and into the grassy field where everyone was parking. The silhouettes of dozens of people danced around the bonfire, throwing objects into its stomach, feeding the massive flames.

When I opened the passenger door a loud cheer rang out through the night as the flames suddenly burst in intensity, growing ever higher. Even at a distance, I could feel the heat.

Russell pulled the seat forward, and Kevin and Cat crawled out. He came around to my side, as I leaned back against the door, put his arm around my shoulder, and gestured toward the pyre. "Isn't it beautiful? I love fire."

"Yeah, and I was getting sort of hypnotized by it. Staring at the shapes, all that orange, angry heat... when something catches fire, it just suddenly loses all sense of what it once was."

"Feeling poetic tonight, are we?" he teased, hugging me closer. "Did you know that in our culture, we call this *Samhain* (he pronounced it sa-win)? Tonight is the end of summer, the harvest, which technically means the end of a year. Tomorrow begins a whole new cycle."

"So at midnight, you yell 'Happy New Year'?" I joked.

"Nope, we just turn back into pumpkins," he teased, and started leading me towards the gathering. "Come on, let's see who's here."

We passed through the field of cars, where some guys were sitting in the back of their pick-up truck, tailgate down, swinging their legs, drinking beer and catcalling any girl that happened to walk by.

As we approached the farmhouse I noticed the windows were just empty wood frames, the broken glass probably destroyed decades before. Through these portals I could see people's shadows milling around the keg, and lit candles atop old milk crates.

People were using the windows as alternate exits, because the front entrance was a log jam of underage teens trying to get a beer.

At the front door, there wasn't a porch or step. The gap between the foundation and the ground was about two feet, so the only way inside was if people pulled you in. I didn't like the idea of being hoisted up into that place, filled with strangers, doing who knows what inside.

"Hey Russell," I heard Mike's voice call out from the proximity of the fire. We turned towards the sound, and scanned the silhouettes of dancing teenagers. "A Town Called Malice" by the Jam was blaring from a boombox nearby. He came forward out of the shadows, beer in hand.

"Mike!" I heard Cat call out as she and Kevin came up behind us.

"And you, you little shit." Mike shook his head at her. "I see some of your little friends milling about. Why'd you have to tell them about this place? Now it's going to be over run."

"Yeah, we'll have to call an exterminator," Erik yelled out, coming up behind Mike and reaching around to slap Russell on the shoulder. He then noticed me there and slurred flirtatiously, "Ohhhh, Gwen! Helllloooo."

"Hey," I replied scooting in closer under Russell's arm.

"What's so special about him anyways?" he asked pointing at his friend. "Look at what you're missing!" He pulled his arms open wide swinging around in circles laughing.

"That's enough, Erik," Russell chided politely, apparently knowing his friend meant no harm. I wasn't so sure, with the way he kept leering at me.

"Where did you see my friends, Mike?" Cat asked. Mike turned around and pointed to the opposite side of the fire. She then proceeded to pull Kevin behind her as she made her way in that direction.

"Come on guys," Kevin called out as he was being dragged away.

"You want me to get you a beer, dude?" Mike asked Russell.

"Not tonight, dude," he answered.

"Seriously? Dude!"

"Mike, chill. Maybe later," he responded, a little more forcefully. "You don't want anything do you?" He asked me, suddenly realizing I may have had a different response.

"I dunno, maybe?" I answered. This surprised him.

"Really?"

"What? I can be cool too, ya know... dude!" I teased.

"Who's saying you aren't cool? Hey, why don't we see who's here you might know, okay?"

As he pulled me behind him through the crowd, I was bumped by people left and right. Between the competing sounds from the individual boomboxes, the strange shadow play from the bright moonlit sky, and the light from the fire, everything began to blur together.

With every bump and brush against one person after another, a barrage of visions washed over me. Assaulted by the continual flutter of hazy and vague scenes rushing by, the sense of vertigo wormed its way from my head to my stomach and back again. Along with the random imagery, there was a constant ringing in my ears, like a thousand souls were trying to talk at once. I wasn't sure why it was so overwhelming that night. I'd been in plenty of crowds before, but never had I experienced anything like this.

I was getting totally disoriented, when suddenly, the chaotic flicker of scenes flooding my brain simply washed away to reveal a single, steady picture...

An empty room, in the back of a barn, with graffiti all over the walls: satanic symbols, curse words, and vulgar sexual pictures. In the center a single burning candle - its red wax pooling like blood across the aged wood flooring...

Another jostling of the crush of teenagers, and as quickly as the solid vision appeared, it was gone. I immediately looked left and right, trying to catch sight of the source. All I could see, however, were the backs of the people who had passed by, simply too many to know which person it could have been.

Though the vision had vanished, the giver's essence still lingered: dark and violent. It sat in the pit of my stomach... sour... vile.

Something bad was going to happen.

"Come on, Gwen," Russell encouraged as my sluggish pace was slowing us down.

I tucked myself in, making myself as thin as possible, to avoid touching anyone, as we navigated our way through the crowd to the other side. There we found Jennifer, Liz, Kelly, Craig, Drew and Brian gathered on a giant blanket. They were huddled up together, against the cold wind kicking up, their faces aglow from the reflection of the fire.

The full moon was starting to rise, cresting the mountain range in the distance and lighting up the center of the sky. Someone had put on "Spellbound" by Siouxie and the Banshees and it echoed out eerily across the fields.

"Hey guys," Kelly called out to us.

"Come on over," Jennifer offered. "We brought tons more blankets."

"Earth to Gwen!" Kelly exclaimed over the sound of the crackling and popping of the enormous pit of flames.

Overwhelmed by just getting through the crowd, and trying to process the image of the room in my head, I felt a bit off kilter, but managed to respond, "Thank you, don't mind if I do."

Cat and Kevin were already sitting on the one available corner of the blanket, so Russell and I sat on the opposite available end.

He sat down first and motioned for me to sit in front of him, between his legs. He then wrapped the blanket over his back, and like bat wings, wrapped me up in a cozy embrace.

"What was that about back there? Are you okay?" He whispered in my ear. "Did you see something?"

"Yes, but I don't know what. I have a bad feeling that…"

"Gwen, did I hear you say you have a bad feeling? No bad feelings! There's to be none of that tonight!" Liz declared. She then handed me a cold bottle that looked like it was filled with Kool-Aid. "Here try one of these. They're berry-flavored. Craig brought them."

Even with the fire and the full moon, I could barely focus on the bottle's label. "What is it?" I asked, untwisting the metal top, and taking a sniff.

It kind of smelled like my mom's cheap Gallo Wine she kept in the refrigerator, but sweet. I took a sip, and immediately felt a tingle of warmth spread through my extremities. It did almost taste like a berry Kool-Aid with the kick of a cough syrup.

At first I wasn't sure I liked it, until I took the second sip. "Yum, that *is* pretty good."

Russell took the one offered to him, and unscrewed the cap, "Go easy, Gwen. It tastes like punch but it'll sneak up on you." He then took a swig.

Brian chimed in, "Dudes! Check out my righteous Halloween mix tape. They're oldies but they're goodies!" He chuckled to himself as he put it in the boombox and hit play.

The first track got everyone in the spirit, "Monster Mash" by Bobby "Boris" Pickett and the Crypt-Kickers. Loud cheers of approval swept through the groups surrounding us, and everyone sang along. When "I Put a Spell on You", by Screamin' Jay Hawkins came blaring through the speakers a few minutes later, it was greeted with equal delight.

"Speaking of being bewitched," Russell leaned over, and whispered in my ear, "Would you like to toast our anniversary?"

"Anniversary?"

"It's been one month since our first date!" he answered, shocked I didn't remember.

"It has? Oh, cheers!" I said lifting my bottle, and clinking it against his.

"*Slàinte Mhath* (he pronounced it slanj-a-va)!" he responded. "And may there be many more."

"Yes! And many more!" I smiled as he leaned forward for a kiss. His lips tasted of berries, and the continued flow of alcohol kept my insides warm and tingly. "Mmmm, you taste so good."

"Gwen, is that you?" I heard a female voice call out. I pulled away from the kiss and stared up to the shadow in front of me. I tried to shield my eyes from the light of the fire to see whose face it was.

She leaned down and came closer - it was Andrea.

I reached out and hugged her, pulling her into our laps. She laughed as she fell on top of us. "Gwen! You naughty girl! Do I smell wine coolers?"

"Why yes, yes you do. Would you like some? It's deeeeeeeeelicious."

"Ryan has a beer he's holding for me. I just wanted to come over and say hello! We haven't hung out in so long!"

"I know! We should totally do something soon!" I responded, feeling giddy. The psychedelic melody of "Wicked Annabella" by the Kinks crept passed my ears.

"Cool songs! Whose mix is this?" Andrea asked. Everyone pointed at Brian, who was oblivious to the compliment, busy digging through the Styrofoam ice chest.

She looked up into Russell's face as she tried to scramble back off our laps, giggling. "From the looks of it, things are going well."

"You've never met Russell?" I asked, it only occurring to me then, that I had no idea if they knew each other.

"Not officially, no. Nice to meet you," Andrea said, finally standing up. "I've heard about you, of course. And of course there's Erin's rumor mill. You know how she is? I know better than to believe most of what she says, so don't worry."

"Please tell me she isn't here!" I said louder than I had intended to.

"No, no, you're good. It's too bad how it all just sort of fell to shit between you two this year."

"It *is* too bad, but I'm pretty over it now."

"You heard that Chris broke up with her right? Finally came to his senses and realized what a manipulating monster she was being."

This was news to me. I tensed and sat straight up, trying to process what she'd said. I didn't know how I felt about it.

The song "Witchy Woman" by the Eagles began in the background with its heavy beat, and at the same time I felt Russell squeezing my thigh in reassurance.

"No, I hadn't heard," I relaxed back into his arms, and put my hand on top of his, holding it tightly, in my own way thanking him for being there. "Well good for him. I wish him well."

"He's here, by the way," she replied.

"Chris?" I asked.

"Uh huh," she confirmed.

Russell interjected, "Andrea, do me a favor, will you? Find him and bring him over. I just thought of something that might help all of you."

"Um, help us with what?" she asked, clearly confused.

"Just bring him over, okay?" he asked again, sitting up, and taking the blanket off. He picked up his pack, and pulled out the books, the Ouija board, and the doll. He then stood up and laid them out before us in the dirt.

Eventually Chris and Andrea walked back over. Chris looked uncomfortable. I stood up, not sure what Russell had in store.

"Hi, Chris," I said quietly, also feeling uncomfortable.

"Gwen, Cat, Kevin and I went back to the house a couple weeks ago, and we helped free the spirits that were trapped there," Russell explained.

Andreas's eyes widened. "Did it work?"

Just then the soulful guitar strings of ELO's song "Strange Magic" began echoing around us. I thought to myself *what a fitting soundtrack for our discussion.*

"We hope so," I answered. "Our nightmares have stopped, so that's a good sign."

"I was having nightmares too," Chris suddenly admitted. "But they stopped a couple weeks ago. So that was you guys?"

"Yeah! We performed a cleansing ritual that took all damned night!" Cat chimed in. "It was exhausting."

"Yeah, dude! It was rough!" Kevin agreed.

"I'm sorry I didn't go with you guys," Chris responded, hands in pockets gazing at the ground. "Someone should've told me."

This response left me a bit stunned.

"Dude..." Kevin responded, shaking his head.

"I know. I've been a mess," Chris replied, looking up. "Gwen, I'm really sorry about the last couple months. I really am."

My chest exploded in that moment, and before I even blinked an eye I threw myself at him and wrapped him in a hug. "I've missed you so much, Chris."

"Same here," he replied and hugged me back. I immediately felt a wave of his emotions: relief at first, then a burst of happiness.

"Awwww, dang it guys," Andrea said, and wrapped her arms around the two of us - a big love fest.

"Hey look at that - the gang is all back together," Kevin remarked from the comfort of the blanket, not bothering to get up.

"Andrea... Chris... I want to ask the two of you to join us in our final act of banishing the negative energies from that house," Russell said.

"What do you plan on doing?" Andrea asked, suspiciously. "Nothing scary, right?"

Suddenly a scream ripped across the night, and heads all around popped up, listening intently. A chill went down my spine, the hair rose up on my neck, and my entire body covered in goosebumps.

"Did you hear…"I began to ask Russell, but just then, howls erupted, and like a wave, starting at the house, made their way through each group, circling around the bonfire.

"Bad Moon Rising" by Creedence Clearwater Revival had begun blasting from Brian's boombox, and everyone cheered, lifting their drinks to the sky.

Russell shook off the distraction and looked back at Andrea, continuing, "No! Nothing scary. The full moon, especially on Samhain, is a powerful shift of cosmic energy, and the bonfire acts like a purifying element. We're going to throw all the bad things from that house in the fire, and as the smoke goes up, so will all the negative energy and entities."

"I'm totally in. I would love to burn something from that place!" Chris exclaimed, and a smile crossed his face, the first one I'd seen in ages.

"Does anyone have paper and pen? Everyone can join us," Russell called out to the group around him. "Just write down on the paper what you'd like to let go of, or what you'd like to invite into your life, and then throw it into the fire. It's the time for letting go, and a time for new beginnings."

As the girls rummaged through their purses for something to write with, the boys scrounged scraps of random flyers and debris from around the property to write on. Floating over the scene, the haunting synthesizer and soft percussion of Santana's song "Black Magic Woman" elicited hoots and hollers of approval.

Kevin and Cat picked up the books and handed one to Andrea. She didn't want to touch it at first, until Cat assured her she'd be fine, especially after she got to throw it into the flames.

Chris picked up the Ouija board, looking at it warily. He appeared to be flashing back to the attic.

I walked over and reassured him, "We cleansed that room, and we fought hard to free the spirits, including the mom and the daughter you saw in the mirror. Throw it in the fire, and as you do, think about putting it all behind you. Watch it burn. Let it go. Yell out, *'I release you'*, if you want."

"So... you believe in all that stuff now?" he asked, a little shocked at my statement, but with a grateful smile on his face that I understood where his fear was coming from.

"Yeah, you can't go through what I've been through this year, and not be. Remind me to tell you about it some time."

Cat went up to the fire first, and tore pages from the books and threw them into the flames. I turned back around to watch them immediately light up, twist, turn, and then WHOOSH into a flurry of ash. It was mesmerizing.

After a few pages, she just decided to throw the whole book in, followed by another. "All you negative energies and evil spirits, leave us now. *We release you!*" she yelled out!

Cheers went up amongst the group formed around us: Brian, Drew and Craig were on one side, and Liz, Kelly and Jennifer on the other.

Then "Don't Fear the Reaper" by Blue Oyster Cult started, and everyone paused to listen and reflect, as they stared into the flames... the guitar and cowbell echoing out into the night.

Kevin then did the same with his books. Afterwards, Andrea followed with hers. They each, in turn, repeated what Cat had said.

Our group of friends started to take turns tossing in their pieces of paper with a variety of choice words at what they wanted to get rid of in their lives.

Chris came up last, and tossed in the Ouija board. "Fuck you, spirits!" he yelled. "Now get the hell out of here!" This brought about a rowdy response of "Fuck, yeah!" and "Right on, dude!"

Russell then came over, and placed the doll in my hands.

I gazed at it, thinking about Jane Elizabeth's bound spirit within, and as I threw it into the flames, I yelled out, "You can never do harm again to anyone! Leave us now, Jane Elizabeth. *We release you* from this world!"

As the doll's hair and clothing quickly caught fire, the sound of cracking and popping intensified, creating a wall of white noise.

Then the plastic began to melt. It was hard to not think of it like skin peeling away from a skeleton, and I had to remind myself, it was just a doll. However, I couldn't help but picture Jane Elizabeth's real face. I had to turn away.

"It's okay," Russell said, as he came up behind me and wrapped me in his arms.

I turned back to stare into the heart of the fiery beast, worried that it hadn't done its part to purge the past, or dispel the spirit of the angry child. I wanted desperately to believe we'd done everything we could.

"We did," Russell whispered, in answer to my unspoken question.

As it quieted down, the smooth melody of "Moondance" by Van Morrison came on, and unconsciously Russell and I began to sway back and forth in each other's arms.

Hearing the lyrics, humming along as I stared up into the night sky, I thought to myself, *it is the perfect night to be dancing under the moon with...*

"My love..." Russell sang, finishing my thought, and then leaning in to kiss me. It was a wonderfully long heartfelt kiss, filled with the hope of good things to come.

Thank You

To my parents: for reading aloud to me as a child, taking me to the library, feeding my imagination, and fostering in me the love of all genres of literature.

To my superhero team of editors:
Miss Moneypenny - Able to leap over to the post office in a single bound, willing to work on an ice cream budget, and with speed and dexterity can dispense red ♥s and LOLs amongst a flurry of edits.

☯

Captain Pedantic - "Ever Unafraid to Offend", able to toil over every detail, and question everything without tiring; the arch nemesis of the Creative, and a necessary evil against the threat of mediocrity. Your mighty wordsmithing sword can rest until the spring.

And:
The Infamous R.M. – Ever resourceful, eternally patient, and with prolific proficiency able to bring beautiful cover art to life!

Coming in 2022:

Across the Dark Stream

…there was a coven of witches.

Made in the USA
Las Vegas, NV
07 November 2021

33923595R00177